ECLIPSING APOLLO

Loves Of Olympus – Book Three

SASHA SUMMERS

*'Love will dare to make men die for their Beloved –
love alone;
And woman as well as men.' ~ Plato*

For a love that endures death and time...

Prologue

Apollo, do not desert me now. Guide me. Show me the way.

Apollo heard Coronis' prayer, though she uttered no words aloud. His curse was muffled for he knew his fate was sealed. Denying her was impossible. He glanced at the only woman who threatened everything he stood for. It would be easier to still the very blood in his veins than to turn from her when she called upon him.

"Apollo, King Phlegys thinks us gone, he'd expect no aid from us. Our time as mortals is done. Olympus waits," Hermes cautioned. His friend would know his mind, know it was pointless to add, "This is not our fight, brother."

Help me bring honor to my father. Save me from shaming myself. I ask you...I beg of you.

Beg? Coronis? This proud, fierce woman. His chest ached with unfathomable longing as his gaze feasted upon her beauty and vibrant spirit. For it was her spirit that drew him in and bound him to her.

Hear me, Apollo. Her eyes closed in prayer. Yet her hands fisted, pressed rigid against her hips and revealing her distress... *Please, I give myself to your care... I give myself to you.*

Her words consumed him. Damn this weakness she stirred in him, he had no choice.

"Apollo," Hermes all but growled.

"You were always the wiser." He clapped Hermes on the

shoulder before striding through the crowd.

His presence was noted amongst the spectators. From jubilant approval to hostility at his interference, their reaction varied. But silent prayers were offered. Many sought Apollo's aid, many worried over the threat Damocles posed against their good king. The prayers of his people. He was their God, not just Coronis', his duty was here-- to all of them. Even if none knew him as an Olympian.

When he stood straight and proud before Coronis' father he spoke clearly, his words ringing out in the now hushed clearing. "King Phlegys."

Coronis' amber eyes flew open, her sudden intake of breath sharp and unsteady. Was that delight upon her face? Or did his wishes cloud his vision as well as his judgment?

Apollo knelt. "I offer my strength, in your champions' stead, oh King."

Silence fell.

King Phlegys could refuse him. He'd made no secret that he and his queen wanted Apollo gone, away from their daughter. And yet, Phlegys loved his daughter dearly... too dearly to give her to the fool Damocles without a fight.

He glanced at the mortal King-a good man-and saw relief upon Phlegys face. Phlegys' queen gripped his hand, drawing her husband's attention. Her nod was quick but enough for Phlegys to answer, "Your offer is accepted, most heartily, Apollo."

Apollo nodded and rose. The crowd jumped as he clapped his hands together, rubbing them together with childlike enthusiasm. "The games were through before I'd had my fill. 'Tis a fitting way to end such celebrations, is it not, Damocles?" Arching one golden eyebrow, he smiled at his opponent.

He heard her again, the sweet satisfaction in her silent prayer. *My thanks, Apollo.*

Apollo could not stop himself. He turned, his gaze fastening upon her. She blinked, but met his gaze with a defiant tilt of her head—as was her way. If she knew he was the same Olympian she prayed to, not a mere man named to honor her city's deity, she would never again seek his aid.

Her amber gaze held his, blazing with disdain... defiance.

He smiled. No. She would not. And he would miss the sound of her voice.

He winked at her, knowing his irreverence would gall her and chase away his grief for the moment.

And, oh, how she balked. Her face revealed all. Her control, her relief, vanished—replaced with wide-eyed incredulity, then consternation. Had she not chided him before for his lack of humility... of decorum? How he had laughed, as he longed to do now. She was too easy to bait, and react. Her anger was quick and glorious. He reveled in the heat of it.

He smiled broadly, letting his eyes sweep over her. He did not care if all saw his admiration for this woman. She was worthy of it, deserving of it.

And tomorrow he would be gone. His hands fisted, briefly. Tomorrow.

Her nostrils flared, the muscles of her jaw fighting to hold back what he suspected would be an admirable diatribe. But she succeeded—much to his disappointment.

Damocles low breath, almost a growl, caught his attention. The mortal was livid, his face blood-red and his body coiled for battle. It would be a good match—one all here would remember.

Do not let him fall. Her prayer startled him. Urgent. *Give your namesake the strength to be victor this day. Apollo must win. He will honor you.*

His gaze met hers. For the first time in his existence, he wished he were mortal. Regret, something he'd little experience with, all but choked him.

"Go with Apollo, Coronis." Phlegys bent closer to his daughter, whispering something in her ear.

She nodded, her gaze still locked with his. "Yes, father." Her final plea was heavy with desperation. *Do not let him fall.*

Apollo smiled broadly, his brow rising high. Could this prickly, haughty woman care for him?

"Coronis," Queen Talousa grasped her daughter's hand. "He saves us all, daughter. Take care."

Coronis nodded at her mother's words, tearing her gaze from his as she descended the steps, her long stride carrying her to her father's tent. Apollo followed, watching intently, noting the flex and shift of muscle beneath her gilded skin. Yet, the lush swell of both hip and breast left no doubt of her femininity. 'Twould be easier if he could deny it, for then leaving her would offer no challenge at all.

He followed her into the tent, waiting for her reprimand, her fight. Yet she held her tongue, setting to work. That her father had sent her to help him bathe, to anoint him with oil, before his match with Damocles was a gesture he'd not expected. Phlegys was indeed thankful.

As was Apollo.

She shivered, her long fingers trembling as she lit a lamp and cast the tent in long shadows. He heard her draw in a deep breath, her slight pause as she set the taper aside. Was she truly troubled? For him? Or did she doubt his prowess and fear the claim Damocles would make upon her if he lost?

She was not a fretful sort. He'd no desire to see her so.

He moved closer, searching out some words to soothe her. He would win, he knew it. But such claims would make him a greater ass in her eyes—if such a thing was possible. So he waited, unable to pull his gaze from her lithe form. His gaze traveled down the back of her neck and over her shoulder. Her arm was strong and trim, pouring water from a large pitcher into a beaten copper basin with ease. When the ewer was full, her long fingers grasped a bottle of oil. With another deep breath, she turned to face him.

He frowned.

She did not meet his gaze, staring all about the tent—save at him. He smiled, the ache in his chest surprising him. With one step, he removed all but a hairsbreadth of space between them, allowing him the luxury of staring down at her.

But she simply regarded his chest, her lips pressed flat, her breath shaky.

"Do not fret. You've not broken your vow. You said you would never ask for my help. And you did not."

When she looked at him, he fell silent. Her gaze bore into his very soul. He would promise all to this woman, give all to her... for her.

But she was not his. And would never be.

He did not reach for her, no matter how his hands ached to touch her. Instead he whispered, "You will never have to ask. I give it to you freely. I always will."

her. To be separated from her—her favorite child—for the better part of a year was painful. And when Persephone was returned, the shade Erysichthon lurked in every shadow ready to steal her away forever. If Demeter was at her wits' end, he could hardly fault her. But he knew better than to ally himself with whatever schemes the Goddess had planned.

"There was more to Hades' bargain than just the dead king, Demeter," Hermes attempted reason. "She must divide her time between the Land of the Living and the Land of the Dead to keep the balance, Demeter. You know this."

Apollo frowned. All knew it. Yet Demeter refused to accept it.

"Perhaps. But, Hades loves her." Demeter shook her head. "He will give her up. When Erysichthon is caught, he will side with me. And Persephone will be free of the Underworld."

Apollo remembered too well Hades' adoration for his young wife. "Does she want to be?" Apollo asked, knowing his words were futile. Demeter would not listen, she did not want to listen. She only wanted her daughter.

Ares added, "I've seen the spark in her eyes when she speaks of her husband—"

"How can she know what she wants? She is still a child. *My* child."

Apollo heard the desperation in Demeter's voice and pitied her.

"She will always be your daughter, Demeter." He spoke softly, entreating. "But she is, proudly, Hades' wife."

Hermes spoke carefully. "Hades will deliver her soon. Savor the time you have with her. Bask in the sweetness of her smile, her laughter. She is happy. Surely that is a boon to any mother's spirit?"

Demeter sighed. "She was happy before him."

"But can she be happy without him?" Hermes asked.

"Whether you have our support or not, the Fates blessed their union." Hera interjected.

"The Fates can be persuaded otherwise," Demeter continued, turning wide and beseeching eyes upon him.

"I will not go against the Fates." Apollo shook his head. This was not the first time Demeter had come to him, seeking his aid. "This is my final answer."

"And Erysichthon?" Demeter snapped.

He kept his tone neutral. He'd learned the importance of diplomacy long ago. "You doubt my loyalty? We have, all of us, pledged to hunt the shade."

"You go too far, Demeter." Hermes had no qualms revealing his affront. "He has grievously offended Olympus. For that, he will face justice."

"She wants more than justice, Hermes." Ares turned an assessing eye upon Demeter. "You seek vengeance, Demeter. A task best shared by those who know it well."

Demeter smiled at the God of War. "I accept your offer, Ares."

"Hades is a most able protector." Apollo shook his head, ignoring Ares' dismissive snort.

"Vengeance?" The frustration in Zeus' tone caught Apollo's attention once more. "Why seek out such trouble when there is peace. Athens is strong and whole once more. Your crops flourish. Our people are stronger than ever. Apollo and Hermes leave for the Pythian Games..."

"And Erysichthon continues to threaten my daughter," Demeter interrupted. "How many innocents have died, Zeus? Not on the glorious battlefield, but cowering from the shadows of night. We rule the mortals, yet he threatens our dominion. The mortals fear *him*. Children whisper *his* name and tremble with fear. He has power. A power we enable by doing nothing."

Apollo saw the faces of his brethren then. Demeter's words struck a chord.

"I am done with words. What good have they done? You may stand and speak of peace." Demeter's voice broke, her shoulders heaving in her fury. "I will stand by no longer." Her gaze speared Poseidon. "Find me Erysichthon's daughter."

Erysichthon's daughter? Apollo frowned. Years had passed since Erysichthon's death. Why would Demeter want the mortal now?

Even Poseidon was surprised. "I've... I've no knowledge of her whereabouts."

"Of course, you're finished with her. What charm could an aged mortal woman offer the likes of you?" She shook her head, regarding Poseidon with pure scorn. "Left her to fend for herself these years, himself. Save a pretty face and a body the Gods would admire, she'd seen little reason for him to own such arrogance. Were it not for his carelessness, the deer would not have suffered. And the lion would still live, majestic and free.

"*You* are neither light on your feet, nor skilled at the hunt," she bit out.

His smile vanished, replaced by such incredulity she almost laughed. "I see your arrow is not the only weapon you possess."

She smiled. "The Gods gifted me with more than a deadly aim."

"What need have I for such gifts when you are so capable?" She had not expected the hint of humor in his eyes, gold-copper-and dazzling in the setting sun. "The Gods favor you, lady. And their favor makes you a gift to all that look upon you."

She snatched the arrow from him, his fingertips brushing hers. It was the slightest touch, yet something passed between them—something invigorating and warm. His gaze remained fixed upon her, so heavy its weight was almost tangible upon her skin.

She glared at him, tilting her head defiantly and crossing her arms over her chest. Let him look his fill at the woman that saved *his* life. And he did, a most thorough inspection—from her head to her dusty bare feet. Assessing... exploring. *An arrogant ass, to be sure.*

"Your men are coming? To assist you?" He stepped forward.

She stepped back, needing distance from this man and the disquieting affect he had upon her. She glanced at the sun before setting to work on a make-shift litter she could pull back to her stallion Charon. She didn't answer, but cut cleanly through a sapling tree. He may be arrogant, but she would be foolish to underestimate his strength. He need not know she was alone.

"Then I offer my aid."

She stopped then, turning on him with narrowed eyes. "There is no need." A foolish declaration considering daylight waned and both animals would be near impossible for her to pull.

He cocked an eyebrow.

"Apollo," another man arrived, looking red-faced and agitated. He led a most resistant Charon. "Damn brute bit me more than..."

Her horse knocked the man down, stilling only when it stood before her, blowing into her hands.

"He has no tolerance for strangers," she spoke to the men, feeling steadied by her horse's presence. She was no longer outnumbered. For Charon would protect her if she needed.

"Are we strangers still?" The golden man asked.

She arched a brow. "We are."

"We need not be. We are travelers come to Delphi for the games." The other man spoke, wiping the dirt from his chiton. "At your service."

"Travelers without names?" She focused her attention on this new arrival. He appeared a more genial, less demanding sort. Coronis found him a vast improvement over his companion.

"I am Hermes," the companion offered. "While the hunter is Apollo."

"Your parents were most loyal to the Gods." Coronis let her eyes travel over one, then the other. "What a burden to have such names."

"Burden?" Apollo asked, his forehead furrowing ever so slightly.

She considered Apollo. He was well named—for he looked just as she imagined the Olympian Apollo: a near perfect male specimen. And gold, as the God of Light would be. His parents must be pleased then, though she would not dare say such a thing aloud. "Man's purpose is to achieve honor and glory, his birthright. Your honor and glory must be that and more—worthy of bearing the names of the Gods, I would think."

Hermes' smile was warm. "I am, alas, named for a messenger. My burdens are the lighter of the two."

Coronis returned the smile, regarding Hermes anew. Hermes had bright eyes—a quick wit perhaps—and an eager smile. Such a man was always a welcome addition to her father's fire during the games.

"I suppose it would depend upon the message?" she offered.

Hermes nodded. "True, true. I've no stomach for gossip or intrigue."

"A shame." She sighed. "I would invite you to my father's tent to dine. But he is most fond of a good intrigue."

"Oh?" Hermes smiled. "Well, then, I might recall a story to tell."

"One or two?" Apollo scoffed, laughing.

She felt the weight of golden eyes upon her, but did not turn to him. While Hermes' nature was pleasing enough, Apollo unsettled her.

"Come, then. Let us help you bring your prizes to camp," Hermes offered. He glanced at Apollo asking, "Which did you..."

"I've loosed no arrows this day," Apollo spoke. "Or cut any throats. The lady is a most impressive hunter."

She saw no insult or teasing upon Apollo's too handsome face, only respect. She did not care for the pride his words offered her.

"Your father's pride will know no ends," Hermes offered.

She tore her gaze from Apollo to pull the knife from the lion. Her father would thrash her if he knew she'd ventured so far into the woods, alone. "Perhaps," she murmured.

She did not resist their help as Hermes lifted the stag onto Charon's back behind her. Even though the best course was to leave the lion, and leave her parents unaware of its part in this hunt, she could not bear to part with it. And as the weight of the lion upon Apollo's shoulders seemed no burden at all, she did not stop him.

Once she sat atop Charon, some distance from her newfound companions, she felt no qualms about assessing them. Rather, assessing Apollo. What she saw confirmed her suspicion. He appeared to be a warrior, the width and breadth of his frame and muscles left little doubt on that score. And since his face was a work of masculine perfection—without scar or blemish—he was either a truly skilled warrior or one who'd never tested his strength. He'd come to win the games, claim the prize, and woo the women. Many a man did as much. And while she admired their physical prowess and their pursuit of glory, the *man* was often found wanting.

"You've come to compete in the games?" she asked as they cleared the tree line.

Apollo looked at her. "To win."

She arched a brow at him. "To win what?"

"All, lady." Apollo winked at her, his smile strong and sure.

She shook her head. "Which is your best event?"

"Archery," his answer was quick.

"Well, then mighty Apollo—" she savored every word, "—we know who will win."

He stared up at her, once more astonished. "*You* compete?"

His question ended any curiosity he might have offered.

Whether he questioned her right to compete or her ability to do so mattered little. She had no reason to dislike him, save his arrogance. But, for her, that was enough. She had enough of arrogant men bent on bringing her to heel. Or worse, to wife. She would not be distracted by a pleasing form, no matter how pleasing. She felt a frown mar her brow and saw Apollo's brow furrow in kind.

"He *will* win. But I come to challenge myself," Hermes spoke, laughing. "And the revelry."

She blinked, turning from Apollo to Hermes. "A noble notion, Hermes, to better oneself. I applaud *your* goal. And your humility." Her father's house would be too crowded to be overly bothered by Apollo. Doubtless he would find entertainment elsewhere. She turned a smile upon Hermes, nudged Charon forward with her knee, and motioned for them to follow. "Come. Father is doubtless hunting me even as we speak."

Neither men commented on the pace she set, but it was only once they'd left the forest that she realized how low the sun set. Her father would be furious with her. Beyond furious if she arrived after dark with two strangers—strangers both handsome and capable of mayhem at that. Her tributes and her hunt would pale in comparison.

Her mother... No, her mother would not be pleased. Her devoted father loved her mother so that her emotions would rule his. So he would not be pleased.

As indulgent as her parents were, they were fiercely over-protective. Even as a child, she was shadowed by a nurse or companion. When she grew too fast for a human companion, they'd given her Balek the Beast, a massive dog that let no one within reach of her. She'd left him tied at camp—he ruined all her hunting sport. Then there was Charon, her horse. He let no one touch him, or her. If someone tried, he bit hard and didn't let go. Hermes was lucky he'd escaped so little damaged.

The camp was alight with torches and fires by the time she arrived. They rode on, through the ever expanding tent village, to her family home. While the house was removed from the city proper and surrounded by vast lands for olives and grapes, the games saw her home surrounded by tents and travelers. It was her father's responsibility to reward those that earned it, keep the peace amongst the competitors, and ensure the games were fairly judged. His mind was consumed with these tasks—yet the small group of horses waiting outside her father's house warned her of what was to come. Indeed, even as she drew Charon to stop, her father stalked out onto the steps of the house, his gaze searching the horizon... And falling on her.

"Coronis-" He broke off. His stride was barely restrained as he made his way to her. "You are late," he all but hissed.

She slid down before him. "Forgive me, Father, the hunt..." She smiled, knowing he loved her smile more than anything.

The severity of his features eased, his rigid posture easing. "And what a hunt." His gaze shifted from her face to the stag upon Charon's back. It was only then that Hermes' and Apollo's presence was noted. "These two as well? Did you lure them into service?"

She laughed. "I did no luring. That is a skill I do not possess."

"Threaten then?" her father answered.

Hermes and Apollo laughed.

"And you are?" her father asked, appraising each with narrowed eyes and a painfully thorough inspection.

Coronis glanced quickly at Hermes, but her gaze lingered on Apollo. Why did he look at her, now? Her father was a man of importance.

"Hermes, of Athens," Hermes offered.

"And I am Apollo." Apollo did regard her father then.

"You've come for the games?" her father asked. At their nod, he continued, "And welcome you are. I am Phlegys and this is my daughter, Coronis."

She saw the surprise on their faces, followed by a quick bow and murmured apologies. Hermes was quick to make amends, "King Phlegys, we welcome your greeting and offer apologies for our lack of-"

"Come, come. Tonight I am a father too pleased by the return of my only child to worry over such formalities," her father interrupted. "I bid you good evening and look forward to your showing at the games. I must take my daughter to her mother, for she is beside herself with worry."

She glanced at Apollo, still carrying her lion. He reached for it, clearly intending to offer it to her father but she shook her head, ever so slightly. She could not claim the kill, she valued her hunts too much to give them up over vanity. If her parents knew she brought down this glorious beast, that she'd gone against her father's dictate and gone deep into the forest, her hunts would be a happy memory.

Apollo cocked his head, a small smile on his lips.

She scowled at him.

He winked at her.

She stared. What impudence? What gall... Her anger near choked her.

"Coronis, let us find your mother." Her father's hand encircled her upper arm, leading her away from the infuriating man she dreamed of teaching humility to.

Chapter Two

H is temple, in the quiet of dawn, was a magical place. This time of day he might savor the solitude and peace of the world waking. Such a setting offered him freedom to clear his mind, receive any prophecies, and embrace the day before him. The prayers of a thousand people bombarded him, gathered for the games and seeking glory. Others sought health or happiness, but all turned to him. From his throne on Olympus, it was all too easy to forget how loyal these mortals were to him, and his brethren.

Mortals like the faithful Phlegys and his... vexing daughter. Even her prayers confounded him. She was a woman, yet her prayers were neither sentimental nor pleading. She simply asked for the strength of her people, the health of her father, and Apollo's continued favor. Other than her family she mentioned only one man—Damocles. While her need for strength and patience so as not to kill the fool with her bare hands amused him, it provided little insight into the woman. A woman who'd weighed too heavily upon his dreams the night before. A woman he'd be wise to set aside. One did not bed the daughter of a king, no matter how tempting she might be. Even if the brush of her fingertips against his was akin to stroking a living flame.

His gaze wandered the countryside, appreciating how little the view had changed. He'd been a child when he'd first come upon Python, a child playing at being a man with weapons he'd yet to master. He'd heard of Poseidon's plans to conquer the great dragon and deigned it a task that might gain the approval of his brethren. He'd thought, at the time, that the dragon would devour him. He bore the scars of that battle, the puncture of the dragon's bite leaving four perfect indentions-two on his stomach and two on his back. Somehow, the dragon had lost and Delphi was Apollo's.

The announcement had earned a variety of responses from his fellow Olympians. He was young, his presence new and most unwelcome by Hera. While Zeus and Ares, even Athena, applauded his skill, Poseidon was furious. After losing Athens to Athena, yielding such a prize as Delphi galled the God. It chafed Poseidon still that he'd lost such a bounteous land and devoted people to a youth. And while Poseidon had yet to seek some sort of vengeance or retribution against Apollo for stealing Delphi, Apollo remained wary of the God of the Sea.

Yet, even with the threat of Poseidon looming, Apollo had never regretted his impetuous actions. Delphi was a glorious site, the weight of import and air of prophecy obvious even to those who doubted the benevolence of Olympus and those that ruled there. It was the heart of Greece and he loved it dearly.

He drew in a deep breath, shivering from the crisp morning air. The day was full of new opportunities and he would make the most of it. He spied his crows, their white feathers a bright spot amongst the spruce and fir trees foliage. They were his most loyal informants— most helpful when dealing with matters of diplomacy. Or wooing a reluctant woman. Their beautiful song made him smile—and made women swoon.

He set off, following the path beyond the tent encampment and the fields, to the caves beyond. Few knew of the Olympian Springs, for the trek was long and difficult. One had to scale the sheer front of a mountain before finding the cave's entrance. But once the journey was made, the rewards were great. A thermal hot springs encased in a crystal-lined cave. Alabaster walls, illuminated by the dazzling gems in the rock. A handful of shafts cut through the mountain into the caves, allowing sunlight to spill inside. In the morning, the waters were a refreshing way to start the day-or soothe fatigued muscles. But at midday the cave was almost blinding—too hot for mortal flesh.

He'd expected to savor the hidden springs alone. A great grey

delay our union this time, Coronis?"

She froze, glaring at him with unconcealed contempt. "I see no one worthy of my hand."

Damocles' eyes narrowed as he stepped closer.

But Balek growled, inserting himself between them.

"The time will come when your opinion no longer matters. Your father won't live forever and you cannot rule." He shrugged.

"Until that time comes, you know my answer." She forced herself on towards her father's house before she unleashed her mounting anger.

"Coronis," Ichthys ran to her side. "I've been looking for you."

She smiled at her dearest childhood friend. "Have you? Last I saw you, you had eyes for only fair Antinea."

"Tell me you will be mine and Antinea is dead to me," Ichthys promised.

"Fickle lover indeed," Coronis shook her head. Even Ichthys toyed with women? "I pity poor Antinea."

Ichthys stopped then, his brown eyes sweeping her face. "What has happened?"

She shook her head.

He snorted. "No, no, I know that look all too well." He sighed. "You've seen Damocles?" Ichthys glanced over her shoulder. "He arrived this morning, loudly, as is his way."

She did not follow Ichthys' gaze but headed up the steps of her father's home. She nodded at the attendant inside before leading Ichthys into the inner courtyard of her family's home. "Let us leave talk of unpleasant things outside, Ichthys. I'm in need of a distraction."

"Why?"

She wrinkled her nose, glancing at him. "Nothing of note."

"Yet you seem ready for a fight."

"If I wanted a fight, you would know it." She smiled sweetly at him. "I do not."

He laughed. "Fine. I will leave well enough alone."

"You shall," she agreed. "Let me change and then we can see what tasks Father has for us."

"Us?" He shook his head.

"What else do you have to do? Find some manly preoccupation

or Antinea will lose interest." She entered her room, but called out. "Father relies on you, as you know."

"I do," he answered. "And I consider it an honor."

Coronis changed quickly, accepting the help of her aged attendant, Pina. The old woman had been with her since childhood. A victim of the long-ago Persian raids, Pina's tongue had been cut out and her leg badly broken. Her mother loved Pina so that she'd nursed the old woman until she was well. And Pina loved Coronis so dearly she hid all evidence of Coronis' less ladylike endeavors. Coronis adored her for it.

Pina draped a clean white tunic about her, clasping the shoulders and draping the extra fabric. When Pina was satisfied with Coronis' robes, she turned to Coronis' hair. Her nimble fingers turned Coronis' tangled locks into an elegant cascade of woven braids and ribbon.

"Thank you," Coronis murmured, brushing a quick kiss to the older woman's well-lined cheek.

Pina nodded at the door.

"Ichthys is here with me," she answered Pina's unspoken question. "I know," Coronis nodded. Ichthys was Pina's choice of husband. And her mother's as well. Truth be told, he was the only man Coronis hadn't rejected outright. And the only man who had yet to ask for her hand.

"All is ready for the Holy Ceremony," Ichthys spoke when she entered the room. "Will you accompany me?"

"To the Holy Ceremony?" She paused. The event signaled the beginning of the games. A re-enactment of Apollo's duel with the dragon Python, the very battle that brought about the games. It was a great celebration—rallying all those gathered together for the first time. Those that wagered on competitors would get their first glimpse on those competing. As well as those parents seeking husbands for their daughters. Attending such an event with Coronis might curb Antinea's enthusiasm and insinuate something more at work between him and Coronis. "And Antinea?"

He shrugged.

"Is she leading you on a merry chase?" She teased.

"You're a hunter—you know the thrill of the hunt." He smiled. "Is there finer prey than that of love?"

The thrill of the hunt. She frowned, her thoughts shifting toward Apollo. "Love?" She scowled at Ichthys. "Give me an angry wolf or a charging boar in its place, I beg of you."

His dark brown eyes searched her face. "I look forward to the day you are brought low by love."

"I thought you were my greatest friend."

"I am," he assured her. "But I know which hunt has the sweeter rewards. You, fair Coronis, have much to learn in matters of the heart."

Poseidon's head fell back against the tree, his hands tangling in Daphne's hair as she sucked him into her mouth. She had a most skilled and thorough tongue. And her hands, the scouring of her nails along his outer thighs and buttocks. He quivered, his body tightening for release. But her mouth lifted.

"Do I please you?" she rasped.

"Is it not evident?"

She smiled, stroking one finger down his throbbing length. "Such a sight pleases me."

He pushed her onto her back and pushed between her thighs. He slid deep, groaning as her heat encompassed him.

She sighed, her head falling back with a smile. "Stay awhile." Her hands gripped his hips and held him close.

A nymph was meant for pleasure. To bed one was an exhausting fete, for once their pleasure began they would stay in its throws until they were too spent to move. The diversion she offered was more gratifying than his search for the shade tormenting Persephone. Daphne had been quick to draw him in, sliding her scented limbs about him and pressing a most inviting kiss upon his lips. And when her hands grasped his cock, he no longer cared about Demeter's need for revenge or the fruitless quest he was on. He would gladly take what she offered.

He drove into her, draping one of her shapely legs over his shoulder. It took no time. The intensity of his thrusts grew, making him more frantic. Daphne's nails pierced his back, her face twisted with raw passion. When she cried out, he ground deep, his release shaking him.

He lay at her side. "Tell me why Apollo's favorite nymph showers me with such affections?" He stared down at her, appreciating her ample curves and eager disposition.

Tears gathered in the corner of her eyes. "He is tired of me."

He arched a brow, his finger caressing the pebble of her nipple. "Of this?" He shook his head.

"He said as much." She closed her eyes as he continued to fondle her.

"What did he say?" he asked, leaning forward to lave the tight peak of her nipple with his tongue.

"He said nothing," she gasped. "His body said all."

Poseidon looked up at her, curious. The lover Apollo, whose endowments were legendary and his exploits many, was unable to love a most enthusiastic and willing nymph? This was news indeed. News that might be of import later.

"There must be another, fair Daphne. One who's wrung him dry. Fear not, he'll tire of her and return to you." He would have to learn the identity of such a creature—mortal or no. A mortal lover could not compete with a nymph. But for now, he would enjoy what Apollo would not. "Until then, I will happily occupy your time." He rolled over her, entering her with one hard thrust.

Chapter Three

"She is most comely," Hermes murmured, assessing the round wench serving wine. "As is she." He nodded at a maid with flowing black hair. "And that one."

"You've a most discerning eye," Apollo teased. "What makes a woman comely to your eye? If she is warm and willing?"

Hermes laughed. "I see beauty in them all."

Apollo nodded, leaning against an aged oak tree. The day of feasting lasted too long for his liking. He stood now, watching the comings and goings of those visiting Phlegys and his family before partaking in the abundance of food and drink. He hoped that tomorrow, when the games began, this restlessness that gripped him might ease.

"You've come for more than sport on the field, Apollo." Hermes nudged him. "There are too many warm and willing to woo without setting your sites on one that is not. You will not win *that* one."

Apollo glanced at Coronis, drinking deeply from his wine skin. She sat, illuminated by torches, inside her father's tent. At her father's side... Hermes was right. He'd do better to ignore this passing fascination with the King's daughter and seek out a woman who would welcome and appreciate his attention.

"And who should I win?" Apollo glanced at his friend.

Hermes smiled. "There are two women that study you the way you've been studying the lady Coronis."

Apollo pushed Hermes, laughing. "And they are?"

"The buxom Khloris." Hermes nodded at the women as he spoke. "And the full-lipped Erato." Hermes leaned closer. "While Khloris assets are clear, there is a look of spirit about Erato that suggests she would be a most passionate lover."

It was true, Khloris had a bountiful chest that promised to fill his hand and then some. He was fond of a large chested woman and soft curves he could lose himself in. Her eyes went round when she discovered his inspection. The flush of her cheeks was most becoming.

"There would be no resistance from that maid," Hermes chuckled.

Apollo nodded at the maid. Her answering smile was invitation enough. She was a fine woman, tall, with pale wheaten hair, ample curves, and no hint of haughty indifference. No, she would likely welcome him into her bed. But she did not stir his blood.

His gaze shifted to Eratos—who openly glared at Khloris. She was a small thing, with bright eyes and a full mouth. Her chest could not compare to Khloris' but she had a certain grace about her. Where Khloris was light, Eratos had the blackest hair and a gilded hue to her skin. And while looking upon her was pleasurable, he felt no urgency to have her.

"It's not like you to be so..." Hermes paused, "selective."

Apollo shoved Hermes again. But his friend's words were true. Apollo had a lusty nature easily roused and quick to reignite. He'd drawn the nymph Daphne into his bed just this morning, to ease the frustration that riddled him. But even her skilled hands and mouth could not make him rise to the challenge. And the more desperate Daphne's attempts to make him hard, the more agitated he became.

"What ails you?" she'd asked, her whispered words brushing across his waist. Her hands cradled his length, stroking his skin with feather-light caresses.

What indeed? A most skilled and beautiful creature caressed him, drew him into her mouth, and whispered words of encouragement. Yet he felt... nothing.

He was not a temperamental sort, yet his mood went from grey to black in that instant. He refused to accept that his fascination for a fiery, impertinent, stubborn mortal was the cause for his impotence. He would not give such a notion credence.

"Leave me, Daphne. Perhaps we've been too familiar too long. Find your pleasure elsewhere," he'd growled, setting her away from him and leaving his tent.

A peel of laughter drew his attention to the mortal in question. Coronis laughed and smiled, conversing freely with one more boy than man, a *boy* that was too often at her side. When she'd arrived at the Holy Ceremony with her parents, he had been with her. While she sat riveted, watching the scene of a young Apollo kill Gaia's child, Python, with arrows until the dragon lay dead—he watched her. And the boy. If Apollo had not known Coronis was an only child, he would have thought the boy was her brother for there was an intimacy between them.

Was he her betrothed? Was Coronis intended for such an unimpressive specimen?

"I have heard your competition tomorrow," Hermes continued. "Ichthys there," he pointed at the object of Apollo's assessment. "He plays the aulos."

"Does he?" Apollo asked. "For it would appear that is the only contest he is fit to take part in."

Hermes laughed. "He is friend to the king's daughter and her family."

Apollo said nothing.

"He has made no claim upon her hand or spoken to her father about a match, so you've no need to do the poor man harm." Hermes paused, clapping Apollo on the shoulder. "I've heard he woos the fair Antinea. But the mighty Damocles is another matter." He nodded in the direction of one of the largest mortals Apollo had ever seen. "He is determined to win Coronis, and her kingdom, though she's refused his offer more than once."

There was no denying Damocles was a warrior. His body was heavily muscled, bearing scars of battle. He would be an intimidating adversary—for a mortal. But it was the way Damocles stared at Coronis that vexed him. The giant was too proprietary, regarding her with both hunger and impatience. "And what does her father say?" he asked Hermes.

"The king and queen dote on their daughter. They will not force her hand." Hermes shrugged. "As Phlegys is young and virile there is no need to rush such things, I suppose."

Apollo did not argue. Phlegys was both those things, but he was still mortal. Coronis should be matched, if not married, by now. For the sake of his people and his daughter's well-being. "And how do you come by this information?" he asked.

"Mara is a serving maid in Phlegys' house." Hermes smiled. "A few cups of wine and I knew much about the king's household and those in it."

Apollo arched a brow. "And what did you learn of Mara?"

"A sweet girl. An innocent." Hermes frowned. "And none of your concern."

Apollo glanced at his friend. Hermes has an odd sense of nobility when it came to mortal women. He prized virginity as something to be preserved versus something to be taken. Apollo considered virginity, freely given, a prize to be treasured.

Coronis' laughter rang out again, demanding his attention once more. She had never known a man, of that he was certain. As fond as she seemed of this Ichthys, she did not regard him with a sensual eye. A relief, to be sure. If she had, Apollo feared he might rip the boy limb from limb.

"Apollo?" Hermes asked. "Drink more, brood less. It is unlike you and makes for boorish company. You rival Hades with your frown. What of our wager?"

Apollo groaned. "Have you bedded a woman?"

Hermes shook his head. "Not yet."

"Then you cannot bid me lose in archery," he argued. "That was your wager, was it not? The first to bed a maid picked the contest the other must lose in?"

"It was." Hermes smiled. "And I will do so in the morning."

Apollo laughed then, drawing the attention of the fair Khloris, the spirited Eratos, and the sharp-tongued minx Coronis. He gave the first two a broad, knowing smile. He would no longer think on Coronis.

"Which will it be?" Hermes asked. "Either would be delighted by your attention."

"Both," Apollo ground out, tossing back the contents of his cup.

Coronis stroked Balek's ear, her attention wandering to Apollo and his companion Hermes. She should be savoring the evening's feast. She should join in the gaiety and amusement of those gathered. And yet, hers was forced. Her dreams had been most troubling—all because of him.

She had kept her distance at the Holy Ceremony, taking note of where he was before sitting at her father's side. While he seemed enraptured with the re-enactment, she grew distracted. She found pleasure in the curve of his smile...and the play of muscle in his arm. Never had she seen such masculine beauty. Never had she gleaned such enjoyment from a man's appearance. Her dreams had been most troubling.

Tonight she would not gape at him. She would leave that to the other women feasting upon him with their eyes.

That her mother's maid Khloris fawned over him was one thing—for she had no man. But the sly Eratos' interest was clear, even though her intended worked now in the stables.

When Apollo smiled at Khloris, Coronis turned away, swallowing against the knot in her throat.

"Will you read tomorrow?" her mother asked, taking her hand in hers. "Your new poem will elicit tears and laughter, I think."

Coronis smiled. "You love me too well to think otherwise."

"It is good, Coronis," Ichthys agreed. "I've been forced to hear it again and again, and am still moved by your words."

She laughed. "Again and again? I shall not read tomorrow, to spare your poor ears."

Her mother frowned. "Coronis, I beg you to reconsider."

She patted her mother's hand but made no assurances. It was far easier to throw a javelin or shoot an arrow than read her own words aloud before such a large and varied audience.

"Will you play tomorrow, Ichthys? I hear our newest competitors will take part in the musical competition," her father spoke, offering a platter of figs to his wife.

Coronis said nothing.

"Which? The one with the affable smile? Or the one the women believe descended from Olympus itself?" Ichthys teased.

She snorted.

"Coronis," her mother chided.

"You may well dislike him, daughter, but I see one who might finally teach Damocles a lesson," her father spoke. "What did he do to earn such a low opinion from you?"

All eyes regarded her.

"Is his ego not enough?" she answered.

Her mother's gaze drifted to the man in question.

"You are a hard woman to please, daughter. His ego?" Her father sat back in his chair, staring at her. "Will I live to see you married? I dream of taking my grandchildren hunting, of teaching them to track—as I taught you when you were young."

She smiled at her father. "If I am hard to please, you and mother are to blame. Your bond is strong and true, I will settle for nothing less."

Her father's gaze settled on her mother, his affection plain upon his face. Her mother, however, still regarded Apollo with a growing panic.

Coronis frowned, turning to see what had so distracted her mother. Apollo was speaking to Hermes and Damocles. "A distressing sight, to be sure," she sighed. "Beauty, wit, and brawn together."

Her father's laughter boomed, drawing all eyes toward them. Including the very man she sought to avoid. But his golden gaze scarcely acknowledged her. Instead, he bowed low in salute to her mother and father.

When her parents were occupied with tributes and well-wishes, Ichthys stooped low and whispered, "You treat him as low as Damocles without reason. Why?"

She glanced at her friend. What had he done? He had ruined her hunt, hardly an act worthy of persecution. He'd teased her, something Ichthys did regularly. When he'd found her at the Olympian Springs... The echo of his touch seared her fingertips. It was that simple touch, an offer of aid-no more, that gave her pause. Why did *this* man stir her so? "Nothing."

Ichthys' brow furrowed as he regarded Apollo. "Coronis-"

"Leave it," she hissed. "Go find Antinea, woo the lady's parents."

"Perhaps I should speak to your parents, woo them instead?" he swallowed, his expression severe. "Your father's request and the wishes of your lady mother-"

"No." She stared at him. "Ichthys, do not say it." She stood, staring blindly about the tent. If he asked for her hand, she would be forced to accept it. But such an arrangement would make neither of them happy. She wandered to a serving table, filling her goblet with fresh water from the mountain spring.

"Lady?" Apollo stood, his face sweeping over her face. "Are you well?" He spoke with concern.

She drained her cup, wishing she'd filled it with wine instead. But muddying her mind with drink would further complicate matters. And, faced with such a man, she knew she needed her wits about her. "It is a warm evening."

He nodded, his gaze still heavy upon her.

She glanced at him. "How do you find Delphi?" she asked, hoping an exchange of civilities might ease the strange tension between them. Her mother would expect her to be a gracious hostess to all of their guests, no matter how disconcerted he made her.

"It is beautiful country." He stared into his cup. "Peaceful, yet revitalizing."

She nodded. "Have you never visited before? On a pilgrimage?" Did such a man pray to the Gods? "Perhaps your family made the trek, to speak with the oracle?"

"Many years ago," he answered. "I find the land unchanged, as prosperous as before." His gaze found hers. "But it is the people of Delphi I find most intriguing."

"Oh?" She refilled her goblet, offering to serve him as well. "How so?"

He smiled, shaking his head.

"Coronis," her mother called. "Come child."

"Your lady mother calls," he murmured.

She nodded. "I wish you well tomorrow."

"Do you?"

"I do." She smiled. "For I am not competing." She left him, her smile growing as the sound of his l

Chapter Four

Coronis watched those gathered on the field. She must not be discouraged. The best had come to partake of the Pythian Games. And she was one of them. She'd come in fourth in the foot races, no small accomplishment. True, her javelin showing had been too poor to note but it had never been her best event. Now, with her bow in her hand and her quiver on her back, was the time to make her father proud… and show the mighty victor Apollo he would not win all.

She could deny it no longer, Apollo was a man amongst men. The strength of his body was only slightly less surprising than his musicality with the lyre. With each new event, he'd proven himself the fiercest competitor. And it galled her that his ego might be warranted.

She was confident in her skill with a bow but she prayed nonetheless. *Apollo, I would bring pride to my father and my name.*

Her parents sat across the field, from the best vantage point. Her father spoke to those great gentlemen that came to watch the day's events. He'd been in a fine mood since the dawn for this was his favorite day of the Pythian Games. He preferred the test of a man's strength and will to any other. And while tomorrow's chariot races brought the biggest crowds and most showmanship, Coronis agreed that the hardest challenge man could face was against himself.

"Are you ready?" Damocles asked, smiling at her.

"To beat you?" she asked, smiling in return.

He chuckled. "I look forward to ridding your tongue of its barbs Coronis."

"A task that will not fall to you." She sighed.

Apollo drew near. "The man that wins such a prize would seek not to remove the barbs, but to work his way in, amongst the barbs, until he is surrounded and embraced by them."

Coronis and Damocles stared at him.

"Why would a man do such a thing?" Damocles scoffed.

"Have you not seen the way she defends her father? Her family and people?" Apollo spoke to Damocles, impatience lining his words. "A husband would be honored to have a wife so fiercely loyal."

Coronis stared at Apollo, sifting through his words for some hidden dig.

Damocles snorted. "She shames her father with such displays as this..."

Coronis' fury was quick. But she had no time to react, for Apollo was quicker.

"You forget who is host here." Apollo's voice was so sharp that both she and Damocles recoiled. "Your words disrespect King Phlegys and his daughter. If the king were to learn of such a slight, he would not tolerate it."

Damocles scowled at Apollo, bowing up and stepping closer. "Tell him then, so that discord reigns and I might take his country by force. Tell him."

Coronis moved quickly, her heart in her throat. "Such matters are unimportant on days like today. We must not forget why we are here, on this field. None would anger Olympus or Apollo by disrupting the games for such a trivial thing." She placed a hand on each man's shoulder.

Damocles face was red, every muscle in his body taut and ready. "You will leave," he hissed. "When next the games are held, I will sit in that chair," he pointed at her father. "And Coronis will sit meekly at my side." He glanced at her before stomping away.

She watched him go, fury and fear warring within her. "If I were a man..."

"He would try to kill you, not wed you," Apollo finished.

"He might try, but I would welcome the challenge." She jumped when his hand covered hers, still resting on his shoulder.

"You would defeat him." Apollo confirmed.

She pulled her hand away, alarmed by the warmth of his touch and the delight his words stirred. "You flatter me?"

He grinned. "Perhaps it is strategy? I have seen your gift with a bow."

She shook her head. "I wonder which is the greater threat? Damocles, with his bumbling words and wandering hands or you?"

His grin vanished. Indeed, he looked offended. "Me?"

She nodded. "I know what Damocles wants with me, he tells me daily. But you..." She shrugged.

They were not alone, a score of men milled about on the archery field. Yet she was overwhelmed by him. All of him. His unwavering gaze intent, the slight furrow of his brow, the tightening of his jaw. When he stepped closer, his subtle scent filled her nostrils and weighted the air in her lungs. She felt small staring up at him—but safe. As if she were encircled in his presence.

His gaze was relentless, studying her face until her skin grew heated and her heart was thundering in her chest. "Shall I tell you what I want of you?"

"Apollo?" Hermes voice rang out.

She blinked, instantly aware of their situation. They stood far too close together, in front of her father, mother, and all those gathered. But before she could move, he was heading toward Hermes.

She cast a furtive glance at her parents. Her mother was horrified. Her father, amused. And Ichthys, perplexed. Perhaps she had shamed her father this day, by the spectacle she'd made of herself with Apollo.

But the judges arrived and the games were called to order. She'd set aside her worries to win. And, after Damocles' insults and her display with Apollo, she must win. She did not watch the other competitors, they did not matter. All that mattered was hitting the small red dot in the midst of the sails stretched taut over mounds of hay. If several managed to hit the mark, they moved on to a target at greater distance. And then another. Her father had never seen the tournament go beyond four rounds, for the target was too small for accuracy.

The first round, she hit the mark with ease.

The second was no more of a challenge than the first.

As they prepared for the third round, the sky crackled with thunder. She glanced at her rivals then, knowing some feared Zeus' thunderbolts and Poseidon's rain. She found them invigorating. Apollo's face was set, determined. There were two others. Cadmus, she knew to be a strong archer. The other was unknown to her. As the first drops pattered against the packed dirt at their feet, she let her arrow fly straight. It hit the mark as a bolt of lightning cleaved the sky.

Did Zeus approve? Or was he as Damocles, censuring her participation?

Apollo, too hit the mark.

When the others were done, the judges inspected the target. Cadmus was off the mark. And the other, Jedrick, was so close a great debate ensued while the rain picked up.

"Lady," Khloris arrived, carrying a brown cloak. "From your mother."

Coronis glanced down at her tunics, the layers of white fabric hanging heavily about her. Her mother had already insisted she wear a full tunic instead of those worn by other female competitors. In addition to its length, Pino had been instructed to add an under-tunic as well. "Give my mother thanks, but tell her I have no need of its cover or the extra weight," she muttered.

But Khloris was paying her no attention. No, her smile was for Apollo alone. And, in the pouring rain, it was Khloris' garb that grew immodest. Apollo, and Jedrick, were delighted to look upon her massive chest.

"Return to my mother, Khloris. Your presence is a distraction," she barked.

Khloris turned a bright shade of red before hurrying off the field.

"Some might welcome a distraction if it gives them the upper hand," Jedrick mumbled.

"I need no distractions to win," she snapped back, her gaze shifting to the sky above. A patch of blue appeared. She could only hope they'd have a chance to finish before the dark clouds overcame them.

The judges returned, excusing Jedrick from the field. The

rain continued, light but steady, as she and Apollo prepared for the fourth round.

She closed her eyes, focusing on the beat of her heart and the patter of the rain. She drew in a deep breath, clearing her mind. Her arms lifted the bow, the arrow threaded and ready. She waited, pressing the arrow shaft to her cheek before opening her eyes. She focused, narrowing her eyes and releasing the cord.

Her form was perfect. Her slender arms were sure, the muscles gracefully guiding her arrow home. Apollo did not need to follow the arrow to know she'd hit her mark. The smile on her face said it all. He'd never seen such a smile. There was no hint of self-satisfaction or boastful pride. No, she radiated joy, pure and unfiltered. And he was mesmerized by it.

He knew his fate. Hermes had won their wager and he must lose. The smile on her face made such a loss unimportant. But he must be careful. He would not steal her accomplishments with a poor showing. She would expect him to do his best. She would want to win honorably.

He turned, readying his bow as he'd done a thousand times before. It was all too easy to miscalculate, to skew his arrow a hairsbreadth from the mark. He released the arrow, stunned when it hit the target.

The crowd reacted instantly, applause and cheers breaking the silence.

He looked at Coronis, stunned by the slight smile on her face. "Why do you smile?"

"Father says there's never been more than four rounds." Her smile grew. "We shall make history."

He smiled in response. "Winning is no longer important?"

"Winning is everything," she argued, incredulous. "Surely you see that."

In that moment she was not just a woman. No, she was a competitor. An adversary to respect. He nodded, puzzling over the affect this woman had upon him.

Once the field was cleared and the targets were place, a silence fell upon the spectators. He would lead this time. The target was miniscule, an easy miss...

Coronis scarce waited for his arrow to fly before releasing hers.

The crowd waited as the judges ran the length of the field to the targets.

From the corner of his eye he watched her. She stared at the ground, her hands clasping her bow as she shifted from foot to foot.

When the judges pulled her arrow from the target and held it high, the crowd erupted with cheers and applause—to be drowned out by rolling thunder. Rain fell down in torrents, lightning split the sky in quick succession, sending all in the stands in search of shelter. He would have followed the others, but she stood, staring up at the sky, smiling. So he remained at her side.

He would touch her, pull her against him, and hold her. Instead, he stepped closer and took her hand in his. Only then did she look at him.

Lightning pierced the sky, striking a great tree at the edge of the field. He'd scarce heard the crackle and snap of its mighty trunk before the air around them whistled and the tree began to fall. He did not think, but pulled her tightly against him, sheltering her with his body. When the ground shook with the force of the fall, he held her still. Her back was pressed against his chest, her scent tickling his nose, while his arm cradled her waist. His hold eased once he knew she was safe, but the feel of her curves against him was a heady thing. If not for the chill of her wet tunic on his skin, he would have held her until she forced him to release her.

He swallowed, taking in the tree. If he'd not pulled her aside, Coronis would be dead—pinned beneath the tree. His chest felt heavy, weighted by a most crushing pressure. The feel of her, trembling against him, was the greatest comfort. He drew in a deep breath, running his hands along her arms. "You are cold," he murmured, his nose brushing her ear.

She shivered, pulling from his embrace. She glanced at the tree, the realization of what might have happened clear upon her pale features. She stared up at him with a face so conflicted he would draw her close once more. Instead she ran from him, toward the safety of her father's house.

"You stand here, dripping wet, longing for that?" Poseidon waved the storms back.

"I wondered if you'd a hand in this." Apollo smiled. "What brings you to Delphi? To rain upon my games?"

"Boredom." Poseidon grinned. "I am besieged by wailing women. First Demeter, then Daphne."

"Daphne?" Apollo frowned. The two, together, could be troublesome.

"She is most distraught at having lost you to another. And your... plight as a result of this mortal." Poseidon stared after Coronis. "After seeing the mortal, I wonder at the fascination?"

"So you bring a storm?" Apollo clarified.

Poseidon shook his head, pointing at the fallen tree. He laughed, his pale blue gaze meeting his. "The storm had a purpose." He shrugged. "You were too quick."

Apollo stared at Poseidon. He was the reason Coronis faced danger? And for what—to pacify a nymph? Coronis life was no toy... But he could not speak. The roar of fury in his ears drowned out whatever Poseidon was saying. Apollo struck out, his fist catching Poseidon solidly in the jaw and knocking him flat in the mud at his feet. Poseidon was too stunned to react when Apollo straddled his kin, content to pummel Poseidon's face into a bloody pulp. Even after Poseidon lay still, his blood mixing with the mud beneath them, Apollo continued his attack.

"Apollo," Hermes was there then, pulling him off of an unmoving Poseidon. "He is done."

"He may be, but I am not," his voice shook, the depths of his anger beyond his control. "Take him from this place."

Hermes sighed. "Calm..."

"Hold your tongue, Hermes," he warned. He flexed his hands, drawing air deep into his lungs.

"It is Poseidon's nature to seek out mischief—"

Apollo turned on Hermes, silencing his friend with a look. "His idea of mischief differs greatly from mine."

Hermes nodded. "What did he..."

Apollo shook his head. "I cannot speak of it or I will rip him apart." He looked at his brethren. Poseidon's features were bruised and battered, his face covered in blood. It was a small victory for Poseidon was a proud deity. "I begin to understand Hades abhorrence. And Athena."

Hermes frowned.

Apollo stooped, swinging Poseidon over his shoulder and setting off across the field.

"Where are you going?" Hermes followed.

"I would take him far from this place," he paused. "And from Coronis."

"I will take him, brother," Hermes spoke. "King Phlegys will look for you tonight. You've won all today, save archery. You are a champion and will be celebrated as such. Where should I put him?"

"I would throw him into the ocean," Apollo offered. "And aim for the rocks."

Hermes laughed. "I shall take him to Olympus."

Apollo nodded, dropping Poseidon on the ground. "Warn him not to return here... And never, ever, to seek her out again."

"I will," Hermes assured. "Go."

Apollo did not look upon Poseidon again, or Hermes. The fever in his blood unnerved him. He was not a vicious sort, or prone to fits of temper. But Poseidon's actions had set his blood boiling and his body thrumming for violence.

"Where is our champion?" Her father asked her, his face alight with good wine and company.

Coronis gaped at her father. "Why ask me?" Her eyes narrowed as she surveyed those gathered around her father's fires. "Seek Erato or Khloris for they've been doe-eyed and pink-cheeked since he arrived." All three were absent from her father's tent.

Her mother stared at her.

He'd saved her today, she knew that. She should be grateful for that. Yet her agitation ruled her and laced her words with venom. What did she care if mighty Apollo took Erato or Khloris or both to his tents? Perhaps such attentions would tire him, preventing any more of his self-inflated speeches or superior smiles.

"Daughter?" her father smiled, broadly.

"Let us send Ichthys instead," her mother's long fingers stroked the inside of her father's arm.

Her father leaned back in his chair, covering his wife's fingers with his hand. But his tawny gaze was fixed upon her, studying her.

"Hurry, Coronis, so our invitation is not too late."

She glared at her father as she rose. "If he'd wanted our company, he'd be there," she snapped, pointing to Hermes lounging comfortably atop a pile of furs directly across the great fire pit. "Doubtless drinking your wine and speaking too loudly."

Her father attempted to hide his laughter with feigned laughter, causing her to scowl all the more. "Go, entreat our guest to join us, Coronis," he was still amused, though his words were not a request.

"Coronis," her mother warned. "Your father bids it."

She could argue. She longed to argue. The idea of fetching Apollo, of entreating him to join her family, chafed at her. But that would hardly change the outcome. Her father asked so little of her she could hardly refuse him.

With a sigh that left no doubt of her displeasure, she swept from her father's tent to the celebrations outside.

The cool night rumbled with the swell of music, laughter, and overlapping voices from the hundreds gathered for the games.

She nodded, returning the smiling well-wishes and "Kalispera" she received on her way through the tented settlement surrounding her father's temporary dwelling. Her frown was lessened by the music, the songs of joy, and the squeals of delight by those dancing together. It was too fine a night to let one mortal man affect her. True, he was a conceited oaf—too pretty to be blessed with the physical prowess the Gods had seen fit to grant upon him. But watching him made it impossible to deny, he was, indeed, named well.

She turned, glancing up at the stars overhead. In two days, the games and all gathered would be gone. And she'd remain inside the walls of her father's house—a well-appointed cage. If not her father's house, then Ichthys', no doubt. She fought against the ache in her chest. As much as her father loved her, he knew she needed to marry... To carry on his family basileus and to ensure the protection of the people he ruled. She was not ready.

Her gaze wandered to Apollo's tent, at the edge of the encampment. To be free like Apollo, like any man, she supposed. Such a freedom she would never know.

Laughter spilled out into the night, feminine and coy. Coronis froze, disappointment and anger warring within her.

She chose temper as victor.

Was it not custom for champions to spend even the briefest moments at her father's fire? Was it not customary to thank him, for the benevolent host he was? Apollo was a fool, but even he would know the way of it. He'd not even bothered to tie the tent shut. She could see... He was naked... And he was not alone. She swallowed.

He sat in a metal tub, one leg dangling over the side. He was talking, of course. The man seemed to think his every word a gift from the Gods. Erato, who was on her knees washing his foot, laughed as if she agreed. Stupid cow.

Khloris appeared then, pouring water over his shoulders from a large earthen jug. He sighed, shivering slightly, as Khloris set the jug aside and began to scrub his neck and shoulders. Her pale fingers clasped a thin rag against his gilded skin, sliding it over the impressive curve of his shoulder.

Coronis swallowed again, her hands fisting inexplicably.

He looked at her then, startled. But instead of looking ashamed, his brows rose, his lips curved in that smug grin, and he waited.

She wanted to yell. She wanted to hit him, to slap that look from his all-too-handsome face... To demand his apology for putting his baser needs before the respect he owed her father. He should not sit, smug and waited-upon, when she'd been sent to fetch him. She was not a common servant. She was certainly better than the two *serving* him. Oh, how she longed to tear the cloth from Khloris' pudgy fingers and knock Erato aside...

She stopped then, stunned by rage twisting her insides.

She was a fool, too, to waste time expecting more from the likes of him. He may be named after Apollo, but was a man. An irreverent, lustful, peacock of a man...

She cocked a brow in return, not bothering to hide her disdain as she spoke. "I will inform my father that you're too busy for his company this evening."

Erato gasped, Apollo's foot sliding from her hands, while Khloris dropped the rag in the dirt at her feet. With mumbled apologies, they both hurried from the tent, scurrying past Coronis into the night.

He dared laugh. "Stay, awhile, fair Coronis. These maids were simply attempting to make me fit to visit your father's home."

"I fear it would take far more than a... bath to make you fit company for my father."

Apollo stood, still smiling. "You would win any contest of words, Coronis." She refused to look at the heavily muscled thigh or the angular plane of his stomach. "Your tongue is lethal, sharp and ready."

She pressed her lips together, then. He goaded her, as if he gleaned some sort of satisfaction from her ire. If he gained some sort of pleasure from it, she would not give it to him. Apollo wrapped his chiton about his lean hips before looking at her again.

A drop of water ran down his throat, slowly trailing the contour of his chest—tracing each chiseled edge of muscle that lined his stomach. When the water disappeared beneath the cloth at his waist, she could scarce breath. And when her gaze met his she was near singed by the heat in his glorious eyes.

He was a fine specimen of a man, of that, there was no denying. That was why she stared... but no more. "I will tell my father," she murmured, breaking the hold his molten gaze had upon her to hurry back to her father's tent.

She stopped, not two tents away, furious once more. She would not run back to her father because she'd found his body worth admiring. Was not a fine painting worth study? Or a lovely piece of music in need of an audience? She admired his form, the gift the Gods had given him. For that, she would not be ashamed.

"Coronis?" Thick hands gripped her upper arms, pulling her against a wall of muscle. The smell of wine and sweat, soil and stink, filled her nostrils.

"Damocles," she muttered, pushing against his chest. "You've enjoyed Dionysis' vine a great deal this night."

His hands did not release her. "It is my right to celebrate the games. And the blessings Apollo has bestowed on us all."

"Then Kalispera to you, Damocles-"

"Have a cup with me," his voice was a low growl. One massive hand slipped from her shoulder to cup her cheek. "Please."

She stilled. One glance at the set of his jaw and the flare of his nostrils. He was not asking. "My father..."

"Has guests," he finished. "You shall be mine." He gripped her forearm in his fist, leading her to his tent.

Damocles had always been a brute, but it had been years since he'd dared exert his strength over her. If he'd not wreaked of drink, she might have reason to fear. As it was, she relished the challenge he gave her. Perhaps putting Damocles in his place would alleviate some of her frustration over Apollo. Her stomach tightened, images of Khloris' hand roaming over Apollo's shoulder taunting her. Her temper flared, hot and welcome. She dug in her heels, using all her weight, all her strength to stop the giant. She roared, "Damocles you forget who I am..."

He yanked her against him, his hands bruising her shoulders. His mouth pushed, his teeth nipping her lip and prying her mouth wide. She yelled, but his hand grabbed the nape of her neck, holding her in place. She slapped him with all her might, but his head scarce bounced. She kicked out, but his knee slipped between her legs, one hand gripping her buttock as his tongue invaded her mouth. She gagged, her bile rising as his tongue stroked hers. She fought, struggling in his arms, yet his grip tightened and her anger waned... replaced with something akin to fear.

No. Apollo...

A crash. A grunt. And she was free. Falling to the ground, but free.

Damocles lay, motionless, at her side. She shook her head, vaguely aware of the shattered bits of a large earthen jug about Damocles' head.

She blinked, stunned.

"You should have waited." Apollo crouched beside her, his gaze traveling over her face, searching, assessing.

She looked at him, unable to speak, to think. He'd saved her from the worst debasement... Damocles... What had near happened, she shook her head, shuddering and horrified. Her arms, her shoulders, the echo of Damocles' touch was hot on her skin. She rubbed her arms and neck, near chafing the skin to remove the lingering sensation, then stilled.

Apollo watched her. And on his face she saw the undisguised rage and disgust that churned within her. His jaw clenched. His nostrils flared. And when his gaze fell to her mouth, his chest shook as if his lungs failed him.

He stood suddenly, offering her his hand. Yet she sat, staring at his hand, disoriented by what had come to pass and his reaction.

"Coronis," his voice was low, husky and entreating.

She stared up at him. Whatever emotion had gripped him but moments before were gone. His brow was lifted, the hint of a teasing smile upon his lips. And in his gaze she saw only comfort, safety, and warmth. She took his hand, shivering as his fingers closed around hers. He pulled her to her feet, holding her hand only long enough to ensure she was steady. Once he'd released her, she flexed her fingers... seeking...something. The night air felt frigid.

With a sigh, Apollo regarded Damocles still form. His hands fisted briefly before he drew in a deep breath. "You owe me a jug." He nudged the broken pottery with his toe.

"I... You..." She sputtered. "I... A jug?" He thought of his pottery? Now? What of her well-being?

He nodded, looking at her. "You are most welcome."

"What?" she cried, outraged anew. He was the most... exasperating man. "I-I am?"

"Or was this a rendezvous?" He was smiling broadly now, his hand on his hips. "Is he," he glanced at Damocles with pure contempt, "...your lover?"

She wiped her mouth with the back of her hand, wishing she could cleanse the feel and taste of Damocles from her. "No."

"So the kiss? It was not given freely? It would pain me to know I've parted two lovers."

She spat on the ground, wishing she'd been the one to bring Damocles to heel. "No." Bile burned the back of her throat, bitter and hot. "No."

"Here." He offered her the wine-skin at his waist.

Coronis glared at him, snatching the skin from him and gulping down mouthfuls of the sweet, rich drink inside. It helped, some.

"It angers you that I saved you?" He was astounded, she could hear it in his voice. "Again."

"I did not ask for your assistance," she argued, refusing to answer his question.

"You needed it," he countered.

"I did not." She shot back.

He frowned then, shaking his head.

"Do not stand there, shaking your head at me," she yelled. "You... you..." she sputtered.

His smile returned, albeit reluctantly. "I have offended you."

She paused, thinking about his words. He'd done nothing wrong. Her reaction made no sense. If it had been another woman he'd defended, she'd have praised him for his actions. So why did it gall her, outrage her, that he'd done the same for her. If he had not, doubtless she'd be fighting Damocles in his tent even now. Taking a deep breath, she looked at him. As difficult as it was to admit he'd done her a service, she must. She need say nothing more than thank you.

"If I'd known Eratos and Khloris presence would affect you so, I never would have accepted their offer to help me bathe." His brows rose. "Did your father send you, I wonder. Or were you seeking a private audience with Damocles and are too reluctant to admit it?"

He mocked her.

"My father requested your presence. Why, I have no notion." Her anger choked her, she could barely speak. Her anger erased all thought of praise or consideration. If his words had not stung so, the absolute delight on his features would have. She clenched her fists, ignoring the need to strike him. She would not, could not, lower herself in such a way. Instead she stepped forward, ignoring the tremble in her body and voice as she spoke. "I have never asked for your aid." She paused, drawing in another breath. "Do you hear me?"

He nodded, his eyes narrowing and his smile waning. "I do."

"Then know this. I vow you will *never* hear such a request from my lips." Her added, "Ever," was a strangled hiss. Without another look, she marched back to her fathers, uncaring if he followed or not.

Chapter Five

She was the most magnificent creature he'd ever seen. He heard her words and knew she meant them. She would not have thanked him for sympathy, she was too proud for that, no matter how he longed to comfort her. The bastards attack had rattled her, for good reason. She prided herself on being capable and strong, yet she was no match for Damocles. Better to rouse her spirit with taunting than to see her wounded by the brute. And while it grieved him to know she reviled him so, he was proud of the strength and conviction she carried.

He followed her to her father's tent, though it took him time to shake hands and accept the congratulations of those that had seen him crowned victor of the games. In truth, his attention wandered, seeking her out in the sea of faces... Assuring himself she was safe. He needed her safe. First Poseidon. Then Damocles. He swallowed.

He'd not expected Damocles to act so. True, the man was more muscle than wit but his actions were those of madman—or a man overcome with drink. When her prayer reached him, the anger Poseidon had unleashed rose once more. If she'd not been present, Damocles would have suffered severely.

He watched her slip into her father's massive tent and considered turning around. He was too quick to anger this evening. Was it wiser to risk offending Phlegys by staying away? Or to hope the night's entertainment might distract him?

In time, he made his way inside Phlegys' tent. He would honor the king, as was right, for Phlegys was a good man. It was stifling inside, crowded with revelers chatting about the games past and the races set for tomorrow. When he spied Hermes, he joined him, sitting at his side and drinking deep from the cup of rich wine he was offered. Hermes placed a tray laden with succulent lamb, nuts, fruit, and sweet honey cakes between them.

"More wine?" Hermes offered.

Apollo shook his head, leaning back on the furs to rest on his elbow. Try as he might, he could not keep his gaze from searching out Coronis. He should have stayed with Khloris and Eratos. But then, who would have stopped Damocles. He sighed, popping a fig into his mouth.

Hermes nodded. "You still seem ill at ease, brother."

Apollo glanced at his friend, sighing. "I am."

A peal of laughter, free and lively, drew his attention to Coronis once more. Her skin was golden in the firelight. The flames moved over her, caressing her curves in a most distracting way.

"Apollo," Hermes glanced at Coronis as he spoke. "Do not act rashly. That is all I ask. She is a proud woman."

"She is," he agreed. *Proud, strong, beautiful, and loyal...*

He glanced at the cup in his hand, heeding Hermes warning. The games had offered him the challenge he sought. Even losing to Coronis had been sweet, for the smile upon her face had been more thrilling than any victory he'd experienced.

Her happiness pleased him so. Her happiness made him satisfied.

He glanced at her then. She was listening to Ichthys, her face animated. Why did he hunger for her to look at him so? He did. He wanted her, carefree and laughing, to himself.

He swallowed, his vision wavering with prophecy.

A boy, laughing and strong, was running along the cliffs. Apollo called to the boy and grabbed him up, carrying him in his arms. He was a solid child... and he had his mother's amber eyes and blinding smile.

"Apollo?" Hermes nudged him.

Apollo sat forward, his breathing hard and fast. He knew this boy. His heart thundered, so full of love and hope... The boy was his son. He knew it.

Apollo let himself stare at her then. His visions promised nothing. Yet he knew she was his. He would have her, he would love her... No... He did love her. As new an emotion as it was, he recognized what it was and welcomed its power. All would be well.

A son, a boy he knew already. Their son would do great things.

Her eyes met his. She did not shy from him, though he sensed her agitation. He could not stop his smile for it was from his heart.

Her eyes widened, startled perhaps. She swallowed, her skin flushing as his gaze held hers.

"Apollo," Phlegys summoned him, breaking the spell that gripped them and demanding his attention. "You are a mighty competitor."

"Do not encourage his ego, my King," Hermes said. "For it is a sizable thing already."

Phlegys laughed. "He has earned such praise."

"More time on the archery range would see him champion all events." Coronis spoke, laughter in her voice. "I would be honored to help?"

"Coronis... Yours was an impressive display, to be sure." Phlegys shook his head, laughing at his daughter. And yet, Apollo saw the proud smile upon his face. "You do honor to the very Olympian you're named for, Apollo. Archery aside." He nodded at his daughter again.

Apollo smiled, savoring her enjoyment.

"You wear the laurel wreath well. I have no doubt this is not your first crown?" Queen Talousa asked.

Apollo shook his head, ignoring Hermes laughter. "No, my Queen. It is not."

"Tell me, then," Phlegys asked, "what would you wish to receive, in place of laurels?"

He felt eyes upon him. Ichthys, Phlegys, Hermes—all those seated around the King's fire. But it was Coronis that drew his attention once more. One fine brow was arched, waiting for his answer. He suspected she would have an eager retort, something sharp and cutting, but he could not stop the words.

"Your daughter is the finest prize a man could hope for, my king." His eyes held hers as he took a sip of wine.

He was not surprised by the quiet that followed. Nor was he

surprised by the outrage on Coronis' face as she stood, scowling at him.

Phlegys was amused. "She is not a prize, Apollo. She is a woman."

"Yes. I've noticed that." Apollo nodded.

"She will be wed when she chooses," Phlegys continued. "To a man worthy."

"You are a rare father to give her a choice. Most fathers would use such a prize to barter for gain." Apollo saw her mouth fall open and her eyes narrow to slits.

"I have no need to barter. I have everything I want. She is *my* most prized possession. I would not dare to sacrifice her to a man I did not know." He paused, regarding him carefully. "A man that might be unworthy."

Apollo tore his gaze from her and turned to Phlegys. "I drink to you, King Phlegys. You are a worthy leader of men and a wise father." With that, Apollo raised his cup.

Coronis would have preferred to leave. Her victory was a dim memory compared to this evening's events. After Apollo's toast, she'd lingered at her mother's side, smiling when needed but saying little.

"Coronis?" Her mother squeezed her hand. "You seem… distant this evening, when you should be celebrating."

She forced a smile to her lips. Her mother would grow distraught over Damocles. And furious over Apollo's insolence. Or worse, feel indebted to Apollo. No, she'd rather the rest of the night was uneventful. She was quick to reassure her. "I am well. Content."

Her mother's brow dipped. "Content? That is a word I've never heard from you before." She shook her head. "Truly, I grow concerned."

Coronis laughed. "I sought to soothe you."

"Well, stop it." Her mother frowned. "I know your spirit too well. You are of high spirits or low spirits, but rarely in-between. I would hear what has affected my headstrong daughter."

"Damocles," she confessed, but offered no more.

Her mother nodded, searching the crowd. "I fear he grows

bolder with age. He wants to reign—and you are his means to accomplish that."

Coronis nodded, remembering his threat of war all too well. "Advise me, then."

"Marry." Her mother's smile was small.

"You cannot want me to join with that man?" She blinked, horrified. "Would he take care of Delphi, Apollo's Temple, and our people as Father has?"

"No, no," her mother patted her arm. "Not Damocles. But someone. I know you balk at such talk, but if you were to find a husband now, he would have many years to learn from your father—to become a good king and husband." She nodded at several guests as they moved slowly around the tent.

Who then? She knew her mother favored Ichthys. It was because she loved him so that she could not marry him. How could she explain that to her mother? Who else was there?

Her mother paused in front of Apollo and Hermes. "My husband says you are of Athens? Do you have family in the great white city?"

Coronis scarcely acknowledged Apollo as he stood before her mother. Hermes, however, received her warmest smile.

"I do. My father is a councilman," Hermes offered. "While Apollo has a vast holding in the country surrounding."

"Fertile land, heavy with olives and lavender." Apollo paused. "The Gods have also granted us a mighty flock of sheep."

"You are blessed by the Gods, indeed." Her mother was impressed.

"Even if we are burdened with such names," Apollo spoke, his deep voice beckoning her.

She frowned, unable to refuse his baiting. "You have earned it, Apollo." Her gaze locked with his, drifting in his golden eyes... until thoughts of Eratos and Khloris and Damocles made her frown and tense once more.

"While I have yet to earn mine?" Hermes laughed.

She laughed too, pleased to find some distraction from Apollo. She must be mindful of her behavior with her mother's shrewd gaze upon them.

"Are the games for glory alone? Or do you seek wives as well?" her mother asked, forcing Coronis to regard her mother with new eyes. Was her mother seeking new suitors for her?

"Is a wife not her husband's glory?" Hermes offered.

Her mother smiled. "If he is a good husband, yes."

"Yours seems the best of husbands." Apollo nodded in the direction of her father.

"He is," her mother agreed. "And the best of fathers."

Coronis nodded, smiling at her father. He was an uncommon man, she'd known that from the start. His temper was slow to rise, his mind quick, and his word unwavering. He loved her and her mother openly, loudly, and with great relish.

"Those seeking wives would do well to learn from him." Her mother nodded before leading her away from them.

Coronis held her tongue until they were once more seated by the fire pits, at her father's side. "That was a most direct conversation, Mother."

"Was it?" she asked. "I have yet to meet a man who does not need guidance."

"You cannot mean *that* man?" Coronis frowned at her mother. "I have heeded your warnings about a man too proud. And a man too beautiful-"

"Because such a man does not hear." She nodded at her father— and Apollo making his way to her father. "But a man who hears, one who takes advice from those older and wiser, even with such an abundance of both pride and beauty, can be forgiven." She smiled.

"Can it?" Coronis murmured, grappling with her mother's approval of Apollo.

"Does such a man truly disappoint you?" her mother asked.

Disappointment was not the right word. He was pleasing—too pleasing—to look upon. His form and strength were equally as so. No, it was the way he looked at her, only her, that troubled her. He was too intense, too overwhelming. With a single glance, she felt unsteady and lost. Or angered, for her temper burned brighter than ever before when face with his teasing condescension. "He is... he is infuriating."

Her mother's brows rose. "Is he?"

She shook her head, turning from her mother.

"What has he done to rouse such passion this evening?"

If her mother was so insistent, she would gladly tell her what sort of man Apollo was. "I found him in his bath earlier this evening. Khloris and Eratos were both... attending to him."

Her mother laughed.

"Mother," Coronis hissed, her frustration mounting.

"He is a man, Coronis," her mother scolded her. "Unmarried, with no intended. A truly handsome man. I'm hardly surprised that either would wish some time with him." She paused. "I am, however, greatly surprised that such a thing affected you... so powerfully."

Coronis crossed her arms over her chest, scowling first at her mother, then at the man in question.

"It angered you?" her mother asked. "To see him with these women?"

Yes, she was. It angered her that he could draw her to him, protect her, to speak with such tenderness that her heart ached to stay in his arms... Only to find him enjoying Khloris and Eratos touch hours later. Why had he not come after her... She stiffened. Such thoughts were most troubling.

"Coronis?" her mother probed.

She shook her head. "No. It angered me that Father waited and I was subject to such a display."

"It was only a bath?" her mother asked, studying Apollo.

"Yes." Though the memory of Khloris eager hands upon his broad chest made something hot and hard settle in the pit of her stomach.

Her mother's smile was far too amused for her liking. In truth, she would retire—escape the crowds and warmth of the night to clear her mind and cool her temper. It was not to be. While she did her duty exchanging pleasantries with those come to give their respects to the keeper of Delphi—Apollo stayed at her father's side. He laughed and talked with an ease that both impressed and further galled her. Her mother seemed most pleased by this turn of events.

By the time she retired, she was most dismayed.

Sleep was elusive, taunting her then plaguing her with a tangle of troubling images and fears. Apollo was there, holding her close and smiling down upon her. She basked in his love and knew it to be true. She felt such happiness... Then such grief. Apollo was frantically searching for her—calling out her name. Try as she might, she could not answer him. But she wanted to. She woke, trembling. Balek's great head lay on her stomach, his whimpers no doubt what roused her. She stroked his ear, drawing in deep steadying breaths. "A bad dream, nothing more," she whispered.

It was all too easy to imagine Apollo's face smiling upon her. His arms holding her close. It was a most pleasing thought—one that warmed her. Balek yawned and rolled over, his tongue flopping from his mouth as he closed his eyes. She smiled, rubbing his stomach as she stared through the large window. The sky was streaked with the rising sun, the chirp of birds welcoming it to its place in the sky.

Today the chariot races took place. The crowds would grow, for they were a favorite event for many. Perhaps it was the thrill of the race, the chance of danger heightening the stakes? Many who stood no chance at victory with discus, javelin, bow, wrestling, or the more aggressive pankration would race for a laurel leaf or olive branch.

The horses were another matter. Coronis loved their majestic beauty. The coupling of grace and strength was something she appreciated above all else. And there would be much to see today. Some names she knew, while others dared to make their first run at the games. Even Damocles boasted of his new team and the lightness of his chariot. And, of course, Apollo would race. She sighed, puzzling over her dream and the impact it had upon her. There was denying it, or the mix of emotions that pressed upon her heart and mind when she thought of him. Apollo. She sighed again, shaking her head.

Once the games were over, Delphi would empty. Apollo would leave.

She sat heavily, running her hand along down Balek's head when he pushed under her hand—whimpering. "Shh, Balek, all is well," she soothed.

Pina must have heard them for she arrived with a comb and clothing. On this day she would sit beside her mother and father, bedecked in fine robes of white, yellow, and gold—to honor Apollo and his own fiery chariot.

But today was something more. As winner of the archery contest, she would fire the ceremonial arrow that started the chariot races. It was a great honor, something she'd dreamed of since she'd fired her first arrow.

Perhaps that was why Pina took care to make her braids more elaborate, winding gold threads and yellow ribbons throughout. When that was done, Pina placed a large beaten gold necklace about her throat. Today Coronis was not just Delphi's princess, she was favored by Apollo himself. The old woman stepped back, smiling her approval.

"Will Damocles win today?" she asked Pina.

Pina shook her head emphatically, hearing all.

"Will Favros?" He was the favored one.

Pina shook her head again, pointing out the window at the sun. A smile lined her well-wrinkled face.

"Apollo?" Coronis asked.

Pina nodded.

She frowned. "Has he won all other events?"

Pina nodded.

"All save one," she could not keep the satisfaction from her voice. Her victory was all the sweeter knowing she was the only one to defeat him.

Pina patted her cheek, bobbing her eyebrows playfully.

"You think him handsome?"

Pina's eyes went wide, nodding emphatically.

Coronis sighed. "Yes, yes, I know."

Pina patted her cheek again, frowning.

"Do not fret, Pina," she spoke softly. "I agree, he is a fine champion." She said no more but went in search of her parents. The procession of the chariots would begin shortly and she'd yet to have her breakfast.

Chapter Six

Apollo stood in his chariot, assessing the field. At least a dozen chariots stood ready, the sound of stomping of hooves, impatient snorts, and the snap of reigns drowning out all else. Anticipation filled the air, thrumming in the blood of both man and beast.

All turned to watch Coronis, radiant in her finery, take her place on the platform. She lifted her arrow, waiting as it was set aflame, and aimed for the large ring that sat atop the arena's edge. The ring represented the sun, her flaming arrow the light he shed upon the mortals that were devoted to him. While all else watched the path of her arrow, his gaze remained fixed upon her. The roar of the crowd assured she'd done her job, as did the joy of her unfettered smile. Such elation left him breathless.

He blinked, the scene surrounding him fading as divination descended upon him. It was Coronis... but not as she was now. Tears streamed down her face as she ran, her hair flying out behind her and her tunic hanging from her bare shoulders. She stopped, looking back over her shoulder but whatever she saw forced her on, gasping for breath and frantic. She stumbled, falling to her knees and calling out. "Please, no, I beg of you..." she sobbed before calling out his name. His name. Just as quickly she faded, leaving him once more in his chariot, surrounded by the people of Delphi and the sounds of their excitement.

"Apollo," Hermes voice reached him. "Beware, Pyrios looks ready to take a chunk out of your competitor."

Apollo slapped the reigns on his horse's flanks, absentmindedly, overcome with the images that played out before him. Coronis. Begging for mercy. From who? It was his name she'd called out... Would he do this to her? Fear gripped him then. That such a thing was possible—that he might be to blame. No, surely not... Then who? He was trembling.

"What is it?" Hermes asked. "What did you see?"

Apollo stared blindly across the arena, seeking out Coronis as she returned to her parents. His hands twisted in the reins, cutting the palms of his flesh.

She sat at her father's side—well, whole, and smiling. The urge to go to her, to feel her warm and solid in his arms, gripped him. He would never hurt her, to think of such a thing injured him deeply. His gaze pinned hers, silently demanding she look at him—such was his need for reassurance.

She did, her brow furrowing as she regarded him. She shifted in her seat before standing. She crossed the covered platform that housed Phlegyas and his guest, her hands gripping the balcony as her gaze searched his face. He should not stare, openly. But it was necessary to ease his soul. Dread weighed heavily upon him—and helplessness. He could not look away or ease his grip upon the reigns. It was too much to bear, seeing her now yet fearing what was to come.

"Apollo?" Hermes was at his side. "What ails you, Brother?"

The horn blew, bringing those in the first contest forward.

"Apollo?" The urgency in Hermes' tone was sharp. "Can you ride?"

Apollo nodded, forcing air into his aching lungs.

King Phlegys called Coronis, severing the hold her gaze had upon him. Still, he watched her move to her father's side, saw the redness bloom in her cheeks as her father spoke to her. It was only when she regarded him again, rigid with hostility, that Apollo could breathe once more. To see her strong and rebellious offered him comfort.

How could he see his son and know him as such? And then see Coronis suffer so? What could two so differing visions mean? That he would have her, with or without her consent? He swallowed against the self-loathing that roiled in his stomach. Her pain was not to be born. No, no. This would not come to pass. He must remember this was a vision of what *might* be. He would do whatever was needed to change it.

He tore his gaze from hers, drawing in a deep breath. King Phlegys and his Queen Talousa regarded him closely, concerned perhaps. He bowed low, knowing that hardly excused his behavior.

With a slight shift of his reins, his team stood on the line. The anticipation he'd felt this morning had vanished, replaced by this almost crippling fear. It no longer mattered that he rode against Damocles and his blacks, a boy with a promising team, and Favros with his champions. His heart was not here. But his team was ready and eager, pulling against their reins with tossing heads and pawing hooves. If nothing else, they demanded his steady hand.

When the horn sounded again, they tore ahead.

Damocles team surged, the blacks' wild eyed as they passed them on the track.

Apollo let them go. He might be a God, but his animals were not. Immortal, yes. But they had no more power than any other horse. He would not see them tire early when they hungered to win.

Another chariot flew past—the driver's face young and eager.

Favros, Phlegyas' champion, waited, his team keeping pace with his own.

At the turn, the boy lost control. His chariot slid across the packed dirt, making a bone-shuddering impact against the stone walls of the arena. The wheels bounced, landing on the rim, before pitching the basket of the chariot to the side. The boy sat, bloodied and disoriented by the wreckage before collapsing in a heap.

Apollo and Favros exchanged a glance. It was not uncommon to lose several riders, especially those with little to no experience. Fast horses did not ensure a win. No, patience, control, and trust between master and beasts were needed. Hopefully this boy would live to learn from his mistakes today.

The final lap was upon them, and both he and Favros loosened the grip on their team. It was only then that Apollo realized his hands dripped with blood. His palms were cut deeply from his hold upon the fine leather. It mattered little, he would heal.

His team matched Damocles', making the giant fool tighten his grip on the reigns until Apollo feared for his horses' mouths. He frowned at the mortal, but did not slow his team. Pyrios had found his stride and would lead the others home.

Through the cloud of dust, Favros matched him, and the two raced toward the victory line. But at the last Favros' chariot faltered, his left wheel tilting at an odd angle before sliding from its' spoke. The basket of the chariot hit the ground, while Favros clung to the reigns.

Pyrios threw his head, as if demanding more from Lampos, Actaeon, and Phlegon. Together, the four horses led, running with a determination he could not inspire. Damocles continued to whip his horses, but he lagged. Apollo's victory was swift, leaving Damocles stunned and the people of Delphi cheering.

His gaze searched until they found her. The delight on her face was all the prize he needed. He would hold on to this, her beauty and strength. He would etch the curve of her smile and the grace of her body into his mind so that he could leave her.

Coronis stood, rigid with anticipation, her gaze searching the crowd. The races were over, the victor crowned. Watching her father place the final laurel wreath upon Apollo's head left an ache in her chest she was unfamiliar with. He would come for her, she knew it. He would ask for her hand and her parents would expect her to accept. This beautiful, proud, passionate man wanted her— his behavior today left little doubt. Surprisingly, such a notion did not displease her.

Perhaps it was her dream or the weight of his gaze upon her, but she felt changed. His eyes had beckoned her, holding her as if his arms bound her tightly to him. In the depths of his golden gaze, she felt warmth… and so much more. Affection, respect, appreciation and hunger. And alarm… True concern. For what? What troubled him, she knew not. But she would find out, so she might comfort him. The desire to comfort him was both troubling and exciting.

And yet the thought of being bound to such a man terrified her. How could a man with such appetites be satisfied with one woman? Did she dare to wonder what sort of husband he would be? What sort of King? Would he be a gracious ruler, loyal and just, wise and patient? Would he love her? And could she love him…

"What do you seek, daughter?" her mother asked.

Coronis jumped, so engrossed in her search that she'd almost forgotten the presence of her parents. "No one."

"No *one*?" her mother repeated. "Then you may accompany me to the house. Tonight all of Delphi will descend upon us."

Once more, she searched those milling about them but there was no sign of Apollo. Disappointment pricked sharply, surprising her. It was unlike her, to be so erratic. But the crowds seemed naught but noise and distraction. She needed a moment to pray and reflect upon this unexpected turn of events. When her father joined them, she asked, "May I go to the temple first?"

Her mother's hand cradled her cheek. "You seek guidance from Apollo?"

She nodded. It would be wise to focus on her God, and not the mortal.

A slight furrow creased her mother's brow. "Are you well, daughter? My counsel may not be as all knowing as Apollo, but I offer my wisdom to you if you would have it."

"I will come to your chambers when I'm finished with my prayers." She hugged her mother. "Come Balek," she called the dog to her side.

"Home," her father spoke, "before the sun is gone. Tonight I would have you close to me. If you've more to say to our Olympian than time allows, I shall escort you to the Temple in the morning."

She smiled. "Yes father."

Balek led the way, head held high and ears alert. He had no qualms baring his teeth to anyone that stood too long in her path. Perhaps he sensed her restlessness and sought to please her. Whatever the reason, they reached the hilltop and Apollo's temple in short time.

"Welcome," Apollo's high-priest greeted her. "Your visit is an unexpected treat, Princess."

"I would offer thanks to Apollo for the games. And the safekeeping for those that participated." Favros' had broken his leg and arm—minor when compared to the two lives lost this day. She smiled, commanding Balek wait upon the steps before adding, "After all the chaos, the peace of the Temple is a welcome relief."

"You are loyal to our Apollo." The priest led her inside. "He will smile down on you."

Once she was alone, she drew in a deep breath. The night sky was clear, sparkling with the brilliance of an endless cast of stars. Through the glistening white columns of the temple, a cool breeze carried the sounds of the comings and goings outside. The last feast was a bittersweet time. After a week of time spent forging or strengthening alliances and friendships, parting was difficult. Four years changed much.

She stared at the temple dais, alight with long white tapers reflected on a golden mirror. Through the main antechamber was the Oracle's chamber. A chamber empty until the games were over. But she had no need of the Oracle.

She knelt on the marble floor, staring up at the frieze of Apollo and his mighty chariot above the dais.

"Apollo, hear me," she murmured. She would not speak her prayers aloud, Apollo would hear them. "I give you thanks for the games, for the victories were many with few injuries to speak of. I give you thanks for my father, for his kind goodness serves your people well—and makes me proud to be his daughter." She took her time, offering praise over her mother, her station, her gift with the bow, and her blessed life before pausing. She continued silently, the only sound in the Temple the hiss of the torches and faint crackle of the tapers wicks aflame. "Your counsel is needed... I implore you... Guide me, show me my path." Her eyes lingered on the chariot as she searched for the right words. "It is a daughter's duty to marry well, to increase her family's basileus, to provide heirs... And while I am a daughter, I fear my skills at being a woman often fail me. Perhaps I should turn to Hera, but my life's devotion has been to you." She stared around her, taking in the bountiful offerings. "A man has come to these games, a man you would be pleased by—I think. He stirs something within my breast, something that frightens me. He frightens me, though I'd never admit it. Not for the breadth of his chest or strength of his arms, though that is truly impressive. But by the way he... consumes me with his gaze. I fear I could be swallowed alive in him and forget who I am." She blinked, the sting in her eyes startling her. "Worse yet, I do not think I would mind if such a thing happened." She shook her head. "If this is your will, I give myself over to it. If it is your will."

Her prayers were done yet she stayed, grappling with the truths she'd spoken. Apollo would show her, her faith in the God of Light would not fade now. She must resist her own erratic bouts of temper and... awareness. She must be prepared for what her Olympian would want.

The shadows stretched far across the marble floor when she stood. She could stay no longer, indeed her prayers had given her a sense of expectation she'd not had when she arrived.

Balek greeted her with the thump of his long tail and a massive yawn.

She made her way through the encampment, smiling at those who greeted her. And with every step, her anticipation grew. He would be there this evening, celebrating his final victory. His golden eyes would seek her out, noting her whereabouts as she moved about the party. He would offer her his dazzling smile and arched brow when she looked upon him. Yet she knew his gaze was upon her even when she pretended his notice was of no consequence for the warmth of his steady gaze heated her skin.

Her mother greeted her, helping Pina change her garments. She listened to her mother chatter, excited by the return of their daily life. She found the games an exhausting event. Her mother was neither fond of crowds nor the attention the games brought to her family. But the love she bore her husband helped her endure both. Coronis raised her arms as they wrapped and tucked her finest tunic, woven with the softest lavender thread and trimmed in gold. When that was done, Pina unbraided her hair to cascade in gentle waves about her shoulders. Her mother placed her golden laurel crown atop her head and stood back.

"You are a vision," her mother sighed. Pina nodded, clasping her hands together. "Did your prayers ease your spirit? You seem less troubled."

Coronis smiled. "I suppose I am."

"I envy you the peace you find in Apollo's temple. You and your father. Does that make me less loyal? That I prefer to *do* than pray?"

"No mother. Not at all. For all that you do, you do to please Apollo and Olympus," she assured.

Her mother searched her face, stroking her hand upon her daughter's face. "You are a rare child, Coronis. So strong... so headstrong..." Her mother drew in a deep breath.

"Like your father?" Coronis asked-loving the stories of her long dead warrior-grandfather.

Her mother nodded. "Perhaps. Though you favor your father most." She cupped her face, pressing a kiss to her cheek. Coronis felt her mother's slight tremor as she drew her into a quick embrace. "Come then, our guests arrive." Her mother took her hand and led her into the inner courtyard. This house was large, meant for entertaining during the duration of the Pythian Games. It was also ornately furnished with detailed tapestries, shallow pools, and luxuriously covered reclining klines. If all the seating was taken, piles of pillows littered the floor. Father had spared no expense, bringing in musicians and entertainers as well as an impressive array of food and drink. There was no denying the guests' astonishment, or their gratitude. Her parents were most devoted hosts and considered their service to Apollo and his games of the most import.

"You look like you've descended from Olympus," Ichthys held her hands wide. "A nymph at the least. I have never seen you so... so womanly."

She frowned at him. "If that was flattery, I shudder to think of your insults."

He shook his head, appearing both mystified and admiring. "Forgive me, Coronis, I beg you. You caught me unawares, your appearance is so-"

"Lovely," Hermes interrupted, bowing deeply. Apollo was not at his side. "You may have stolen victory from those daring to compete against your bow, but tonight you've stolen the hearts of every man here."

Coronis could not stop the giggle that welled up inside her. She'd never had a man weave such a web of fawning on her behalf. "You go too far, Hermes. Your words are far too pretty to serve any purpose but to reveal your gift of prose. You forget there is no crown to be won here tonight."

"I need no crown." Hermes smiled. "Or meat or drink. This evening my eyes could feast upon you and be well satisfied."

She shook her head. "I would not see you starve on my account." She was all too relieved when her father appeared.

"Come, daughter," her father slipped her arm through his.

"Your mother seeks your company."

Apollo took the cup of wine offered, emptying it before King Phlegys and his daughter arrived. Perhaps he longed to delay the inevitable. Tonight would be the last time he looked upon the fair Coronis. No matter what argument Hermes offered, and there were many, Apollo's mind was made up. If Coronis faced danger, it would leave when he did.

"May I say that you've honored the very Olympian you're named for," Queen Talousa spoke to him.

He offered her a deep bow. "You honor me by saying so, oh Queen." His gaze lingered on the woman's face. There was little in the way of resemblance to Coronis. This woman was lovely, to be sure, but she had none of Coronis' confidence. Where Coronis' eyes flashed fire, Talousa was meek.

"Now that you've conquered all of Delphi, what will you do?" Talousa asked. "A man like you, from a good family, gifted with strength and a sharp mind, has an enviable future. And, undoubtedly, will need a fitting wife."

"I see only the return trip home, my queen." Did she hear the bitterness that laced his tone? If she did, her expression revealed nothing. Her surprise at his declaration, however, was clear.

"Home? Soon?" she asked, her eyes searching the room.

"Hermes and I depart at sunrise," he confirmed—wishing this night might last forever.

"Tomorrow?" Coronis' voice.

He hesitated, gathering all his control before he turned to face her. It was not enough.

She glowed, as if the Fates had gifted her with an aura to rival any of his Olympic brethren. The gold that adorned her head and throat further warmed her sun-kissed skin. Her brow was furrowed, her amber gaze intently searching his face. "You are done with Delphi?"

He swallowed, knowing what she meant and hating the words that slipped so easily from his mouth. "I am. The games are done." He could say no more.

If it was hurt that crossed her face, she masked it instantly.

Indeed, she would not look at him. "I wish you safe travels and the God's favor," she murmured the formal parting. "Father, Ichthys calls."

It was better if she put distance between them. He knew it. Yet the urge to pull her to him, to cradle her cheek and taste her lips fought his ever-crumbling control. He longed to shake her, to ignite the temper he'd come to admire so. To tell her who he was, that she belonged to him. To admit the need he felt for her made leaving unbearable—too unbearable to be parted this way... He stepped forward, staring down at her, knowing the memory of her as she was now would haunt him forever. Without thought, he clasped her hand in his. He'd no right, he knew as much. As did Talousa and Phlegys, yet none stopped him.

Yet the look of Coronis' sweet face gave him pause. Her face, tilted toward his. Her lips parted, cheeks blooming with color. Her gaze locked with his, searing his heart and challenging his resolution to leave her. Moments before her glorious gaze shone with fury, he'd seen something else. She stared at his hand—at him—with something akin to true longing. And the sight of that was more potent than anything else.

If not for Talousa's delicate cough, he would have forgot his purpose. "I bid you a most fond farewell, lady. May the Gods watch over you and keep you safe."

She opened her mouth but did not speak. Her fingers tightened around his hand for but an instant. Was this the only embrace he would have from her?

"Apollo?" It was Hermes. "You have won all but one game, it hardly seems fair that you would try to win the fair Coronis as well."

Apollo released her hand, bowing low before her. "I would not dare attempt such a thing. The lady deserves better."

Coronis eyes narrowed at his words. She thought he mocked her. Perhaps it was best that way, for her to think on him with nothing but scorn. He suspected she would not think on him much once he was gone. While she would haunt his every day. He smiled at her, savoring her beauty and the heat of her anger before she joined Ichthys.

"You've bested my champion and those from every corner of Greece," Phlegys spoke. "You've the wit of an educated man, and the manners as well."

Apollo said nothing, he was too fascinated by the rigid tension of her posture. And the line of her arm as she reached for an offered cup.

"Delphi is a land of plenty," Phelgys continued.

"Because you honor your God above most mortals," Apollo spoke with feeling. "In all my travels, I've seen few so devoted. Olympus rewards loyalty above all else, do they not? And so, the evidence of your loyalty is reflected in the Delphi's bounty."

Phlegys nodded but Talousa regarded him closely—too closely.

"Can we not persuade you to stay?" Phlegys asked.

"Perhaps we should not press him, husband." Talousa slid her arm through her husbands. "Perhaps it is the will of the Gods that he go."

Chapter Seven

"**K**ing Phlegys!" Damocles voice rang out, disturbing the quiet of their morning meal. "Oh King?"

Her father stood, sighing. "If only *he'd* left this morning."

Her father's words stirred unwanted images of Apollo. The man seemed to revel in her discomfort. One minute he seemed transfixed by the touch of her hand, the next he was quite satisfied to lounge on pillows surrounded by far too many willing, doe-eyed women. She didn't know which troubled her more: the tender warmth his touch inspired within her or the urge to slap him soundly when he laughed—loudly—over one of those languishing at his feet.

Damocles' yelled, "Mighty King of Delphi!" chased all thoughts of Apollo away. Instead, she was greeted with her mother's concerned expression. "Mother?"

"I'm sure it's fine." Yet she could not meet Coronis' eyes.

"What's happened?" Coronis asked.

"Did... Did you hit Damocles over the head with a vase?" her mother asked.

"Is that what he said?" She was surprised. Why would he let her take the blame for such an assault instead of Apollo?

"It is what's *being* said. Leave matters to your father, Coronis," her mother warned. "Damocles' temper needs little encouragement."

Coronis hesitated inside the doors of the house, finding no comfort in her father's smile as he went to greet Damocles on the steps of the house. She waited, a dreadful foreboding clenching her stomach.

"It's too early for an audience, Damocles," her father's voice was elevated.

"I come with a challenge," Damocles returned. "I will not stand by and have my name tarnished by your insolent daughter. It is time we put this matter to rest. I will marry your daughter and ally our people."

Coronis pulled open the doors, astounded by the man's disrespect. Her mother's distressed, "Coronis, no," was drowned by the hot thrum of angry blood in her ears.

At the sight of her, Damocles smiled. "Good morning, Princess," Damocles voice rang out, ensuring none misheard him. "I challenge you, Coronis. Since you insist on being treated as an equal, let us settle our... disputes as men. Pankration."

Coronis drew in a deep breath, her loathing hot and quick. Damn his pride. He goaded her, smugly, knowing she must yield. In front of... her gaze swept the gathered crowd. He'd left her no choice— her father no choice. If she resisted his challenge, her people would fight for her. If she accepted, she would lose to him and be forced to marry him. She could not win this. Yet every muscle tightened and anticipation coursed through her, eager for his challenge.

She would not bend to him. She stepped forward, even as her father sought to lay a restraining hand upon her forearm.

"You cannot accept, Coronis," her father hissed, standing at her side. "You will not." He turned, offering a placating smile to Damocles hulking form. "Damocles, such a jest-"

"It is no jest." Damocles shook his head once, smiling. He surveyed the crowd, all too pleased to be the center of attention.

She swallowed, surveying the crowd as well. *I must remain calm.* But oh, how she longed to strike the goading smile from his wretched face.

"My *daughter* cannot accept such a challenge, you know this." Her father's hand tightened upon her arm. She felt his slight tremor, and glanced at him. It was her temper, her pride, which caused worry to line his beloved face. When would she learn restraint? Obedience?

"Your champion, Favros, is too injured, King Phlegys. Will someone stand in his place?" He turned, assessing the men within his audience. He shrugged, then turned back to her father. "No?" He smiled, almost sympathetically. "Marriages are often arranged in such manner. It is past time for such a union to take place." His tone, already tinged with victory, sickened her. There was no hope for a peaceful resolution, she knew this.

Damocles sought vengeance... from her. He would see her utterly humiliated—defeated before all. Their marriage would guarantee both.

To defend her honor meant defying her father... Blasphemy. But to turn from Damocles challenge and succumb to him...Nausea roiled with her. She could not. She closed her eyes, praying earnestly. She drew in a deep breath, pouring her anguish into her silent plea. *Apollo, help me bring honor to my father, my family, and... to myself. I ask you... I beg of you... Help me.*

The noise of the crowd shifted, voices rising and falling, some excited, others angry. She opened her eyes.

The mortal Apollo stood before her father, golden and proud in the morning sun. "I offer my strength, in your champions' stead, my King."

She found it difficult to breathe. He was here, smiling his damn smile. Relief found her, swift and sure. He would leave with the dawn, he'd said. And his words tormented her. She'd never known a night so long. From panic to emptiness, knowing he was gone left her aching with too many emotions to name, let alone understand. When dawn found her, she was still tossing on her mat-denying the need to find him and bid him stay. Seeing him now filled her with... joy.

Then fear. For Damocles looked at him with murder in mind. She need not fear, he would certainly not thank her for it. He had the skill to defeat Damocles. While she found his arrogance insufferable, he was a champion. And she needed a champion.

My thanks, she prayed silently.

Apollo's eyes found her, gold–startling-as they fastened upon her. He winked. He *winked*. His lack of humility, of decorum, was exasperating. Whatever other emotions this man might inspire in her, frustration was constant. And yet, he was the only one that had come forward to defend her. No, not just her. He would defend her father, her people. And she was indebted to him. Such a realization was both unnerving and exciting. To accept his offer—what would he want in return?

His eyes swept over her, unmasked admiration crossing his handsome features. Apprehension knotted sharply in her stomach.

Her father's voice rang out, in answer to Damocles and Apollo alike. "Your offer is accepted, most heartily, Apollo."

Apollo nodded, clapping his hands and rubbing them together with childlike enthusiasm. She watched, enthralled in spite of herself. Was he not the slightest bit intimidated by Damocles? If so, she saw no sign of it. No, he smiled at Damocles, arching one golden eyebrow as he quipped, "The games were through before I'd had my fill. 'Tis a fitting way to end such celebrations, is it not, Damocles?" Was it wrong to find such confidence admirable? She did. She admired him far too much.

Damocles was far less impressed. His face was mottled and red with fury. Every muscle in his massive body was taut, coiled for battle. This would be no gentleman's match; that much was clear. And while she knew Apollo was stronger than most, she offered another prayer—suddenly desperate. *Give your namesake the strength to be victor this day.* She could not bear to belong to Damocles. Worse, she could not bear to lose Apollo.

She sucked in a wavering breath. It would be worse to lose this man. *Apollo.*

Damn her weakness. Damn his smile, his face, his voice... Damn him. She swallowed. He should have left this morning. If he'd left she would have nothing to fear. No thought of him injured or slain at her expense... Anxiety gripped her, settling cold and hard upon her chest. It was a new sensation, most unwelcome. *He must win. Do not let him fall.*

"Go with Apollo, Coronis." Her father gripped her arm, drawing her attention. "He is your champion, treat him as such."

Her father's words filled her head. *My champion.* Against Damocles—who hated Apollo only slightly less than he hated her. "Yes, father."

"Coronis." Her mother grasped her hand. "He saves us all, daughter. Take care."

Her fear increased, making it hard to breathe. *Do not let him fall.* She turned, her stomach tightening as her gaze met Apollo's.

You must win. You must.

Apollo smiled broadly, his brow rising high.

She pulled her gaze from his, walking past him to the competitors' tent. He would follow her, she knew it. They had little time to prepare. She must help him bathe and anoint him with oil before he met Damocles in the ring.

Her champion. She shivered, pushing into the tent. She lit a lamp and drew in a steadying breath. She was not a fretful sort, so why was she so afraid? Why did he unsettle her?

She knew the answer but refused to address the ache... the yearning that tugged her heart.

No, no.

She poured water into a beaten copper basin, grabbed the bottle of oil, and turned to him. His gaze caught hers and he cocked his head, assessing her.

An amused smile wreathed his too-handsome face. "Do not fret Coronis. You've not broken your word to me. You said you would never ask for my help. And you did not." He moved forward slowly, towering over her. His smile faltered as he studied her, intently... possessively. "You will never have to. I give it to you freely. I always will."

She stared up at him, astonished. Her suitors flattered her with pretty words, poetry, even song. But no man spoke to her so plainly. Or dared to look at her as he did.

His gaze wandered over her face. He seemed to linger over every feature, tracing the arch of her brow, the curve of her forehead, the seam of her lips, and angle of her jaw—before pinning her gaze with his. "Do I frighten you, Coronis?" his voice was low, almost a whisper.

She stared into his eyes, fathomless and golden. What was he asking? Was she afraid of the depths of emotion he stirred within her? Was she fearful of how her body trembled, anticipating the moment when they might touch? Or that she dreaded his departure so that she could neither eat nor sleep. She shook her head, unable to answer.

She was a proud woman, he knew as much. But he would have

the truth from her. He wanted to believe she spoke the truth—that fear did not exist between them. But that was not true. For the first time, he was terrified. Was his fate to wound her? Could there be a future for them—without fear?

She reached for the clasp of his chlamys, but he stopped her. He'd thought Phlegys meant to honor him, sending his daughter to tend the champion. Now he wondered at the man's actions. Perhaps Phlegys meant to test him? The thought of her hands upon him, anointing him with oil, seemed a far greater threat than the one Damocles offered. He ignored the small furrow on her brow, freed the clasp of his cloak and jerked the fabric from his shoulders. She stared at him, the furrow turning into a frown as he sat upon the stool by her side. He hands fisted on his thighs, his every muscle tightening, as he waited.

Her gaze remained fixed upon his chest, the rapid rise and fall of her chest revealing her discomfort. The furtive glance she cast him seemed to answer whatever question she silently pondered. She moved behind him, close enough to fill his nostrils with her tantalizing scent. He stiffened when her hands slid through his hair. He did not move as her fingers combed his locks from his shoulders and tied it back. But when her oiled hands rested upon his shoulders, he could not stop the shudder that wracked his body. She hesitated, her fingers curling into his skin—the slight whisper of her breath caressing the back of his neck.

He stared at the candle, how the flame danced and leapt. He must clear his mind, think of Damocles, of Phlegys and his people. He must not lose himself to her touch. Or wonder what she might do if he reached for her. How he longed to reach for her.

Her hands moved, sliding along his shoulders to cradle the sides of his neck. Her thumbs stroked upward, her forefingers running along the underside of his jaw. He closed his eyes, resisting the urge to lean into her touch. It would be all too easy. To kiss her palm, the inside of her wrist...

"Pina," Coronis voice was soft. "Did mother send you?"

Apollo scarce acknowledged the older woman. He should be thankful for her presence, for Coronis seemed easier. But the woman's presence did little to temper his response to Coronis' touch. Her hands still moved over him, still heated the blood in his veins.

His sight faded, the details of the candle-the tent-wavering as a vision gripped him.

Coronis lay spent, naked and glorious in his arms. Her smile was that of a woman well satisfied. His hands stroked the silken curve of her hip, moving leisurely up her back to smooth her tousled hair from her face. The feel of her body delighted him, but it was love that fulfilled him. When she tilted her head towards him, freely offering her mouth for his kiss he did not stop himself from professing, "I love you." His words were a whisper. And while his vision vanished, his words still hung in the air.

Coronis stared at him, as did the woman, Pina.

He stood, towering over her. He'd not meant to reveal himself in such a manner, not now. But he was not sorry. He did love her.

Coronis thrust the copper basin at Pina, facing him once more. Her mouth opened, but no words came out. He'd never seen such confusion, such disbelief. Was his declaration such a surprise? He swallowed, dreading her response. She said nothing. Instead she stumbled over several crates, shaking off his assistance, and hurried from the tent.

He stood, the fool, staring after her.

Pina patted his forearm.

He stared at the silver haired woman, at the smile on her face. She pointed after Coronis and patted his arm again. She placed a hand over her heart, then pressed her hand to his chest, his heart. She smiled again, but Apollo felt no reassurance. While this servant might believe Coronis' heart was his, the only reassurance he had was his vision. Yet this was not the only vision he'd had of Coronis. His heart grew heavy.

He helped Pina, pouring oil into his palms and rubbing it over his face and hair. Once they were done, he smiled at the woman. "Thank you," he spoke.

She nodded, patting his chest again.

He assumed she thanked him. If he'd not stayed, Coronis would have married Damocles to save her people. No, she would have fought him. She would have run...

He paused, his heart thundering. Was that what his vision showed? Did she run from Damocles? And call out for his aid? If he'd not been here, Damocles' challenge would demand an answer. And she'd have no choice but to run. His chest felt light once more, his heart full of hope and love. Now, he was her hero and her people's savior. Soon, he would be her husband and the father of her sons.

Phlegys appeared. "Are you ready?" He paused, searching the tent. "Where is Coronis?"

Pina glanced nervously at him before she waved her hand at Phlegys. Phlegys regarded the older woman closely, watching as she touched her stomach then pressed her hand to her forehead.

"She is unwell?" Phlegys arched brow spoke volumes. "A child that has never been ill is now too overcome to perform her duty to the man who saves her precious freedom?"

"I am here." Coronis hurried into the tent, flushed and wide-eyed.

"You are *recovered*?" There was no denying the bite to Phlegys question.

"I... I needed water," she murmured, her gaze darting to Pina, then, reluctantly, at her father once more. She would not look at him.

Phlegys turned to regard the tall flask of water sitting beside the oil—in plain sight.

The look of shame on Coronis' face pricked Apollo's pride. "Forgive me."

Phlegys frowned. "This man gains nothing today. We do. Is it too much to ask that you attend him? That you humble yourself, here and now, for the man that would save you. From a marriage to the man you deplore above all others. You push me so I wonder why I do not agree to Damocles' offer. You are too headstrong, too reckless." He paused. "I am disappointed, Coronis. And shamed."

Coronis was shaking, her amber eyes wet with unshed tears. She nodded, swallowing convulsively. She turned to Apollo, her eyes downcast and her chin wavering. "Forgive me, sir. I am truly thankful to you." She spoke to him, but she would not look upon him. "I am indebted for the generosity you bestow upon me, my family, and my people-"

"We have no time," her father interrupted. "Damocles bellows to begin. I have rarely seen a man so hungry for blood."

Apollo thought of Ares and smiled. "I have a brother much like Damocles." And while Apollo would never consider engaging in pankration with the ruthless God of War, Damocles was merely an impassioned mortal.

"Do you?" Phlegys regarded him again. "Perhaps it is best he not join you on your next visit."

Apollo laughed. "Let us not keep Damocles waiting." He stared at the top of Coronis' head, willing her to look at him. She did not.

Phlegys led the way, nodding at those that lined the path leading to the arena. Apollo followed, letting the morning sun warm his bare skin. He was ready. He'd enjoyed far too many fantasies about spilling Damocles blood. Today he would enjoy himself.

Two judges circled the ring, holding large sticks. If either he or Damocles broke the rules of the match, the judges would beat the offender until it stopped. He had no intention of biting Damocles or gouging the other man's eyes. But the look on Damocles' face made no such assurances. The man was livid, from past affronts as well as this morning's disappointment.

The crowd gathered was mostly men. Married women were not allowed to attend most competitions as some believed the sight of so much naked male flesh would make wives overcome with desire. Apollo thought most husbands would not mind their wives in a lustful state if they were the ones to reap the rewards. As it was, only unwed or elderly women were present, and few of those.

Apollo did not look for her in the crowd. Her father would demand she attend, as she was the cause of this match. But to see her troubled or distraught would offer too great a distraction. He knelt beside Damocles, at the foot of his statue. The mortal offered up prayers more suited for Ares. Still he heard his opponent's wishes.

Apollo, I come to you with fire in my chest. Help me destroy this man, to crush his body, and tear his heart from his chest. I would erase him from the memory of all gathered here. If you do this, Delphi will be mine, to rule... in your honor. Coronis will be mine, to rule as I see fit. Phlegys is weak, his time is done. Let me be your champion.

Apollo stared up at the figure modeled after him, bidding his temper cool. But he could not set aside thoughts of the Damocles, his large hands gripping Coronis against him while she pushed to get free... He would kill the mortal if he did not calm himself. Worse, he would enjoy the killing. No, he would be wise to control such thoughts.

Apollo stood, taking his place on the far side of the ring. He crouched, waiting, his body poised for the fight. His gaze tracked Damocles, pacing back and forth like a chained beast. The mortal stared at him, his nostrils flared and jaw clenched. While they waited for the judge's signal, Apollo watched the man's fury consume him. Let the fool be blinded with rage, it did not matter. Apollo knew the outcome already. Damocles would *never* have her.

At the judges shout, Damocles moved forward swiftly. He ran at Apollo, dragging one large hand across the packed dirt at their feet—and throwing it into Apollo's eyes before ramming his meaty fist into Apollo's face, his eye. The sound of impact reverberated throughout the silent arena. And the audience erupted. Boos and hissing, cheers and encouragement—all Apollo heard was Damocles grunt as he slammed his other fist into Apollo's side.

Apollo spun, hurling his elbow into Damocles' jaw with enough force to stop the man in his tracks. Apollo did not hesitate, but drove his foot into the man's stomach and sent him sprawling in the dirt.

Damocles lay, stunned on the ground.

No matter the rules or lack thereof, Apollo would not strike Damocles in such a state. But the crowd was not pleased when he extended a hand to help Damocles to his feet. And neither, apparently, was Damocles. He slapped Apollo's hand away and reared up, driving his shoulder into Apollo's stomach. Damocles stood—lifting Apollo high above him.

Poseidon sat amongst Damocles' men, enjoying the wine-skin his new friend Gergo had offered. While Damocles' men were neither witty nor graceful, they were amenable enough. And since he'd no desire to be seen by Apollo or Hermes, he'd best avoid the temptations offered by several fair maids in attendance—putting him in the midst of Damocles men.

He sat back on one elbow, smiling as Apollo went sailing through the air. He knew the oaf of a mortal would not win, but he'd done an admirable job of pummeling his kin so far. It was some sort of balm on his greatly wounded pride.

When Apollo landed on his back, his head bouncing in the dirt, even Poseidon winced. The crowd erupted when Damocles lashed out, kicking Apollo's side so fiercely that the crack of bone was audible. He shook his head. Apollo would not escape this unscathed. Indeed, Damocles landed two more solid kicks against the damaged side before Apollo retaliated.

Apollo's fist struck the side of Damocles right knee, driving the leg into an awkward angle. Damocles crumpled, forced to balance on one leg. It was all Apollo needed. His face was red with fury as he stood, quickly wrapping his arm around Damocles' massive neck. He pulled his arm tight, gripping his wrist with the other hand and pulling. The added leverage and weight had Damocles faltering. Poseidon nodded, he would have done as much.

But Damocles was not ready to give up the fight. His elbow slammed into Apollo's injured side, creasing Apollo's face with unrestrained pain.

Poseidon sat forward, curious. He'd never seen Apollo so... raw. He could hardly fault Apollo. The skin of is side was already blackening, likely from bleeding under the skin, and yet Damocles continued his onslaught.

Poseidon sought out the girl then. He knew Apollo was besotted with the mortal or he'd never have reacted so strongly to Poseidon's... antics. How did she feel?

Coronis. Daphne had told him all she'd learned. Daughter of Phlegys. Unmarried and unattached. While some speculated that Apollo might genuinely woo the princess, Poseidon could not believe it. Apollo would never be bound to one woman—no mortal at that.

Daphne claimed the princess had no tenderness for Apollo, that she hated all man equally. And that was what brought him back to Delphi. He was fond of a challenge. If this Coronis had interest in Apollo, Poseidon would find a way to sway her feelings. If she bore the golden god no interest, then he might be the one to win her heart—for whatever time she held his interest. Either way, he would have his revenge.

Coronis sat as still as a statue, her fingers gripping the arms of her carved wooden chair. Her eyes were fixed upon Apollo. Only the rapid quiver of the front of her exomie, the unsteady rise and fall of the fabric, revealed her agitation. She closed her eyes, her lips pressed tight.

Apollo smiled, his hold easing on Damocles. Apollo was

bloodied and bruised, yet he smiled, and turned adoring eyes upon the mortal woman? Poseidon sat back again, pondering this new development.

It ended quickly. Apollo released Damocles, regarding the mortal giant with open disdain. Damocles roared, his fist descending upon Apollo's face with a mighty force. Apollo grabbed Damocles' fist and sent his own fist into Damocles' jaw. The giant fell, a cloud of dust and dirt rising up around them.

Poseidon's eyes turned once more upon the beauty Coronis. It was her smile that drew him in. For the way she smiled at Apollo made him long to trade places with his golden brethren.

Chapter Eight

"Take this to him," her father's tone was firm. He handed her his finest silks. "Help him dress. Take Pina to tend any wounds, if need be. But bid him join us for our meal, Coronis." He paused. "You owe him much. Ask for his pardon, for your behavior this afternoon."

She frowned at her father. While they both knew she would do as he asked, she would not pretend to be happy about it. Her behavior this afternoon. What of his? What right did he have to speak so freely to her? To say such things... Fear was not an emotion she dealt well with. And while he was a pompous ass, the effect he had on her—his words had upon her—made her truly, deeply fearful. Now her father would send her to him. Alone. When she was more tempted to kiss the smug smile on his too-handsome face than to strike it... Would that not shame her family more than her behavior this afternoon?

"Coronis?" her father sighed, sitting back in his chair with exaggerated disappointment.

She pushed from her chair. "Yes, father. I shall go fetch your champion."

He sat forward quickly. "My champion?" he whispered. "I was not the one he saved today, daughter. I ask you to remember that. I grant you that he lacks humility. But neither does he boast falsely." He sighed. "How is his pride any less frustrating that your own?"

She could not hold her father's gaze then. Her pride. Her foolish pride. If not for Apollo, she would likely be in Damocles' bed, his wife, this very moment. She glanced around the courtyard, taking in the smiles, the revelry of her people. They were safe, protected, when she had put them all in harm's way. Her friends, her family... Ichthys laughing with Mara. Her mother at ease, enjoying the company gathered round. Her father was right. Apollo had every right to be the preening, opinionated, blindingly beautiful man that he was. She owed him much.

She met her father's gaze then, "Yes father."

He nodded, at ease as he sat back in his chair once more.

Pina stepped forward to accompany her. She nodded, gripping the silks her father would gift Apollo to her chest.

She'd not realized how chill the night was until she stepped out of her father's tent. The sounds of night greeted her, the chirp of the cricket, and the hoot of the owl. Overhead a blanket of brilliants shone brightly. Music, laughter, singing, mingled throughout. Tonight was for celebrating, for thanksgiving.

Athena, help me act wisely tonight. Sucking in a deep breath, she straightened her shoulders and set off for Apollo's and Hermes' tent.

It took some time. The city of tents was large. Her father had remarked that he suspected this to be the largest Pythian game in memory. Traveling through the corridors and alleyways that wove amongst the myriad of tents, she suspected he was right. Which made Apollo's victories all the more impressive. All had stayed to see the great battle between Apollo and Damocles. She heard just as many poems and songs dedicated to the morning's match as she had dedicated to the whole of this year's games. It had been a glorious battle, fought by the strongest man she'd ever seen. Fought, and thank the Gods, won. She was proud of him.

His side... The memory of Damocles' shoulder bruising Apollo's flesh. She'd simply prayed that Apollo's suffering end. In that moment, his suffering troubled her more than anything else-even marriage to Damocles.

She sighed, staring at the tent. His tent. She was a fool, then. No better than Eratos or Khloris... Or any handful of women that would gladly trade their dignity for one of his golden smiles. She drew in a deep breath, wishing she could ease the wild beat of her heart.

Pina's hand landed upon her arm, a curious expression on her face.

Coronis smiled, patting Pina's hand twice. She stepped forward, hesitating for the briefest moment before lifting the tent flap.

Apollo lay, sleeping peacefully, upon a mat of furs. His chest was bare, his chlamys draped across his waist to cover him. Not that it mattered. She'd seen him near naked many times. His was a body the Gods would celebrate. She studied him in the flickering light of the candle. A jagged cut ran from temple to jaw. The skin around his eye was brightly discolored-angry looking. Her attention wandered along his neck, noting various scrapes and bruises. His side... She shook her head. His injuries were earned honorably, she should be at peace with that. Yet anger choked her, hot and hard.

"Apollo," Hermes spoke, pushing through the back of the tent. "You must wake if we're to make our good-byes to Phlegys..." His eyes widened at the sight of her. "Princess." He bowed.

Good-byes. They still planned to leave then. "Forgive me," she stepped back, running into Pina. "My father would be honored by your presence this evening."

Pina took the garment from her arms, holding it out to Apollo.

It took effort for Apollo to sit, his pain making her wince. "Pina and I," she hurried to explain, "were sent to help. If you've need of anything?" Her gaze lingered on his stomach as he stood, one hand clasping his tunic about his waist. He stared at her with red-rimmed eyes-smiling as if he was in excellent health. "Had I known you were resting, I would not have intruded."

"You've not intruded," Apollo spoke, one eyebrow arching. "This is for me?" He took the cloth from Pina.

"You are our champion," she murmured. "It is... some sort of tribute, I suppose..." Why did she feel so ill at ease? "Pina has taught me some healing skills, if you've need?" But she could not break the hold of his golden gaze.

Hermes spoke. "His ribs are broken."

"It has happened before, it will likely happen again." Apollo argued, glaring at Hermes. "I need only dress. I've no time for a bath... And have no attendants here to help me." He looked at her then, his smile goading her.

So he enjoyed angering her? "Shall I send Eratos and Khloris to you then?" She spoke sweetly. "Why, I was surprised not to find them here, assisting you with your nap." The sting of jealousy surprised her. And angered her. She was no simpering fool. If he was injured and would not accept her help, there was nothing more she could do for him. She would not stand here, at his beck and call, while he teased her. "I shall tell father you are indisposed and send your companions right away." She raked her eyes over the two of them. "Please, wait here for your... amusements. You've more than earned the right."

Apollo rubbed a hand over his face.

Was he laughing? She didn't mean to growl, the sound erupted without thought. She shook her head, swallowing back her anger. What was wrong with her? She'd no reason for it, no explanation. But she was racked with such a rage she could scarce think.

Hermes turned and left the tent without a sound. Pina quickly followed.

"Since you've not brought my company with you, I suppose I will join your father," Apollo's voice pulled her attention back to him. He released the tunic, unfolding the fabric Pina had given him.

"You... You..." Her hands fisted.

He stood, naked and bronze. Battered—at her expense. The urge to slap his smile once more exceeded the desire to kiss it. "I?" he goaded.

She swallowed, shaking her head. "Are an... ass."

He nodded. "I believe you've said that before, Coronis." He did not cover himself. Indeed, he seemed completely oblivious to his glorious naked state. "Ass or not, if your father summons me, I will come." He draped the silken fabric across one defined shoulder.

She narrowed her eyes. "Perhaps you should bathe first?"

"I did so, before my nap." He laughed, his tawny eyes catching hers. "But I will again and accept your offer of assistance-"

She held her hand up and spun, walking away. Why was she angry? He was injured. If he needed help, it would not be untoward for her and Pina to help him. It shouldn't matter.

"To dress," he finished, walking at her side.

She stopped, glaring at him.

"Please," he asked.

She took the fabric in her hands, holding one end to the ridged curve of his hip. She placed his hand there, to hold the fabric, and walked around him. It would have been a far easier task if his scent did not distract her so. If his presence did not fill her senses. Her eyes feasted on the ridges and angles of his body. Even blackened, cut and swollen, he was impressive. She was proud that her fingers did not slip, that each tuck was precise, each fold carefully arranged.

When she stood back, he was every bit the champion.

He stared at her, his teasing smile gone. In its place, was the same haunted look he'd worn the day of the chariot races. "We shall be late," he muttered, walking from the tent, to her father's house.

She followed, turning her gaze from the impressive line of his back to the clear night sky. She drew in a deep breath and offered, *Apollo, guide me. Help me find peace and light. There is a storm within me I know not how to weather.* Anger. Fear. Apprehension. She could not find her footing.

Apollo turned then. "Coronis," his voice was soft. "Will you accompany me?"

Her chest tightened. Her father had sent her to collect him. He had proven himself to her, to all, today. He teased her, nothing more. Her father teased, as did Ichthys. Her reaction to this man was unfounded... and disturbing. Even if his words were true, that he longed for Eratos' and Khloris' company, it should not matter. She had no claim on him.

She took the arm he offered, wishing she was not affected by his warm skin... the way his muscles of his thick forearm shifted beneath her fingers.

He walked on, his words soft. "I would have sent them away."

Her heart seemed to stumble. She would not pretend to misunderstand him. He spoke of Eratos and Khloris. "Why?" she asked, her voice tight.

But they were at her father's house, and the doors opened wide in welcome. "There is our champion," her father's voice was jovial, welcoming. "My thanks for your presence this fine eve."

Apollo led her inside, seemingly unaware of her. Disappointment welled up. She had no answer to her question. And she wanted an answer.

Her hand slipped from his arm, leaving a startling chill upon his skin. He craved her touch—the loss of it left him aching. She moved from him, so quickly it would have been amusing if he didn't need her so.

He'd not lied to her. He wanted no other woman, something he'd no understanding of. One woman was similar to the next... Or so he'd thought. But now he knew the truth. None compared to her. Coronis was muscle and strength, soft but unyielding, confident and smart, loving and loyal. She was the woman he wanted above all others, yet he suspected she would not yet welcome him into her bed.

His vision offered him comfort. How long he would have to wait for her, for their son, did not matter. He would wait.

"Join me," Phlegys waved him forward.

He walked forward, sitting in the chair at the king's side.

"Bring him drink and food," Phlegys beckoned a girl forward. "I cannot express my thanks, Apollo."

Apollo shook his head.

"I suspect your call to action had less to do with me and my people than my daughter?" He'd leaned forward as he spoke, his words for Apollo alone.

Apollo looked at him. "I'd not let your people fall under Damocles' rule."

Phlegys eyes peered into his. "And I thank you. I've met few that can best him in battle, but he's no leader of men."

He agreed. "His strength is admirable."

Phlegys' gaze darted back to him. "Yet you bested him easily."

His eyes bore into the mortals. "Easily?"

Phlegys' swallowed, his gaze turning to the fire.

Did this mortal suspect? Could he?

"Yet my troubles interfered with your travels," Phlegys continued.

"Delayed but a day," Apollo spoke quickly, understanding then. Phlegys worried over his daughter.

Phlegys sighed, turning his attention to him once more. "Perhaps I spoke too hastily."

Surprising.

"Stay," Phlegys looked at his daughter. "If you wish it."

His gaze sought out Coronis. She sat, laughing and smiling with

Hermes. She laughed with Hermes but scowled at him. When had he become the fool? Besottedly staring after a woman who seemed to feel disdain and fury in his presence. Had her prayer not confirmed such? And yet this afternoon, she'd wanted only to spare him pain.

It was her nature to be so passionate. And it was her nature, her spirit, that had stolen his heart. His hands fisted.

"Apollo?" Phlegys shifted, leaning on the arm of his chair to speak to him. "Her mother was just as... tempestuous. Her tirades were brutal, but invigorating. To see her flushed with anger, so alive and passionate, was a sight to behold." He paused. "I was oftentimes the cause of her temper. She has mellowed with age, and I am thankful."

Apollo smiled, his gaze once more fixed upon Coronis.

"I knew her temper was only as great as her love for me," Phlegys finished.

His gaze turned to Phlegys. "Love?"

The king nodded, a small smile on his face. "You anger my daughter more ferociously than I have ever seen her. She can scarce look at you without trembling from it."

"And you approve?" he asked gruffly.

"I would see her as well matched as I am." He paused. "In you, I see all I could hope for, for my people and my headstrong daughter."

Apollo wanted Coronis, not as lover, but as his wife. And as such, this good mortal need know who Apollo was before such matters were settled. "You truly honor me, oh King. So I must confess all to you." He tore his gaze from Coronis to face the man that would be his son's grandfather.

Phlegys frowned, shifting in his seat. "Confess?"

He nodded, watching the mortal closely. "I have seen the suspicion in your eyes, Phlegys. Your mind is sharp, as is your instinct."

Phlegys hands gripped the arms of his chair. "You are Apollo? Not a mere mortal... named for Delphi's chosen God, then..." He swallowed, standing.

Apollo stood with him, smiling. "I am your Olympian. I am Apollo."

Phlegys' eyes close briefly, resignation upon the man's face. It was only when he'd finished speaking that he realized Coronis stood at his side.

All eyes turned upon them as the gilded tray she'd offered him slipped from her fingers and fell to the ground at his feet. He waited, staring down into her eyes...

She could not breathe. She could not... Surely she'd misheard him. His golden eyes searched her face. He was not... He could not be...

"Leave us," her father spoke to their guests. "Find your beds while I honor our new champion." She knew the house was emptying, but her attention never wandered from Apollo.

Apollo.

"Husband?" Her mother joined them, nervous. "What has happened?"

And yet, Coronis knew.

She *knew* him.

The memory, one cherished above all others, embraced her— pulling her back.

She'd been a child of no more than five—knocked in the dirt, teased and prodded by the boys she so desperately envied. They practiced, even then, for the Pythian Games. As boys, they would all compete, in every event. And when she'd said she would too, they'd goaded her until she'd struck out at one of them.

After that, it no longer mattered that she was a girl. It seemed an army of fists and feet flew upon her. Even with a bloodied lip and a swollen eye, she'd not backed down. It was the arrival of a man, a gilded giant of a man, which finally ended their assault upon her.

He'd scared them away with a single shout.

She'd cowered, waiting for the set-down she knew she deserved. She was a girl, after all. But when she'd looked up at him, she saw only admiration in the giant's golden eyes.

He knelt, cupping her chin in his hand and tilting her head to inspect her wounds.

"You'll live," he'd said, smiling broadly. "To fight another day, no doubt."

"I will," she agreed.

He laughed, startling her. He'd an eager and winning manner

about him. He spoke firmly. "Train harder. Make fury your friend, but never your master. Understand?"

She nodded, repeating his words over and over.

"You're a strong one." He helped her stand, swiping the dust from her thin shoulders. "Own that strength and you will succeed."

She'd stared at him, mesmerized. His eyes were warm, crinkling deeply from the broad smile that wreathed his face. And his words... *You will succeed.*

She swallowed now, staring into those same eyes. *Apollo...hear me...*

His head tilted, his eyes sweeping over her face as the slightest smile formed on his lips.

No, she could not pray to him. Her eyes burned and her throat tightened.

Of course she knew him. It had been him, a giant stranger to a girl as slight as she'd been, that had encouraged her to be the person she was now. How could she forget the man who'd given her the will to fight?

"I remember you," she managed, forcing the words past the lump in her throat.

Her father turned to regard her. "Coronis?"

"What is happening?" Her mother's voice was high, breathy. Coronis was vaguely aware of her father's whispers, of her mother's startled cry, her hand covering her mouth. But Apollo's eyes hadn't left her face. His gaze held hers... searching her eyes with warmth, curiosity.

"I was small then, too small to stand my ground against the boys thrashing me." She glanced at her father, forcing herself straight and tall as she met Apollo's gaze. "You told me... you told me... to own my strength."

Apollo's eyes went round, a slight smile forming. "You were strong, even then, Coronis. I should have known you the moment I saw you, for you've scarce changed."

Her eyebrows rose, wrapping her arms about herself. She should have known him. "You'd no interest in me then, not as you do now."

"If I'd no interest, I'd have left you and your people at Damocles mercy." His hand lifted, as if he could touch her cheek. Instead, he placed his hands on his hips, his jaw hardening.

"You were the one?" her father laughed. "Your counsel was more valuable than mine in such matters."

"That's not true father," she argued before turning back to Apollo. "Do we bow? Offer tributes? How can I repay the constant offense I have made against you?"

"You've never offended me, Coronis." His smile was warm—as warm as the sun.

"No?" she asked, fighting her temper once more. She had prayed to him. About him. And he'd said nothing. How he must have laughed at her... She frowned then, thinking about this afternoon. "You could have stopped this," she whispered. "Why did you go through this... this farce?"

"Coronis!" her mother interrupted, the fear lining her mother's voice reminding her of the truth. She could no longer berate this man. He was no man. He held their fate in his hands.

He laughed. "Do not censure your mind or your tongue, Coronis." He crossed his arms over his chest, tilting his head. "Our son will have your strength."

Her lungs emptied.

She was aware of her father's gasp. From the corner of her eye she saw Hermes cover his face with his hands. But Apollo kept smiling.

She shook her head. "You're mistaken-"

"Coronis," her father thundered, coming to her side and grasping her hands in his. "You will mind your words," he hissed desperately. His hands cupped her face as he whispered, "He is a God—a God, not some thick-headed boy out to salvage his pride. He holds your life in his hands, the life of our people. You will accept him. You will."

She swallowed. There was no compromise in his tone, only determination.

"You have nothing to fear from me Phlegys. If your daughter will not have me, I will seek no retribution." With those words, Apollo erased the tension that bracketed her father's mouth and creased his brow. "It is not my way."

Her father turned, releasing her and making his way to Apollo. He spoke clearly, "You may have my daughter."

"Father," she gasped.

Her father shot her a look, a warning. "We are honored..."

"I would have her say it." He stood before her, too close for her liking. "I choose you as my wife. Will you accept me?"

She swallowed.

"You cannot," he murmured. "Can you, Coronis?"

She had to say something. She had to explain, to convince him. "You are..." She shook her head. "No. I cannot."

He nodded. "No?" His brow arched.

"I—I am mortal. I will grow old. You will tire of me..." She drew in a deep breath. "'Tis no secret that you've a fondness for women—"

"Coronis," her father interrupted.

"Let her speak," Apollo remained calm.

She looked at her parents, how they clung to one another. "If I had not seen the devotion my father has for my mother, then perhaps I could accept less."

"Some would say wedding a God was more," he teased.

Husband? This man? God? She shook her head, her panic mounting. "What you want from me..." She glanced at her father, then Hermes, before leaning forward. "Marriage isn't necessary."

Apollo's brow furrowed deeply, his nostrils flared.

Had she angered him?

"I respect your father, Coronis. I would honor his house, not sully it," his words were hard, biting—offense clear upon his golden features.

"As would I," she agreed. "But when you tire of me-when this son is born-what will become of my honor? Of me?" Would he cast her off? Take their children with him? Return her to her parents? Her fate would be determined by one whose constancy was fleeting.

Apollo reached for her then, his hand cradling the curve of her cheek. "I will guard your honor and protect you, always."

His touch eased her. His words charmed her. From the look upon his face, she knew he believed what he said. And yet, she *knew* him-as did all that were loyal to him. Apollo had loved many and stayed with none. To let him into her heart only to have it crushed... She was not as strong as he thought. Her voice wavered, "I cannot."

"Apollo," her mother spoke. "If... If I may request a brief audience with my daughter. I fear she is... distraught."

Apollo's gaze grew more intense, his hunger and affection challenging her wits and resolve.

"Let her have a minute, Apollo," Hermes interjected. "You've troubled these good people with overwhelming news. How else can a mortal react?"

She looked at Hermes, realization dawning. "Hermes... You too?"

"It is the only way we can enjoy the games." Hermes grinned unabashedly. "Go with your mother, Coronis. Leave me to deal with my brother."

She let her mother lead her from the room, too stunned to think. She crossed the room, leaning against a column as her mother carefully closed the door behind them.

"You must hurry," her mother's voice was soft.

Coronis was in a daze, her mother's sudden flurry of activity no less astonishing than the rest of the evening. It was only when Pina began wrapping her clothes in her blanket that Coronis realized something was amiss. "Mother?"

She'd never seen her mother afraid. No, not afraid, terrified. Her voice shook, "You must run, Coronis. You must. Do not question me now. Do this-"

Her door opened, making her mother and Pina jump. But when they saw only her father enter they returned to their packing. "Talousa?"

Her mother waved at the door, which Phlegys promptly closed.

"She cannot," her mother's cry was a broken whisper. "She does not know Phlegys. She does not know the danger."

"We must tell her," her father hissed, pulling the makeshift bag from Pina's arms to throw it on the ground. "You would have her run? From Olympus?"

"It can be done." Her mother was crying.

Her father sighed, pulling her mother into his arms. "He is not Poseidon, wife."

"Mother? Father? What is this?" she pleaded, taking her mother's hand in hers. "Father... Tell me... What am I to do?"

"You must marry him," her father answered immediately, his face solemn.

"No," her mother argued.

"Talousa, if she rejects him, we will lose favor." Her father held his wife tightly. "If we lose favor, there will be punishment for all. All." He pressed a kiss to his wife's forehead. "But to marry him, to keep him happy. She is wise. We must trust her with the truth."

"What truth?" Coronis longed to scream.

"You are Poseidon's daughter," her father spoke softly. "And your mother is the daughter of the dead king, Erysichthon."

"Erysichthon?" Coronis stared at her parents. "The shade? But he... he is a fairytale, to keep children in bed and out of mischief."

Her mother squeezed Coronis' hand, sagging against her father. "Once, he was a good father, Coronis. He was a good man. Not the stuff of nightmares."

She could not think. "The shade... the shade Olympus hunts?" She turned pleading eyes upon her father. "I don't understand, Father."

"When Erysichthon was cursed, your mother ran—she had no choice. Poseidon... He offered a sort of protection... for a time." He paused, burying his nose in her mother's hair. "I'd loved your mother since I was a boy. It took some time to find her, but I could not give her up. She begged I leave her, worried I'd incur the wrath of the Gods. I would not let her go. So Ione, your mother's given name, disappeared that night. While Talousa—your mother—returned to Delphi as my wife, a widow of the Persian wars."

Coronis stared at them, shaking her head uncontrollably.

"You are Poseidon's daughter." Her mother went on, "More importantly, you are Erysichthon's granddaughter. I fear what might become of you, of us all, if this is discovered."

"Why?" She whispered.

"Erysichthon is merciless in his pursuit of Persephone," Phlegys spoke softly. "Demeter's grief has not eased with time. And since his offenses continue, Olympus has sworn to wipe out his family, to destroy him in whatever way they can."

She stared at the bundle at Pina's feet. "You would send me off carrying such a secret? Such deceit?"

Phlegys released his wife then, reaching for Coronis. "You are my greatest prize, Coronis. I would see you safe, happy, and protected." Worry lined his face. "As his wife, Apollo will protect you. As the mortal that rejected him, there would be no mercy." He sighed, pulling her into his arms.

Coronis drew in a deep breath, seeking the calming scent of her father.

"It is easier knowing he loves you so, daughter. In my heart, I know he will keep you safe—from Olympus if need be," her father's words were a whisper.

Did love matter now? Or her wants? She would do what she must—to protect them. She longed to go to the Temple, to pray for strength and guidance. But who could she pray to now that her favored god sought her hand in marriage?

Chapter Nine

A pollo stood on the steps of his temple, restlessly shifting from one foot to the next. He'd been up well before his sun. His mind would not rest. Anticipation coursed through his blood—more potent than that inspired by any hunt or game.

Today was his wedding day.

How many hundreds gathered round, he knew not. Whether they came to see the ceremony or simply stare upon him—their God—mattered little. They were here, as witness, to this union. He stood proudly, adorned in robes from Olympus, his aura ensuring all knew him for who and what he was. And that Coronis would be his.

Hermes' trip to Olympus had stirred much interest, enticing several of his brethren to make the trek to Delphi, an unexpected but not unwelcome surprise. Hera, Aphrodite, and Demeter stood in the shadows of the temple, content to view the event away from the mortals gathered. Aphrodite had blessed him. Demeter had congratulated him, offering him a rare smile. And Hera offered him the two intricately wrought golden crowns and Zeus' blessing.

"Apollo," Hermes murmured, drawing his attention to the procession arriving.

Phlegys and Talousa led their daughter, swathed from head to toe in the finest white gauze and silks, to the temple. His eyes fixed upon her, missing her prayers and the sound of her voice. She'd been a most devoted servant, her daily prayers as constant as his rising sun. Before he'd come to Delphi, he knew the sound of her voice. Now that she was silent, it troubled him.

Her gaze lifted, meeting his.

If he could not hold her in his arms, he would wrap her in his sun's warmth. The morning sun grew brighter, heating his back and stretching toward her. Its rays surrounded her, bringing a soft smile to her lips. She cocked a brow at him. He bowed in assent.

Those gathered began to cheer as Phlegys led Coronis past them. Some waved olive branches, others laurel branches. After such momentous games and his battle with Damocles, this year would not soon be forgotten.

Phlegys and Coronis began their climb up the steps, but he did not wait for Coronis to reach him. Rather he met them in the middle. While he saw no reason to disguise his eagerness, Coronis seemed bewildered. He stared down at her, well pleased that she was near.

Phlegys offered Apollo Coronis' hand. Apollo took it in both of his, transfixed by her gaze. Phlegys covered their hands with his own, speaking so all gathered could hear, "Apollo of Olympus, God of Delphi and all present, I give you my daughter Coronis." Phlegys wavered, drawing Apollo's eye. The man stared at his daughter with such tenderness that Apollo ached for his loss. "I give you my daughter to sow for the purpose of providing legitimate children and to increase your oikos." Phelgys removed the fine white gauze that covered Coronis, exposing her splendor for all.

Apollo could lose hours exploring her beauty. But not now. Phlegys words were the proper words, as was custom. Apollo knew as much. But this was no mortal union, formed for property and status. He would have it known that this marriage was his choice. And that Phlegys' sacrifice would be recognized. "King Phlegys of Delphi, you honor me with such a gift. I take your daughter as my wife and you as my father. I know of no mortal man as honorable as you." He bowed to the man, eliciting murmurs of approval from the crowd.

Coronis' hand tightened upon his own.

Phlegys stepped back then, releasing them. Apollo held her hand, leading her up the few steps to the waiting priest.

Her hand was cold in his, too cold for one standing in the sun. He lifted it, cradling it against his chest as he waited for the priest to begin. She watched him, he could feel the weight of her gaze upon him. Yet he held himself straight, grappling with emotions too new and overwhelming to name. It was her hand that kept him anchored here, her touch that kept his sudden panic at bay.

The priest lifted the two crowns over his head, then hers. He held the two up, overlapping, then drew them apart so that sun filtered through. The priest spoke, "This union is blessed by Olympus. The Gods themselves have decreed that these two are now and ever shall be one." The priest crossed his hands, holding the two crowns so closely that they appeared as one. "As such, Olympus will honor those that honor them, their union, and their families. Apollo is our God, Coronis is now our Goddess."

Her hold tightened upon his, the trembling undeniable. Only then did he dare look at her.

She stared fixedly at their hands, blinking rapidly. It was not just her hand that trembled, it was all of her. He could think of no mortal more capable of joining Olympus than his Coronis. She would stand against his brethren and earn their respect. Once she had the Gift of Immortality, she would be a true Goddess, his Goddess. His heart swelled at the thought.

He lifted her hand to his lips, pressing a soft kiss to each of her whitened knuckles. Her gaze locked with his. In the brilliant sunlight, he could see the gold and copper flecks in her amber eyes... and that her wondrous eyes sparkled with tears.

He frowned, arching his brow in question. Was she not pleased by her change in status? Or was it this marriage—had her parents influenced her?

His gaze traveled over her face, searching for the words to ease her concern. How could he tell her that the curve of her cheek seemed to invite his touch? That her mouth, parted in surprise, demanded he taste her. He waited until the crowns were place upon them then cradled her face with his hands. He smiled at her, savoring the feel of her against his palms—his fingers. That such a simple touch left him satisfied boded well. Theirs would be a good match. He would show her that theirs was a union above the rest. While their spirits might clash, they were much alike. So alike that he suspected the joining of their bodies would be a wondrous thing. He tilted her head forward, stroking the silk of her cheek and pressing a gentle kiss upon her forehead.

His vision wavered, her scent drawing him into another time and place. His chest felt heavy as he saw the field... The same field, the same vision. She ran, tears streaming down her face, holding the rent fabric of her tunic to her chest. She stumbled to her knees, her eyes staring up into the sky. It was then that he saw the arrows in her shoulder-blood soaking her tunic so that it clung to her skin. A crow—one of his crows—circled overhead, its white feathers a stark contrast to the blackened sky. Black. But there was no storm cloud... Was it smoke? She screamed his name... Desperate, anguished, pleading. The sound tore at his heart.

He opened his eyes to discover she'd covered her hands with his. Her trembling ceased, but he was overcome. He fought the urge to drag her from the steps and into his temple.

Fury choked him... Who would do this to her? Who did she run from? Who would challenge his hold upon her and risk retribution from Olympus? His eyes swept the crowd as he pulled her behind him, needing the shield of his body to protect her from the eyes of one that might harm her.

"Apollo?" her voice startled him.

"To the Temple," he spoke softly, his gaze searching those that watched them.

Ichthys was not pleased, but the mortal was no fool. His hopes for marrying Coronis were destroyed, but Apollo saw an ally in the mortal. When Phlegys passed, Ichthys would be worthy of running Delphi's affairs when he and Coronis could not.

There were others he supposed. A tribe from Larissa had a long-standing feud with Phlegys. A neighboring king with three unwed sons. Even Phlegys' own brother hoped to acquire more property and standing as a result from the union. He'd been bitterly disappointed when Apollo brushed his request aside—but Apollo refused to reward the man on name alone. He'd done nothing to earn any accolades, therefore he would get none.

But what would any of them gain from tormenting Coronis?

His gaze fell upon Damocles, bruised and battered and furious. He regarded Coronis so closely Apollo felt the urge to tear him to pieces. Of all here, Damocles was most likely.

"Apollo?" Coronis repeated again.

How they'd reached the top of the temple, he could not recall.

But they were there. His lady wife smiled, albeit forcibly, while he stood stiff and frowning at his people.

"What is it?" she asked, softly. "I've done nothing to anger you this morning, yet there is no doubt something has pricked your temper."

Apollo drew in a deep breath, regarding his beautiful wife with a smile. "No, wife, you've done nothing but remind me how precious you are."

Her eyes widened.

He winked, his smile growing as her eyes narrowed. "Come, I would make introductions."

"Introductions?" she whispered as he led her into the temple.

She stared up at Apollo. Her husband. The man... no, no man... She swallowed, letting him lead her into his temple. Her emotions balanced precariously, anxiety and happiness.

She'd not expected to feel happy. She'd not expected his kiss upon her knuckles to elicit such warmth, such pleasure, deep inside of her. In truth, the touch of his mouth to her flesh made her tremble with something foreign—and delightful.

Yet her anxiety reminded her of all at stake. She was charged with the safe-keeping of her family. Of her people. No, not her people... She swallowed. Her people were the Thessalian's abandoned by Erysichthon—and Olympus. The Thessalian's that prayed to Demeter, cared for her sacred cypress trees, and were fierce warriors. She was daughter to Ione and Poseidon-

"Coronis, may I present you to the Goddesses Hera, Aphrodite, and Demeter. They could hardly wait to meet you." Apollo's tone was calm, but then he'd spent his life in the company of these immortal creatures.

In an instant, she knew they were immortal. Each was cast in a vibrant aura, encasing their image with an unmistakable glow. She dropped into a deep curtsey, her knees trembling. It was one thing to meet an immortal. It was another altogether to come face to face with an immortal determined to destroy her... If they knew who she truly was.

"Rise, child," Hera spoke. "She is lovely Apollo."

"I see a spirit in her that would rival Athena." Aphrodite spoke. "Has Artemis met her? She will approve." Aphrodite took Coronis' hands. "It is a pleasure to meet the woman capable of making Apollo's heart eager for marriage and commitment. I'd never thought such a day would come."

Coronis knew she should speak. "It is as much a surprise to me, Goddess."

The Goddesses laughed then.

"You have a sharp mind," Demeter nodded.

"And a sharp tongue," Apollo added.

"She will need one, to keep you in check," Demeter continued. "I do not envy you that challenge, Coronis."

Coronis tried not to stare. This woman, with her brown eyes and gentle face, would kill her mother? Would kill her? She cleared her throat. "I wonder if I am up to such a challenge," she admitted, glancing at Apollo. It surprised her to feel as she did. That she longed to move closer, to take his hand in hers, to lean upon him for support.

"From what I hear, you excel at difficult challenges," Aphrodite spoke. "Hermes says you are a champion in your own right."

"You are well matched," Hera agreed, nodding. "One has only to see the two of you together to feel it."

"Where is Poseidon?" Demeter's question put fear into Coronis' heart.

Apollo frowned. "His whereabouts are of no importance to me."

Hera laughed. "Your feud continues then?"

Apollo scowled.

Feud. With Poseidon? Coronis glanced at Apollo's hand, but resisted the urge to take it. She had no knowledge of Apollo's likes and dislikes, who had his affection or his disdain... She had much to learn. But to know Poseidon was their common enemy comforted her. Her mother and father might see Demeter as the enemy, but she understood the woman's need for revenge. If danger found those she loved, she would do whatever need be done to protect or avenge them.

Poseidon... She could not reconcile the anger she felt for the being that was her... father. He had used her mother poorly in her time of need. A shameful act for one who was a God.

"I have no want to see or hear of him on my wedding day," Apollo snapped. "Whatever business you have with him, I ask that you do it far from Delphi." Coronis felt the anger rolling off Apollo and wondered at it.

"I wonder that he would show his face here after the greeting he received when last he visited." Hera laughed.

"You know the business I have with him, Apollo." Coronis saw the haunted look in Demeter's eyes as she continued, "But I will not ruin your day with tales of my woe." She smiled first at Apollo, then Coronis. "I am happy for you both and offer my blessings for a long and fruitful union."

"As do I," Aphrodite agreed, taking her hand. "May the strength of your mind and body rival the strength of the love you bear for one another." Aphrodite placed Coronis' hand in Apollo's.

Coronis relaxed, eased by the contact—then felt the fool. She was surrounded by those who would destroy her—she must remember that. Would these beings bless their union if they knew who she was, who her mother was, and her grandfather? Demeter may seem soft and gentle, incapable of murder or vengeance as her mother claimed. Yet she knew what these immortals were capable of—knew their stories intimately—as all good Greeks did.

"I look forward to seeing you visit Olympus from time to time." Hera smiled.

Coronis blinked. Olympus? Something cold and hard settled in the pit of her stomach. "I... That is too great an honor." She murmured.

"You are married to an Olympian now," Aphrodite's voice was low. "You are most welcome on Olympus."

Her head hurt, a dull throb. She longed to pray, to share her burdens with Apollo... to ask for his guidance.

"Do not overwhelm the poor child," Demeter interrupted. "She's just married this blindingly beautiful creature. That, alone, would be enough for any woman, mortal or not. To bring up Olympus and the rest that comes with it would be positively terrifying."

Coronis found herself smiling, in thanks, at Demeter. It was true. Only yesterday her world was as it should be. Her father was Phlegys. He and his family before him, cared for Delphi, the temple, and Apollo's oracle within. Her mother was Talousa, orphaned then widowed during the Persian invasion. She was their only heir.

No longer—now she was the daughter of a forgotten princess, granddaughter to a specter that haunted children's nightmares and enemy of Olympus. If she could start again, she would beg for ignorance...

"We shall leave you then," Hera agreed. "Do not make her wait too long to meet the rest of your family," she spoke to Apollo.

Apollo nodded, accepting their well-wishes with a tolerant smile on his face.

"Do not fear your husband tonight," Aphrodite whispered in her ear. "Yours will be a most gratifying wedding bed."

To think on her wedding night when so much weighed upon the present seemed an imprudent choice. But now the image of Apollo, in all his naked glory, appeared before her. She'd seen his body many times, as very little was worn on the competition field. And she was no innocent. She knew what happened between a man and a woman. Or an immortal and a woman. And, according to many of the stories about Apollo, he was a magnificent lover. Now he was her lover. She swallowed.

As the Goddesses made their way from the temple, Coronis found it impossible to think on anything other than Apollo... And what waited for her.

"You did well." Apollo smiled down at her.

She nodded, unable to meet his eyes lest he discern her thoughts.

"You've kept your prayers from me, Coronis. I no longer know what occupies your thoughts-or what you want." He cocked his head to one side, the pull of his gaze demanding she look at him. And when she did, she was unable to look away.

Coronis frowned at him. "Am I to pray to you still? Even as my... my husband?" The word felt clumsy on her tongue.

He touched her, his fingers tracing the edge of her jaw. "That I cannot answer." His gaze followed the path of his fingers along her neck and the line of her shoulder. "I've never had a wife."

She shivered, his feather light touch unsettling her. Her stomach felt queer, hollow and hot-aching.

"Tell me," he whispered, "What thoughts are in your head?"

She shook her head.

His brows rose, a faint smile pulling at the corners of his mouth. "No?"

She shook her head again. "You married me as I am. You cannot expect me to yield now."

His laughter rang out in the temple. "Very well." His eyes narrowed. "Will you tell me, if I guess?"

She continued to shake her head. "No, I will not. You've known my mind for far too long. I wish some privacy between us..."

"And I wish nothing between us." His words escaped on a ragged breath. "I would know all in your heart and mind. I would have you think of me as often as thoughts of you find me—it is often, I assure you. When you are near, I would have the feel of your skin on mine—however slight." His hand took hers. "The hunger I have for you consumes all else." He drew in a steadying breath. "Tell me what you want, what you need, so that I may please you, Coronis. It is all I desire."

She could scarce breathe, drowning in his words and the longing in his gaze. "What have I done to earn such a responsibility?" She stared at their joined hands. "It is too much, sir." She was shaking.

"It is," he agreed, stepping so close that there was but a shadow's separation between his body and hers.

Her body throbbed with an ache that forced all thought from her mind. She was connected to this man—this immortal—in a way that both intimidated and thrilled her. His spirit wrapped around her, encompassing her, holding her as surely as his arms. It was maddening, dizzying, this power he held over her. And yet she could not look away, even when she grew light-headed and wavering on her feet.

He held her close then, his thick arms clasping her against his chest and forcing any remaining air from her lungs. She trembled but whether from terror or delight she did not know. All that mattered was his touch upon her. She knew the strength and power he possessed, how dangerous he could be. Yet when he enfolded her in his arms and cradled her against him, it was with a tenderness she'd not expected. His heart thundered beneath her ear, startling her further.

She was no weak-willed woman. She'd never let her emotions lead her, never yielded to impulses without thought. Her instincts were strong, guiding her. Yet something about him... She felt both lost and found, adrift yet anchored—cherished in a way that left her humbled. When he looked upon her, when he touched her, she felt empowered as a woman—warrior or no. "You frighten me," she confessed.

His arms tightened around her, his breath sweeping across her temple. She heard the groan that slipped from his throat before he spoke gruffly, "You need never fear me, Coronis. If I have done something to cause you fear, I ask your forgiveness."

She looked up at him, whispering, "Ask my forgiveness?" He asked for her forgiveness? He'd done nothing save champion her again and again. And now, when she wavered in his arms, he sought her forgiveness. "The only wrong you've done me is taken my God from me."

His gaze held hers. "For one as loyal as you, I imagine it is a grievous loss."

She nodded.

"I am still your God, Coronis," his voice was low.

She frowned. "I cannot pray to my husband and I will not bed my God."

His gaze swept over her face as he cupped the back of her head. His jaw clenched briefly before he bent his head. "Then give your prayers to Hera or Athena." His mouth was soft-firm, fitting against her own and sealing them together. It was a slow kiss, an unspoken request. His lips urged her mouth open, mingling their breath until she swayed into him. A single stroke of his tongue along her lower lip had her eager for his seduction.

His mouth lifted, his nose tracing the shell of her ear, the hollow beneath the lobe. Her hands gripped his shoulder, desperate to stay upright when he drew the soft skin of her earlobe into his mouth.

"Since my arrival in Delphi, you have haunted my every dream," his whispered words tickled her flesh. "You have a hold on me like no other."

Her hands fisted in the silk of his tunic as she stared up at him. "I would release you if I could. I know there are others that would welcome you in my place."

He shook his head. "Is that why you resist me?"

"Resist you? I am in your arms, your wife," she argued, albeit breathlessly.

"Yet you hold yourself away from me. I would have you look upon me with the same longing you hold for your freedom. I want the breathless smile your run through the woods elicits. The sighs of delight roused by your secret baths… I demand the same fervent gleam in your eye I've seen when you find your mark and pull back the cord of your bow." He smoothed her hair from her forehead. "I crave such things—to bring you true pleasure and happiness." His thumb traced her lower lip, an almost anguished rasp to his voice.

His words painted an all too tempting picture. But she was wise, as her parents had taught her to be. She understood men, their nature. Immortal or no, Apollo was a man. "While I dread it," she admitted. "You are a hunter, sir. As am I. What sport is to be found in willing prey? The moment I look upon you with love, with passion and hunger—that is the moment the hunt is over. I have but one heart, my lord. When I give it, I would have it kept whole and cherished. Not returned, shattered, never to recover."

His face darkened then. "My word means nothing then?"

"My faith in Apollo the Olympian was absolute."

"I would have the same faith as your husband," his hands tightened on her shoulders. "I will not give up."

She would not be distracted by his strong brow or the flare of his nostril. She would not admire his perfection or the warmth of his body against her. She would not resist his body, she would not resist his company. But she would guard her heart. "Neither will I, husband," she promised.

His eyes swept her from head to toe, his smile so beautiful it was blinding. "By the Fates you are the most stubborn of women."

She smiled in return. "I am. It has served me well."

He pressed a fierce kiss to her lips. "Come, your parents and the good people of Delphi would celebrate with us before we go."

Chapter Ten

Coronis' words rang in his ears. While he watched her smile and laugh with her guests, he felt the gentle curve of her body pressed against him. While she accepted embraces and gifts, the scent of her hair filled his nostrils. He stared at her boldly knowing his behavior was shameless... He was lost in her, willingly lost in every subtle shift of her lithe body and every hint of emotion on her face.

'I would release you if I could.' Her words tore at his heart. Even now, when she held his heart, she would not love him.

"Today was a spectacle like none have ever seen," Phlegys joined him. "Again, I thank you for the honor you've bestowed upon my family."

"Is taking what I want honorable?" Apollo asked, smiling. "It is no hardship to take such a magnificent woman to wife."

Phlegys smiled. "She is now your wife, but she remains my daughter."

"I have seen the way you treat your queen," Apollo spoke carefully. "Yours is the example I will set for Coronis—she deserves no less."

Phlegys nodded, his face more grave than Apollo had ever seen it. "I will hold you to that."

Apollo stared at the man. If it had been any other mortal, he might take offense. But Phlegys loved his daughter. As did Apollo.

"I have a hunting cottage, on the cliffs at the edge of Delphi. It is a place Coronis holds dear..." Phlegys cleared his throat. "With a few servants, you and Coronis might be quite comfortable—if you were so inclined to delay your return to Olympus."

"I have no intention of taking her there. For now." Apollo regarded the man anew. "You are more than generous."

"I would see Coronis happy." Phlegys shrugged. "The wildlife is plentiful, as is the fishing. It might ease her to have some familiar comforts while she learns her duties as wife."

Apollo's gaze returned to Coronis. She sat forward, her hands clasped by that of an elderly guest. Her amber eyes were fixed on the lined face, earnestly absorbing the woman's words.

"I accept," Apollo murmured. "With thanks."

"Apollo," Hermes hissed. "You may be an Olympian, and newly married, but there is no cause to stare at your wife with such... anticipation."

Apollo blinked, looking first at Hermes, then Phlegys. When Talousa had joined them, he did not know. But he felt a twinge of embarrassment that he'd been caught gawking at his wife so. "Apologies."

Talousa inclined her head, a smile on her face.

"I seek but a moment of your time," Hermes spoke again. "I bid you farewell King Phlegys, Queen Talousa."

Apollo nodded, excusing himself and following Hermes from the hall. He searched out Coronis once before leaving the room.

"You are a man possessed," Hermes sighed. "Akin to Hades when he met his Persephone. Remember she is mortal 'til you've made her otherwise. A mortal doubtless reeling from all that's happened to her."

Apollo nodded, prodding, "This is what you wish to speak of?"

"No, brother, it is not. Yet I see your enthusiasm—all do—and seek to remind you to take care." He sighed. "I would bid you farewell. While you are enjoying your wife, I have been called to help Demeter. I ask, when you're not preoccupied with the delights of your marriage bed, that you keep alert for news of Erysichthon. We will all be happier when he is found and dealt with."

"Demeter? And her vengeance?" He paused then. How would he feel if his son was threatened? The boy in his vision was real, as was the love he bore him. If he were threatened... He swallowed down the fear and fury that rose. Perhaps he should no longer malign Demeter for seeking answers.

"Poseidon brought word of Ione's death. A fisherman says he pulled the body from the sea not long after Poseidon had cast her aside." Hermes shrugged. "Demeter would have proof. Proof I am sent to collect."

"What proof can you give her?" Apollo asked. "Save talk to the dead."

Hermes' brow rose.

"You..." Apollo shook his head. "You go to Hades' realm then?"

Hermes nodded. "He will know the truth of it-or his judges."

Apollo clasped Hermes' arm. "I do not envy you the journey."

"The Underworld is not so dreary as all on Olympus imagine. If anything it is more orderly, more just-as is Hades' way." Hermes continued. "But as Persephone and I are the only two able to travel into the land of the dead, Hades' work and his realm will remain unappreciated."

"As he prefers it." Apollo smiled. He was fond of his sullen kin. Now they shared a common enemy in Poseidon. "Wish him well for me," he added.

Hermes nodded. "I will, brother." He paused, staring into the room behind them. "Coronis..."

"Is my wife," Apollo interrupted.

"She is," Hermes agreed. "I would advise you to treat her as such, with care and kindness."

Apollo stared at Hermes. "Shall I keep an eye on the fair Mara for you?"

Hermes frowned. "If you wish it. Her innocence is a rare gift."

"Hermes," Coronis called out. "You would leave with no farewell."

Apollo was struck anew by the flush on her cheeks and sparkle in her eye.

"No, lady," Hermes assured. "I would have sought you out first."

Apollo watched them, the easy camaraderie between his wife and his dearest friend. He'd no reason for jealousy, yet it was there.

"Father says you leave now?" she asked.

"I am. An errand for Demeter," he agreed.

"Where will this errand take you?" Coronis glanced upon him before asking Hermes, "Somewhere foreign and exciting?"

Apollo smiled. "He goes to Hades' realm, wife."

Coronis eyes went round. "But... why?"

"It is too long and arduous a tale to tell now. I will say only that Demeter seeks the whereabouts of a long lost princess—one who might help bring the shade Erysichthon to heel."

While Hermes seemed unaware of Coronis' peculiar reaction, Apollo was not. In those few seconds of unguarded reaction, her terror had been clear. The knowledge that he'd done this to her, he'd changed her, gripped his heart with an icy fist. When he'd come to Delphi, Coronis was strong and fearless. Yet the last few days had seen her anxious and afraid more than once.

Why she would react so to Hermes' explanation was a puzzle. Was the tale of Erysichthon one she'd heard as a child? Many mortals dreaded the shade and the havoc such a vengeful soul caused... Or was it something more?

"I... I wish you a swift journey," Coronis' voice trembled. "And that whatever answers you find soothe Demeter's spirit."

"I fear only one answer will soothe her spirit." Hermes sighed. "Unless I find Ione, Demeter will not rest." Hermes bent low over her hand. "But I thank you nonetheless." He clasped arms with Apollo, clapping him once on the shoulder, then left them.

Apollo's smile faded when he noted Coronis pallor. She was so pale, her face stark white. Her amber eyes blinked rapidly—warding off tears?

"Coronis?" he spoke softly, drawing her into his arms and tilting her face towards his. "Are you unwell?"

She shook her head, then nodded. "Over-tired, perhaps." Her hands gripped his chiton so tightly he wondered the silks did not tear beneath her touch.

He stroked her cheek, searching her eyes for answers. But she would not hold his gaze, focusing instead on his chest and taking slow, deep breaths. "If I'd known you were so fond of Hermes I would have demanded he stay," he teased.

Her smile was weak. "No... no... I would not keep him from his duty." He felt the shudder that wracked her body.

"Is it his duty that frightens you? His travels to the Underworld or the tale of the shade Erysichthon. When you were a child, did your parents tell you he would steal you from your bed if you misbehaved?"

Coronis stared up at him, her eyes round. "No, never. Is that true?"

He shook his head. "He is a threat to no one save Persephone and those that would protect her—those that take part in the Eleusinian mysteries."

"My parents never spoke of Erysichthon," Coronis relented. "But that did not keep me from hearing the grisly tale all the same." She shook her head. "Why... never mind."

"Ask," Apollo spoke quickly. "All you need ever do is ask. I will answer."

She met his gaze. "Do you mean that?" she asked.

He nodded, frowning. "I do."

"Anything?"

He nodded.

"Why does Demeter seek Ione?" her voice was a whisper.

"She wants Ione to capture Erysichthon." Apollo paused. "The king was her favored servant at one time. So favored she offered Persephone to him in marriage. But before the wedding was done, the king was set upon by a sort of madness and Persephone was forced to flee. He blamed Demeter for Persephone's disappearance and cut down her sacred cypress grove. He was cursed for his blasphemy and died shortly thereafter, but he did not give up his search for fair Persephone. He hunts her, most relentlessly—ruthlessly. More than a hundred mortal girls have died or suffered injuries at the shade's hand."

"Those that take part in the Eleusinian Mysteries?" Coronis asked, shivering.

He nodded. "Demeter hopes that holding Ione might force Erysichthon's hand and end his campaign. Perhaps the shade will surrender if his own daughter is in peril..."

"Peril?" Coronis gasped. "But what has this woman done? What wrong has she committed?"

Apollo's frown increased. "I know little of the poor woman, Coronis. I know she has committed no crime and earned no punishment. Yet she is Erysichthon's only child. And Demeter's last hope." He shrugged. "Demeter is desperate. So desperate that she has enlisted Poseidon and Ares in her hunt. Hermes too, as he is the only one able to visit Hades' realm."

She seemed to consider this, her attention wandering to her hands, still gripping his tunic. She released him then, smoothing the fabric before meeting his gaze once more. "But not you?"

"No." He shook his head. "Hunting Ione is the very thing she's condemned Erishychton of. I admit the answer eludes me-grieves me-but I will not seek out the mortal woman. From the little I do know, she has suffered enough at the hands of Olympus."

He was startled by the satin of her hand upon his cheek. And by the flicker of heat in her gaze. He ached to fan that flame-to unleash the passion he suspected lay within his reach. He eased her closer, so close he could feel the unsteady beat of her heart. "Your father has offered us the hunting cottage, for whatever time we need... to get acquainted as husband and wife."

Color bloomed in her cheeks, delighting him.

"He said you were fond of the place. Perhaps being there, you will become fond of me."

The tale of Erysichton was a grievous one. Coronis thought of her poor mother, the young accolades killed—so much pain and suffering. Too much—with no hope of an easy resolution. She should be fretful... Instead she was helpless.

But cradled as she was in the arms of one that could destroy her, she felt no fear. Coronis could not look away from this man... this immortal. Her husband. After such a day, after so many revelations, she must resist the temptation he offered. She could not love him and keep such secrets from him. She must remember that Apollo is both her salvation and her downfall. Yet now, he held her in his arms, her body most affected, and asked for nothing but her affection.

"I will try," she admitted, her voice tight.

His brow furrowed. "You will *try*?" He sighed. "I will be most relentless in my pursuit."

She could not stop her smile. "Pursuit? Again, my lord, you have won me. There is nothing left to pursue."

"I will not rest until I have all of you, Coronis," he whispered. "Your mind, your body," he paused, pressing a lingering kiss to her startled mouth. "Your heart and your soul."

She shivered. "My soul? What use have you for my soul?"

"You are mine." His lips descended again. "Immortals have no use for souls."

Coronis was still puzzling over his words when her mother arrived, drawing them back into the party. Did he hope to make her immortal then? Her life's path was so altered she knew not what to want or feel.

Yet Apollo's arm, strong and steady, beneath her palm distracted her from the things she would do well to remember. She must fight the pull her husband had upon her, the desire to wrap him in her arms and offer him her heart. His devotion was a temporary thing. She knew of his many lovers-and the depth of their heartbreak when he moved on. She'd grown up listening to such tales of heartbreak and tragedy. All gave in, all submitted to Apollo's whim.

She could not.

When he tired of her, she would still bear the burden of protecting her parents' secret. When he tired of her, those things she'd shared in passion-in the newness of love-could become a weapon used against her mother, father, and her heart.

If the time came she was forced to admit her bloodlines, she would start by telling Apollo who her father was. But as Apollo bore Poseidon no affection, would it matter? Or would such a confession increase her husband's wrath?

She glanced at him, unnerved by the flare of awareness deep in her stomach. A slow ache that increased as she unobtrusively explored the plateaus of his face. She'd seen many sketches of him, statues, and paintings-but none displayed him as he was.

His hair fell long and golden upon his shoulders. He had a strong jaw, the slightest cleft in his chin. His nose was straight, a ridged blade on angled cheeks. Full brows that accentuated the most mesmerizing eyes she'd ever seen. Such eyes. Their color changed: tawny, sand, copper, or gold. And when he turned his gaze upon her, they seemed alight, heating her flesh and warming her from within.

He spoke to Ichthys now, a smile lighting his face. The creases at the corner of his eyes revealed his generous nature. Only a man who smiled wore such lines. He wore them far too well.

He turned his hand, lacing his fingers with hers in a strangely intimate gesture. He did not look at her or pause in his conversation, but he must be aware of her inspection. And, perhaps, her hesitancy.

"Pina and I have all packed," her mother said, startling her. "But I seek a moment, to ensure we've included all you need?"

Coronis nodded, startled when Apollo's hand tightened on hers. She glanced at him, an eyebrow lifted in question.

He smiled at her, both his brows rising in return. He lifted her hand, kissing the inside of her wrist, before releasing her. She stood, bemused, staring at him, until her mother led her away.

"Have we made a mistake?" her mother asked when they entered her room.

"A mistake?" she returned.

"He is so..." her mother paused. "Overwhelming in his admiration of you."

Coronis could hardly refute it.

"Forgive me?" her mother clasped her shoulders. "Forgive me for not telling you sooner. For telling you at all." She shook her head.

Coronis hugged her mother. "My heart aches for all that you have been through Mother. For the fear and worry that has been your constant companion. If there was something I could do to ease it..."

"Be happy." Her mother interrupted. "It is all I have ever wanted. For you to live in joy. To love with your whole heart, free from complications." She shook her head again. "Something I have made impossible now."

Coronis pressed a kiss to her mother's cheek. "Will Pina come with me?"

"And Mara," her mother nodded. "It would seem Hermes favors the girl."

Coronis smiled. "She is sweet. And lucky to have a champion in Hermes."

"Perhaps. But not all Olympians choose to marry when a mortal catches their interest." Her mother drew back. "My heart is happy that he loves you so."

Coronis felt her cheeks heat. "Perhaps. I... I have no skill in the art of love, mother."

"Of course not. He would not expect you to." Her mother smiled. "In truth, I think he would be greatly displeased if you possessed any skills of seduction, Coronis."

"You tease but father has taught me that training and knowledge are necessary to succeed..."

Her mother laughed, covering her mouth with her hands.

She stared at her mother, stunned at her laughter. "Mother," Coronis hissed, turning on her heel to leave the room.

"Coronis, no, stop."

Her mother's call stopped her.

"Child, it is your husband's place to-to train you. You know what's expected when you lie with a man..."

"I do," she snapped.

"It is a joy I cannot express," her mother continued. "You must welcome him, be calm and all will be well." Her mother took her hand in hers. "Now, Pina was most thorough, I think? She and Mara have gone ahead to prepare."

The rest of the day blurred before her. She was aware only of her husband. Once she'd returned to the celebration, Apollo—her husband—had not left her side. Whether he held her hand or his hand rested, large and warm, upon her lower back, his presence was felt upon her. What stunned her was she welcomed it—him.

It was only when the farewells began that she knew, soon, she would be alone with a man who overwhelmed her even surrounded by a thousand people. She shoved such thoughts aside, focusing on the people waiting for her. Some embraced her. Others knelt, asking for her blessing. To some she was Coronis, to others a Goddess. Never had she felt so lost.

"I am yours, Coronis. If you ever have need of me," Ichthys murmured in her ear, his embrace quick and his smile tight. "I will come. In an instant, I will come."

She felt a moments sadness as his dark brown eyes bore into hers. Perhaps he did love her. Perhaps she should have married him the day she'd come of age...

"Coronis," her father drew into his arms. "Send one of Apollo's messengers if you have need of anything."

She hugged her father tightly, burying her face against his neck. No matter that Poseidon created her, Phlegys was her father. His scent was the balm to her childhood nightmares and injuries. His hands had taught her how to aim her bow and wield a knife. His voice had both censured and praised her.

"Your mother will want a word from you now and then—when

you have time," he continued.

She felt his kiss on the top of her head and held on a moment longer. "I will," she spoke, releasing her father and swallowing the knot in her throat. "I will."

He nodded.

She suffered through more of her mother's tears, denying her own. It would not do to fall apart now. Now, when anxiety gripped her tightly.

As her father escorted her down the remaining steps to Apollo he whispered, "Are you safe daughter?"

Apollo's gaze met hers, his smile washing over her. She felt the brush of his gaze as it swept her from head to toe. In its wake her body seemed to pulse, seeking something unknown. She was safe. More than that, she was cherished. And while she could not know how long his devotion would last, there was a certain magic in feeling so adored. "I am," she answered. "Do not linger. I'd say no more good-byes today."

Apollo clasped her father's arm. "I thank you for your generosity. You are a king amongst kings."

Her father smiled, bowing slightly. "One devoted to the God Apollo, even if he is now my son. A son who I charge with protecting my only daughter."

"You have my word," Apollo assured.

Her father released Apollo. "Coronis knows the way." She watched her father nod, saw the hesitation before he headed back inside. She turned away, staring blindly at the view she knew as well as her own hand.

Charon pranced in the dust, tossing his grey head and pushing between her shoulder blades. "Are you eager for adventure?" Coronis asked, smiling.

"As am I," Apollo stood, looking down at her.

"It is no small journey. It might be wise to wait..."

"I cannot wait," he interrupted, pulling her into his arms.

She stiffened briefly, unused to being held so. But the instant his hand cupped her cheek, she eased. She lifted her face to his, offering him her mouth. And he accepted.

This was no gentle kiss but one laden with hunger. His hunger for her. His mouth was firm, demanding, stealing her breath and forcing her lips apart. And still he did not break from her. His tongue caressed hers, stroking deep into her mouth. She moaned brokenly, clinging to him. Her arms slipped around him, anchoring herself firmly to his unwavering strength when she had none.

"You taste of honey and wine," his words brushed her lips. "I would have another taste." He pressed soft kisses to the corner of her mouth, savoring the full pad of her lower lip, before deepening the kiss once more.

With a growl, he tore his lips from hers. His gaze pinned hers as his hands slipped through her hair.

In an instant everything changed.

His gaze grew shuttered, his expression fierce and body rigid. She could not move, his arms pressed her tightly to him. He looked as he did the day of the races, an unrepressed violence that had left her concerned for him. Now, when his hands near tore her hair from her head, she wondered at his altered state.

"Apollo?" She spoke, pushing against his chest with both hands.

His eyes looked upon her, but he did not see her-or so it seemed.

"Apollo, please," she rasped. She had no air in her lungs and had no hope of drawing in breath with his arms so tight about her.

Just as suddenly, he released her. She would have fallen if he'd not caught her. "Coronis..." he whispered, enfolding her so tenderly she forgot the burn of her scalp and ache in her sides. "Coronis."

She drew in a ragged breath. "I am here."

"Forgive me," the anguish in his voice startled her. "Did I hurt you?" He pulled back, smoothing the hair from her head.

She shook her head.

He pressed her behind him, his gaze sweeping the land surrounding them. What he was looking for, she did not know. But there was no denying that something troubled him.

"What is it?" she asked, taking his hand in hers.

He glanced at her, at their joined hands. "I would leave this place."

She moved toward Charon. "Then let us go."

"No." He shook his head, whistling once. "Not that way."

The air shifted, a strange wind buffering down and forcing her to look up. If her world had not been so irrevocably altered, she would have thought herself mad. She knew of Apollo's chariot, all good Grecians did. It set the sun in the sky and carried it away again, but hearing about such a thing had not prepared her for seeing it. She stared at Apollo then.

"That way," he spoke with satisfaction.

The chariot basket was gold and white, etched in bronze or copper. Its wheels shimmered iridescent in the late afternoon sun. Four magnificent horses pawed the air as their manes billowed out behind them. They seemed unaware of their flight. When hooves met earth, they ran steadily toward their waiting master and stopped almost atop him. She held her breath, watching the beasts snort and prance.

"Come." He waved her forward.

"Charon?" she asked. "Balek?"

"We can send for them later, Coronis," he took her hand. "I will wait no longer."

She climbed into the chariot, gripping the gilded railing as he climbed in behind her. He seemed to dwarf her, enveloping her with his size and presence. His scent surrounded her as did his arms.

"You must follow the ridge," she began, pointing to the south. "Veer left at the bent stump. When we come to the cave..."

"Cave?" Apollo asked.

She nodded, glancing back at him. "A break in the rock, a seemingly endless cave." She smiled. "Do I know this land better than you?"

He lifted her hair, draping it over her shoulder. "I have no doubt of it." His pressed the softest kiss to her temple. "I look forward to exploring all of it with you." He lifted the reins then, waiting for further direction.

"At the cave, we follow the left finger of the river," her voice was far too soft for her liking. She cleared her throat. "When it drops from the cliffs, we take the path up to the highest peak."

The horses leapt forward, throwing her into the wall of Apollo's chest. His arm tightened about her, his hand pressed flat beneath her breast. The animals speed was such that Coronis was unable to distinguish any familiar landmarks, whether they traveled over land or through the sky. It did not matter that he said nothing and moved not at all. Something in the weight of his hand upon her overruled every thought and emotion. She could not control the beat of her heart or the quaver in her breath.

The ride was too brief. Such a journey lasted a day, time enough to collect her thoughts and prepare for what was to come. Most had more than a day to reconcile themselves with their wedding and their wedding bed. It made no sense for her to dread the evening. Had she not spent the better part of her womanhood hearing stories of Apollo's prowess? Of what a generous lover he was? His unsurpassed skills.

Her stomach churned.

She felt the play of muscles in his chest and arms tighten as he drew the team to a stop. She stared at the hunting cottage, resisting the panic that welled inside her. What if she displeased him? She was not soft as most women. She was stubborn and argumentative...

"This is no cottage," Apollo spoke. "This will do well."

It was more modest than their home in Delphi, but no less luxurious. Marble columns ran the length and width, as well as the inner courtyard. Most walls were lined with carvings, slats cut through the stone to allow a cooling breeze from the mountains at all time. As it was remote, this was a place Coronis had felt most free. Why, then, did she want to flee?

Apollo stepped from the chariot and turned, reaching for her. She took the hand he offered but was too uneasy to look upon him. Instead of helping her from the chariot, he held her close, pressing his head to her chest and listening to the sound of her heart. She wavered, her hands slowly settling in his silken locks. It helped, to have him soothe her so-to touch him. But then he lifted her into his arms and carried her toward the cottage.

Chapter Eleven

Apollo cradled her body, burying his nose in the silken hair atop her head. The vision was too real, too terrifying. He could not blot it from his mind nor erase the pain it caused him. He must seek the Oracle, perhaps he'd find answers. And he must have answers.

"Apollo." He heard Coronis' plea, "Put me down, please."

"I will," he offered no further explanation.

He'd not recovered from the vision yet, from the terror that gripped him. It started the same as the last. She ran, crying, two arrows in her chest. The rest were fragments, sudden images too hurried to make sense of. His hands bloodied. Her face, contorted in agony as she begged for his help. His crows circling in a smoke filled sky. An incoherent scream-one of pure agony and rage. But not from Coronis. It was he that cried out so...

He'd not meant to crush her or frighten her when he was in the throes of prophecy. Holding her had eased him. He must hold her tightly to keep her safe. Safe and warm and in his arms. He drew in another breath, her scent giving him peace. She squirmed when Mara and Pina appeared, but he did not release her. He could not, not yet.

"Your chambers are prepared," Mara spoke, her surprise covered when Pina nudged her sharply with her elbow. "Follow me," she added, leading them through the inner courtyard.

He did not pause, the house would wait until he was recovered. Right now, he would hold his wife and drown the anxiety that plagued his heart.

The room glowed with candles. An evening breeze lifted the swaths of gauze that hung around the large bed in the center of the room. The air was chilled but a roaring fire crackled and snapped in the fire pit. And before the first pit, a copper tub and clean linens.

"You've done well," Apollo acknowledged. "Bring my lady food and drink."

Mara curtseyed low and left them.

"Will you put me down?" Coronis asked.

He looked down at her and smiled. She was annoyed, her cheeks pink and a slight frown marring her brow. "You are angry with me."

"You humiliate me," she spoke softly. Her eyes strayed from his, though the sight of their chambers did little to ease her temper. When her eyes settled upon the copper tub, every muscle in her body tightened.

"I like the feel of you in my arms."

She stared up at him.

"Kiss me." Whether he asked or commanded, he did not know. Her brow smoothed. "Apollo…"

"Kiss me and I will put you down." The play of her emotions was almost comical.

She leaned forward, kissing him chastely upon the cheek, then relaxing in his hold. He loved the self-satisfied smile she wore. The spark of fire in her eyes lightened his mood considerably. She looked far too pleased with herself.

He smiled in answer, letting her feet touch the floor before tugging her into his hold. "You disappoint me wife," he murmured, lowering his head to hers.

She did not resist him. Indeed, she lifted her face to his, still smiling. But he did not kiss her. He released her. She frowned then, making him laugh.

"I disappoint you?" she bit back.

He grinned. "Never," he murmured, sealing his mouth to hers.

Her mouth was lush and ripe, her lips supple and inviting. That the caress of her mouth emptied his lungs and made him mindless with want was unnerving. He'd had many lovers and many kisses. Such a simple touch should not make his blood roar and his heart race. Yet it did, and he reveled in it. He could not remember a time when love, desire, felt new.

She sighed, parting her lips with no coaxing from him.

He would please her. His hands cradled her face while his lips nudged her mouth wider, the tip of his tongue tracing the inside of her lower lip.

Her arms twined about his neck, her fingers tangling in his hair as her mouth fastened upon him. He'd not expected the sudden hunger in her kiss, the abandon with which she gripped his hair and pulled him closer. He obliged, one arm lifting her so that her curves fitted perfectly against him. She pulled back, her eyes scouring his face, intent yet dazed. There was no denying the startled awareness that rippled through her. She pulled his mouth back to hers, her soft sigh an invitation. Yet, it was her tongue that teased him, her thumb that grazed his lower lip, even as she trembled in his arms.

She broke away, shaken and gasping for breath. "What is this?" Her eyes met his. "I ache. My body, my breath, demands more."

Her words ignited him. "There is much more."

She blinked, her attention wandering to his mouth. "Show me."

He tilted her head back, forcing her gaze to meet his. He reached up, freeing her hair from the small combs that held it in place. His fingers slid through the braids, working patiently until her hair fell in gilded browns and golds down her back.

She watched him closely. A haze of desire hung upon her, but she was not lost to it-not yet.

His fingers fumbled briefly with the clasp at her shoulder, forcing his attention. Once the heavy ornament was removed, his fingers explored the slope of her narrow shoulders, the dip at her throat, and the arch of her neck. His gaze followed his hands' journey, feasting upon her. How he longed to explore her with his mouth, to nip the earlobe as he removed the dangling jewelry. He leaned forward, pressing a kiss to her neck as he removed the last piece of adornment. Even with none of the precious metal upon her, to his eyes she was gilded.

Her under tunic was pinned and tucked, an intricate fall of fabric and ribbon. And while he longed to rid her of her garments, he took the time to memorize her as she was before reaching for the brooch at her shoulder.

Her hand reached up, covering his. "Wait." She regarded him with wary eyes, hesitant once more. "Mara," she murmured.

Apollo turned to see the girl placing a tray of food on the table in the corner. The girl seemed unbothered by them, focusing only on her work. He had no doubt Pina had a hand in that, for Pina had been most displeased by the girls' reaction earlier. Still, be it Pina or Mara, he had no care who was in the room when he held his wife to him. His wife did.

"Are you hungry?" he asked Coronis.

She shook her head, turning from him to stare into the fire.

"A drink?" he asked.

She shook her head again, frowning at him. "I must tell you something," Coronis' hushed words surprised him.

Apollo sat in one of the chairs before the fire, watching his wife. "Tell me."

"I have never..." Coronis stumbled to a stop. "I am a mortal. A woman with no knowledge of man. A mortal husband would find this pleasing. But most mortal men have not loved as you. You have many lovers and many children. I have no skill in such things... I've yet to understand why you've chosen to marry me. Save the child." She paused. "You spoke of a son. He must be of importance..."

"I am pleased." Apollo stood, gripping her shoulders. "If such a man existed, I would hunt him down. You are mine and mine alone. I claim you, body and soul. As you have claimed me."

"I've made no claim," she argued.

"You've no need. I love you," Apollo spoke. "I've made no secret of this. Whether my love is returned matters not. I am yours, woman. And you are mine."

A look of wonder crossed her face. But what truly fascinated him was the flush of her skin, the way her chest shook, each breath quivering and unsteady. He stepped forward, smoothing the hair from her shoulders to trail one finger slowly along the curve of her face, the length of her neck, and across the blade of her shoulder. She flexed her hands as his finger continued its path, along the inside of her arm, brushing the sensitive skin of her inner elbow before encircling her wrist in his hand. He lifted it, turning her hand to trace the lines of her palm.

He was vaguely aware of Pina and Mara hurrying about,

pouring water in the copper tub. But all that mattered was Coronis' gaze upon him. He heard the rasp of her breath, felt the throb of her pulse in her wrist. He would stir her desire, lead her toward true hunger, then show her how he loved her.

He waited until they were alone before freeing her under tunic. His gaze fell from her face, savoring each new inch of exposed skin. She lifted her arms as he unwound the fabric, walking in a leisurely circle. He stilled, admiring the smooth plane of her back. She glanced back at him, her eyes wide and her lips parted.

He dropped the length of the tunic, encircling her waist in his hands. She shuddered, her arms folding over her chest. He swept the hair over her shoulder and bent to kiss the base of her neck. She smelled like his woman, sweet and warm. He ran his nose along her shoulder, inhaling her deep.

"Come," he murmured, leading her toward the fire to avoid the chill of the night air.

She followed, one arm pinning her tunic about her waist to preserve her modesty. When she stood before the crackling fire he smiled at her, his hands lifting hers to his mouth. He kissed each knuckle, his eyes boring into hers. She was breathless, her shoulders' rise and fall accelerated and her gaze uncertain. He could not remember the first time he loved a woman, not her face or name. So much time robbed him of such memories.

If there were a way, he would save this night. The light upon her skin as the gauze of her tunic settled about her hips. He swallowed, overcome by the sight of her.

Her form was exquisite, leaner than most women. Her trim arms reflected grace and athleticism. Her breasts were slight and high, crowned by nipples a dusky rose. He did not resist the urge to touch her. Yet the feeling of her breast filling his hand left him reeling. He wanted to touch her, to explore every dip and valley. A moan escaped him as he regarded his hand upon her. His thumb grazed the tip. Her body responded, instantly tightening, her heart pounding against his hand.

His lips descended on hers, one hand cradling her cheek while the other slid the tunic from her hips. He broke away from her then, a muffled groan escaping him as he cupped her bare hip and held her tightly to him. She was silk, her skin more intoxicating than

Olympus' finest wine. He would drink her in and never tire of her.

Her hands rested on his arms, gripping the thick muscles of his arm and shoulders. "Apollo..."

His name from her lips was the sweetest music.

She turned into him, her mouth seeking his and finding his neck. Her lips were moist, latching onto his, inflaming him. She made quick work of his restraint. Whatever hesitation she'd felt was gone. She seemed most intent on discovering the rest. And with each touch of her lips to his neck, she left a spark of want burning in its wake.

He lifted her easily, smiling against her mouth as she twined his arms around her neck. He met her gaze as he carried her to the large bed. He lay her back, then stood staring down at her. His inspection was most leisurely and thorough. From the soft swell of her breasts, her narrow waist, the plain of her belly and curve of her hip, the supple length of her thighs, and the barest thatch of hair between—she was glorious.

"You stare," she murmured, drawing her legs up.

He stroked her knee. "I do." His hand slid down her calf to gently clasp her ankle. "Do not hide from me, lady. Let me see all of you." He guided her leg down, bending to press a kiss on the inside of her knee. Her body bowed tight and her breath escaped on a strangled gasp. His hand rested on her belly while his gaze traveled lower. "I would learn your body as I know my own." His hand followed, parting her thighs so that he might see the untried treasures of her body. She was gasping then, but so was he. She was his and only his. And it inflamed and amazed him. His gaze returned to her face, fearful that he would lose the precarious grip he had on his control, his want was so great.

Her body was flushed, her breathing ragged, and her amber eyes glazed. She knew not what she craved, but craved it no less fiercely than he.

He tugged his exomie free, throwing it over his shoulder without care. When he climbed onto the bed, she rose up to meet him. She slid her arms around his neck, one hand pressed to the side of his face as he drew her body against his. "I am lost," she murmured.

He shook his head and smoothed her hair from her shoulders.

"I will help you find your way," he promised, shuddering at the crush of her, skin on skin.

She rubbed her nose against his chest, pressing a soft kiss over his thundering heart.

His hand captured hers and held it in place. He need not say it again. He loved her. The rampant beat of his heart echoed his words. Whether she would believe it-accept it-was uncertain. But in this moment, she yielded to him. He gave in to the want that consumed them both.

Coronis stared at her hand upon his chest. No mortal could fabricate such a rhythm. Could an Olympian? And to what purpose? Now was not the time. Whether his love was true, his want of her was. His body tightened and rose—for her. That knowledge was exhilarating.

His hands clasped her to him, his mouth covering hers as they fell back onto the silks and furs covering their bed.

She'd not expected his mouth to explore her so, that he'd nip and suck upon her side or lave the skin on the inside of her elbow. His tongue was feather light, drawing forth a rippling shiver of sensation. His hands were not idle. While his mouth was relentless, he stroked and caressed every inch of her.

When his fingers stroked lightly across the nub between her legs, she turned her head into the rumpled blankets she gripped. Again he touched her, setting a rhythm against that flesh-a source of exquisite yet agonizing delight.

"Your warmth greets me, Coronis," his words caressed her inner thigh, causing her grip to tighten on the fabric she clung to.

The caress of his finger did not ease as he slid a finger inside of her. She heard his choked groan, felt his head fall against her thigh, but could not open her eyes. She'd never imagined such sensations. She throbbed from the feel of him and longed for more.

Her hands drifted, finding his head and tangling in his long locks upon her thigh. She craved the touch of his chest upon her, the heat of his mouth on hers…

Instead, his mouth replaced his fingers and Coronis cried out. Her body bowed, arching back as his tongue urged her on.

Her hands released his hair only to cling to his shoulders. His arm pinned her hips, holding her in place as his mouth and tongue devoured her. She melted, her body succumbing to raw pleasure. It started slowly, a wash of sparks rising from within that gave way to a wave of heat. Each stroke of his tongue, his breath on her inflamed skin, the tightening of his hands on her hips made the waves grow more powerful, gripping her body with a relentless trembling. She held on to him, needing to touch him—to hold him. Then she was drowning, her body clenching with a pleasure that bordered pain. His mouth was insistent, driving her on and pushing her over the edge of sensation. She cried out over and over, mindless in the ecstasy that crashed over her.

She lay gasping for breath as he worked his way up her body. She was shattered, yet his hands and mouth still stirred her. When his lips found hers, she twisted her fingers into his hair.

"Open your eyes," he rasped.

She did.

His jaw was rigid, his nostrils flared, every muscle in his neck and chest were taut. He fought for control... Had giving her such pleasure pained him so? She touched his cheek, stunned by the powerful hunger in his tawny eyes.

"I would not hurt you," his voice broke as he eased himself between her legs. She could feel him, the rigid length of him heavy and throbbing against her thigh.

She pulled his hair, eager for his lips on her but he resisted. He stared down at her, every muscle in his body taut with restraint. Even now, when she knew he longed to claim her as his own, he exercised control. Slowly, gently, he entered her body. His heat and size filled her, a foreign yet elating invasion. Her hands slid to his chest and he froze, searching her face. Her body strained to accommodate him, unused to such pressure. Such sweet pressure. There was no pain, only an inescapable intensity. He waited, watching her. The muscles of his neck and shoulders bulged, his jaw clenched tightly. Yet he held himself still, for her.

When his breath spilled out in a tight hiss, the sound unlocked something deep within her. Had he not proven himself time and time again? Had he not worshipped her body, giving her a passion she'd never imagined? And now he sought relief from the hunger that gripped him. She slid her hands over his shoulders, down his back, to grip his hips.

"You will not hurt me," she managed.

He stroked the hair from her face, searching her eyes for but a moment before thrusting deep. It was uncomfortable for an instant. He rested his forehead against her, kissing her lips softly. When his lips parted hers, she welcomed the heat he stirred within her. She delighted in the feel of his lips and tongue, the mingling of their breath. His kiss, his love, bid her body ease and open for him. He was a part of her, one she craved—one she would miss if he left her.

His hips began to move, the pressure and friction fanning the embers of her newly discovered desire. His hands found hers. His fingers threaded with hers, ensuring he held every part of her. Her body was his to do with as he wanted, a realization that pleased her more than expected. He thrust deep, pulling a moan from her mouth.

"By the Fates, I am yours," he groaned, his movements growing more demanding.

She arched into him, mimicking his movements. To feel him so, moving within her, filling her and laying claim upon her, was freeing—and wondrous. It was blissful—the waves of passion rising once more.

Apollo kissed her, nuzzling her neck, her shoulder, before nipping her breast. His tongue laved her nipple, slipping against its pebbled peak until Coronis was out of control. She was consumed in the fevered sensations, the touch of his hand, his scent, the rasp of his breath, his hand near crushing hers. When his mouth drew her nipple deep into his mouth, she cried out and fell apart, wracked once more with consuming pleasure.

His hands released hers, gripping her hips as his body tightened. She watched, mesmerized by the sight of him. His beautiful face ravaged with passion, his broken groan binding him to her in a way she didn't yet understand. His eyes met hers, boring into her and searing her heart. Every muscle stilled as he pushed deep, forcing a moan from them both, as he came undone. He was beautiful. The rigid length of him throbbed between her legs, spilling his seed inside of her.

She held him, waiting until he melted against her, released

from his need. She winced as he slipped from her body and lay at her side—missing his heat. But then he drew her close and twined his arms tightly about her, pressing a hard kiss against her forehead. Perhaps it was the sound of his heartbeat beneath her ear or the strength in his arms as he held her close that made her burrow into his arms. Perhaps it was the exhaustion following such a momentous day that bid her rest her cheek upon his chest. Or perhaps she wanted to be held by him, cherished by him... She turned her face into his chest, drawing in his scent to blot out all the rest. She was overcome—not just her body, but her heart as well...

"You shiver." He covered them in silks and furs before tucking her against him once more.

She should say something.

"Are you well?" he asked, stroking his fingers along her arm.

She nodded, startled by how easily he prompted her heart's pace to increase.

"Are you tired?"

She shook her head.

"Hungry?" he was amused, she could hear it.

She shook her head again.

He lifted the coverings and came over her. "Speak wife," he demanded. "Or I shall go mad."

She opened her mouth, then closed it.

His gaze seemed to linger on her neck. "Perhaps it is too late to save me from madness." He bent, pressing a kiss to the hollow of her throat. His warm breath fanned her skin, his tongue and lips stirring her once more.

She wanted nothing else. Never had her body ached so wondrously or her heart and lungs been so full yet so fathomless. She needed him, desperately. Now. "Do you need time to recover?" she asked, uncaring that her voice shook. She met his gaze, hoping...

"No," he answered quickly, coming between her legs and filling her once more.

He groaned as he buried himself in her, setting a vigorous rhythm. This time there was no hesitation. No, he was so deep within her she cried out. With his every thrust her body clenched tight, arching off the bed to meet him. She gripped his arms, wrapped her legs around his waist, and stared up at him.

He groaned, tossing the covers from them and rising onto his knees. He braced himself, clutching her hips and lifting her up to take him further still. She could not stop the cry that spilled from her lips, or the frantic buck of her hips. His gaze was fixed upon their bodies-where they came together again and again. A ragged oath tore from his lips, his jaw clenching tight as he paused. He looked at her then.

She was gasping for breath, mesmerized by the look on his face, the hunger in his eyes. She ran one hand down his body, her fingers tracing the heavy muscles of his chest and stomach. His ragged breathing filled the room as he watched the path of her hand. His eyes met hers and she arched into him, asking what she could not put into words.

When he began to move again, her hand settled over his heart. He bent over her, nuzzling and nipping her breasts, her neck, her hands.

Her hands sought some foothold, something tangible, to anchor her. As her fingers twisted in his hair, her body spiraled out of control. She clung to him, holding on as her pleasure engulfed her into pure feeling. He was with her then, his strangled moan the only sound she heard in her dazed state.

Chapter Twelve

Apollo's hand stroked the length of Coronis' back. He waited, worrying of the after-effects from such a night. He'd been demanding of her—too demanding of one so innocent. Still, she'd come alive in his arms. His body stirred at the memory.

She dozed, her arms draped across him and her thigh resting upon his. It was a heady thing, to feel so sated, so at peace. But even after a night of passion, the need to touch her remained. When she turned onto her side, he curled about her back, burying his nose at the base of her neck. His gaze traced the line of her shoulder and hip... He'd seen a thousand women so, but none had transfixed him as Coronis.

His want for her was relentless. His love boundless. She stretched in his arms. She was not so soft, so yielding now.

"Are you awake, wife?" he whispered.

"Am I?" her voice was thick with sleep.

"No," he answered, pressing a kiss to her neck. "Sleep on."

She sighed, relaxing once more.

"Forgive me, Coronis," he murmured. "I'd not meant to use you so."

She looked back at him, a slight smile on her face. "Did you not?"

He frowned. "I was neither patient nor gentle..."

"Last night was truly magic." She rolled over in his arms.

He smiled then. "And for me."

She arched a brow. "Was it?"

His smile grew. "You doubt me?

Her eyes searched his for a long moment. "No."

His hand cupped her cheek, savoring the softness of her skin beneath the pad of his thumb.

"But I am curious..." she paused.

He waited, enthralled by the tones and colors of her eyes.

"What do you want with me now?"

Her question twisted his heart. "You think I'm done with you?" he could scarce manage the whisper.

"Are you?" She blinked furiously. "I..."

His mouth descended upon hers, latching onto her lips with a startling ferocity. He lifted his head when he felt her soften against him. "I am not." His frustration was too sharp to stay as he was. He'd planned to spend the day this way, lost in her. But her question chased such thoughts aside. He would find a way to gain her love and her trust in the love he bore her. He must. "I will call Pina for food and then you may show me all that I do not know of Delphi." His gaze lingered overly long, appreciating the supple expanse of her stomach and thigh, the fall of her gilded brown hair, and sparkle in her amber eyes.

Pina was equally quiet and efficient. She arrived before he could call, carrying a fresh tunic for Coronis.

Apollo washed quickly, leaving Coronis in Pina's care. He'd no interest in exploring the house last night, but now he ambled along the outer halls, taking in the views. On one side of the house, the forest was thick and lush. While the back of the home abutted a cliff, providing a sweeping vista of the rocks and sea below. The cry of the gull and the crash of the sea drew him to the edge. It was a sharp drop, though a set of stairs had been carved into the cliff facing. To Apollo's eye, it was the only way to reach the secluded beach below. He turned his face to the morning sun and sighed. It was a brilliant morn. The trees whispered in the cooling breeze, the air was alive with the song of his crows.

At once his temper eased. He must not be impatient with Coronis. She was a cautious woman, careful and logical. She would not give her heart to him so freely. That was why he valued it so. She was no Daphne or Khloris, as generous with their hearts as they were their body. No. When Coronis came to love him, it would be all the sweeter.

He wandered, appreciating the fine mosaics that adorned the walls of the main courtyard. They were in honor of him, the God Apollo. Apollo the archer. Apollo and Artemis running with the creatures of the forest. Apollo riding across the sky in his chariot. Apollo playing the lyre while a satyr, undoubtedly Marsyas, was playing his aulos.

"Did you really skin him?" Coronis voice surprised him.

He turned to regard his wife. Had he ever beheld such beauty? He smiled, making no attempt to hide his appreciation for her. Her hair fell freely about her shoulders and her plain white tunic was twisted to knot behind her neck. "Who?"

"Marsyas." She nodded at the mosaic.

He sighed. "I've heard many stories about the great Apollo, some true, some nonsense."

"That is no answer," she countered, her brows rising.

"I did," he admitted. "There are times I've done things without thought. That was one of them." He stared at the mosaic, remembering Marsyas all too clearly. "His body became the Marsyas River-a river I threw my lyre into." He shook his head. "I regret such actions. But regret cannot undo what is done."

She regarded him with round eyes. "Do Gods often have regrets?"

Apollo shrugged. "If they do, they'd not admit it." He touched her cheek. "And you? Share one regret with me."

She took the hand he offered her, escorting her to the table Pina had arranged their breakfast upon. "A regret?" Her eyes narrowed as she considered his question.

"You have so few to choose from? Or too many?" he teased.

She smiled at him, arching a brow. "I was blessed to live with little regret in my life." Her eyes focused on the knife protruding from an apple. "But I have one."

Apollo sat back, transfixed by the play of emotion on her face. "Tell me."

"I was younger, weaker than I am now." She took the apple, slicing it. "Damocles was a friend-somewhat. He and Ichthys and I would run free, finding mischief... He was always stronger than us, but there were times he was—I suppose—charming." She tucked her legs up, picking up a slice of her apple. "He offered to help me—wrestling." She shook her head.

Apollo frowned, his blood heating.

"I was a fool, never doubting his intent. Until I was pinned beneath him." She shook her head. "I could not move. I'd never been afraid before that moment."

Apollo stared blindly at the food on the table, her words washing over him.

"He had a dagger at his waist..."

Apollo looked at her then.

"While he pawed at me, I pulled it from his belt. You've seen the scar?" She glanced nervously at him. "I'd aimed for his manhood, but hit his thigh."

Apollo nodded, unable to speak.

"The blade sliced through his thigh, coming out the inside," she murmured, shifting in her seat. "He rolled off of me, bleeding and screaming. And I stood over him, wanting to pull the knife free to end his life." She swallowed, meeting his gaze. "I didn't."

Apollo stared at her.

Her cheeks were stained with color, her posture rigid. She held herself straight, but he saw the quiver of her chin, the tightness of her grip upon the blade she held.

"Come here," he barked, unable to calm himself.

She frowned at him but stood and went to his side.

Apollo clasped her wrist, pulling her into his lap. He pressed her against his chest, letting her scent and touch calm the bloodlust in his veins. "I will kill him."

She looked up at him, startled. "No. It was years ago..."

"Some insults are unforgivable," he countered.

"Yet no true harm was done. I was frightened but not injured. Nor did I need saving," she argued, pulling away from his chest. "I protected myself. Yet I knew I was not strong enough to defeat him without the aid of a weapon—so I trained harder."

"You did not tell your father?"

"Damocles' father lived then, pouring talk of war and alliances into Damocles' ear at every turn." She shook her head. "I could not bring war on our people over such matters."

"There will be no war now." He spoke, forcing the words out. "Let me kill him."

Her brow furrowed.

"If I'd known this..." His throat constricted, ending his words on a groan. "He will be put in his place."

"He has been," she leaned into him, her gaze upon his face. "You have beaten him soundly, husband. If I'd known such a tale would stir your temper, I would have refrained from the telling." She smiled at him, her brow still furrowed. "Let us think on happier things."

Where had he been? What matter of great import had faced him while she fought to protect her honor? It galled him. His arms tightened around her waist, drawing her close to him once more. In his mind, he saw the whole of it. Coronis on the dirt, fighting Damocles. He was proud that she'd protected herself and pleased that she'd wounded him-left her mark of triumph on his skin. Yet, she should never have had to fight so.

"Apollo," she whispered, touching his face. She arched up, tilting her face toward his.

He kissed her, softly drawing in her breath and savoring her sweetness. "You are a warrior, Coronis." He stroked her face. "A warrior of honor."

"I am also a woman," her voice was thick.

"My woman," he agreed, exploring the curve of her face. "The woman I long to take back to bed and lose myself in."

"You should not say such things," she rasped.

"Why?" He smiled. "Because your body craves mine as mine craves yours? Because my words embarrass you? Or inflame you? There is no shame in wanting me, Coronis. Nothing would please me more." His hand slipped beneath her tunic, his fingers teasing the soft flesh behind her knee. "I confess, the only hunger I have is for you." His fingers wandered higher while his gaze remained fixed upon her face.

Coronis could not resist him. She did not want to. She did crave him. Her body demanded she yield to his touch. Being captivated by the fire of his gaze was the sweetest agony. A delight her senses had yet to recover from. His fingers were a light caress upon her thigh, moving ever higher. Her legs tightened, flexing in anticipation.

Her head fell back on his arm, offering him her surrender.

His mouth fell to her neck, his lips trailing along her neck while his fingers reached their target. With one caress of his finger, her legs parted for him. She turned her face into his arm, pressing her eyes shut as his fingers tentative touch set a firm rhythm against her most tender flesh. Her breathing grew heavy, her hands twisting in the linen of his tunic. When he slipped a finger inside her, he growled heavily against her throat.

"You unman me," he husked, his hands lifting from her so quickly she'd no time to argue. But there was no need. He lifted her, turning her in his arms to face him. She straddled him, needing the strength of him beneath her hands as the length of his desire pressed intimately against her. She sucked in a deep breath and grabbed his shoulders, nervously meeting his gaze.

His hands cradled her face, his gaze piercing hers, as they came quickly together. She was sore, his sudden invasion forcing the air from her lungs and releasing her passion. She wanted him, wanted this, oh so much. She bit into her lower lip to keep quiet.

He shook his head. "Keep nothing from me, Coronis. Cry out." His thumb swept over her lower lip, tugging it free. His lips fastened onto her, sucking it deep as his hands guided her hips in a growing rhythm.

Her hands tightened on his tunic. She frowned. She longed to touch his body, to kiss his skin. But then he was thrusting into her and it no longer mattered.

The sight of him wild drove her to the brink. That her body could rule an Olympian was a mystery she'd yet to understand. Yet, had his body not claimed hers? Did she not quiver and ache when he touched her—looked at her—with the slightest bit of passion.

She moved against him, his every sound and expression feeding her passion. He kissed her deeply, sealing her mouth with his and invading her with his tongue. His hands slid down her back, gripping her hips and lifting her. She was helpless in his hold, forced to do nothing more than embrace the raw friction and frantic pleasure. It took no time, his touch stirred her with ease. She came apart. She buried her face against his shoulder to muffle the sounds of her broken cry.

He found his release, his head falling back as he bowed tightly into her. She leaned forward, mimicking his earlier attention. Her tongue, the slight nip of her teeth, and the press of her open mouth. His hands gripped her hips tightly then, as his release continued.

When his grip eased, she melted against him-gasping and replete.

"I'd meant to be gentle with you," he gasped.

"Is it meant to be gentle?" she asked, her words breathless and unsteady. "For it comes upon me almost violently."

His hands cradled her face once more. "I suspect it will ease in time."

She considered his words. "You suspect?"

"Does it surprise you that you'd rouse something new within me?" His words were far too pleasing. He was Apollo, an Olympian. His affairs were the stuff of legend. She would not be so easily led.

Yet there was a part of her that wished his words were true. A part of her that felt pure joy she held a special place in his heart. And it troubled her. Greatly.

"I confess it does," she whispered, wary of his reaction.

He sighed, but nodded. "Words are empty vessels."

She said nothing. That he understood her doubt relieved her. She'd no understanding of what this connection was between the two of them, or how long it might last. But the thought of him leaving... Of being parted from him. Pain gripped her.

He kissed her. "What would you do this day, wife? We have a fine breakfast before us and no end of our leisure. Surely there is something you long to do?"

She forced her distress aside and slid from his lap, rewarded by the hiss of his breath as she did so. "I would eat," she spoke, smoothing her tunic into place.

He arched a brow. "Then let us eat."

She returned to her seat, smiling as he straightened his tunic. She served him, piling his plate with fruit and nuts and lamb.

"When you visited this place with your father, how would you occupy your time?" he asked between bites.

"Hunt and fish." She looked at him. "I shot my first boar in these woods. The woods here are lovely, full of life."

"Your father must have been proud."

"He was," she agreed. "Mother was furious with him."

Apollo laughed. "She does not approve?"

"She worries over me-as a mother will." She shrugged. "She preferred I spend my time exploring, Balek at my side. I suppose that was more ladylike and less dangerous."

"And what would you do on these explores?" He watched her closely. "Methinks your explorations weren't as harmless as you led your mother to believe?"

She smiled but said nothing.

He shook his head. "Finding caves?"

"And the bear that lived there."

Apollo stilled, a scowl lining his face. "A bear? Coronis-"

"It was long ago. And no one was injured, not even the bear." She waved a dismissive hand at him.

"How did you manage that?" he asked.

"I prayed. I was most loyal to Apollo." She smiled at him. "And Artemis as well, never venturing into her wood or hunting those that lived their without seeking permission. I'd not meant to disturb the bear and I'd no wish to be eaten." She drew her legs up, tucking her tunic about her.

"What happened?" He sat back, curious, and steepled his fingers before him.

"Balek and I had been out most of the day. It was hot, so we sought the shade. Balek must have scented the animal for he bounded into the cave. I followed, stumbling and foolish, into the dark of the cave. Only then did Balek quiet. He was at my side, the fur on his back pricking straight up. I heard the bear, saw the faint outline of its massive shape in the dark, and bid Balek stay at my side. I pressed against the cave wall and prayed."

"And what did you pray?" he asked.

"For stealth, so that I might survive. For strength so that I might win if I was forced to fight the bear. And for the bear." She shrugged.

"For the bear?" He smiled.

"It was no fault of the bear's that we'd stumbled into his home. I imagine I'd be prepared to do bodily harm to a stranger that invaded my house as Balek and I had done," she explained.

"You surprise me." His amusement was evident. "You were in danger, yet you pray for the very thing that threatens you."

"It didn't threaten me," Coronis argued. "Balek and I waited until it left the cave then followed. He never knew we were there-a feat I credit Artemis for."

"Artemis?" He crossed his arms over his chest.

"Shall I give you credit then? Even though you've no recollection of the event?" She crossed her arms over her chest in return.

He laughed, holding up his hands in defeat. "My sister was your guardian. Rather, the bear's. My wild sister has no interest in mortal man-unless they are disturbing her peaceful woods or its natural inhabitants."

Coronis felt no offense at his words. "I respect your sister's devotion, Apollo."

"The two of you would be friends, I think." He regarded her.

"Do you? I would like to meet her."

He stood, holding out his hand to her. "Not yet, wife. There will be time enough for such things later." He pulled her against him, pressing his lips against hers. "Much later."

Poseidon watched all, uncertain who deserved his sympathy. Demeter for the brow-beating she was facing. Or Zeus, for attempting order amongst his brethren.

"Enough!" Zeus' voice rolled through the Council Chamber. "Do not cross me on this. No more, Demeter!" He spun, facing Ares. "What cause do you have to threaten our people? *Our* people? Good Grecians. I warn you, the cause had best be steep to justify what's happened."

What had happened? Poseidon watched the color fade from Demeter's face while Ares turned a florid red.

The God of War scowled. "Mortals who keep secrets from their Gods."

Zeus threw up his hands. "Perhaps they feared they'd be skewered in their beds? Have their homes set afire? Why would you do such things? To a fishing village? Were there any arms amongst them?" He shook his head, the veins in his neck protruding as he clapped his mouth shut. He shook his head, muttering, "By the Fates, boy, you've no sense at all."

Ares scowl turned into a mask of fury.

"What have you to add, Demeter?" Zeus leveled a hard stare at the Goddess. "How was Olympus threatened? Greece threatened?" He paused but a moment before booming. "You will stop this campaign!"

"I will not!" She returned, her hands fisted at her sides. "I will not rest until-"

"You will. Most assuredly. Now." Zeus moved in close, his body rigid with an unspoken threat. "If you do not heed me on this, you are banished."

Demeter's eyes went round. "You would not."

"I would." Zeus sighed. "Have you forgotten our purpose? The lots we drew? You would turn our backs on the very mortals that look to you in their time of need? I've no doubt whatever else, they will fear you now. Is that what you want? Did this fisherman have insight? Did he know where Ione was?"

Poseidon saw the slight shake of Demeter's head. What had happened after he'd left? Demeter was most displeased with the elderly fisherman's tale but the mortal had still lived when he left. He'd thought the matter done and set out on the waves, sea foam and carefree-well pleased to be in his own realm.

"What of the fisherman's death?" Zeus' gaze bounced between Ares and Demeter. "A most unfortunate accident? What of those on the docks that came to his aid? The destruction of the fishing village? Have you no shame? You would battle your own people now?" He paused, his anger evident. "You seek answers yet punish those that give them to you. Your behavior is unforgivable."

"Hera," Demeter entreated now. "Make him see reason, I implore you-"

"Demeter, I support my husband in this." Hera's gaze was most sympathetic. "I cannot condone your search now. Not when it endangers the lives of the mortals we rule or threatens their fealty to us."

"But-" Demeter argued.

"This is done." Zeus snapped. "Persephone chose her path. She is happy, even knowing the risks. The Fates approve. You've servants eager and willing to protect your daughter as their own, even with the shade haunting them. Erysichthon's threat grows because of your actions, Demeter. Yours and yours alone. He will have justice eventually. I will have no more talk of vengeance, of hunting this mortal Ione, or of Erysichthon." Zeus spoke to the room. "This is my command."

Poseidon nodded when Zeus looked at him. He saw no point in pushing this matter.

"You've no need to banish me, brother. I leave Olympus," Demeter spoke. "I cannot bear to look upon you any longer."

"Demeter," Hera spoke. "Your heart is wounded now-"

"Now?" Demeter cut in. "It's an old wound, one that will not heal."

"Go then," Zeus was resigned. "You have forgotten who is friend and who is enemy. Return when you've found reason once more."

Demeter said nothing more as she left the Council Chamber.

"Am I banished?" Ares bit out.

Zeus scowled at him.

"Peace," Poseidon spoke. "Ares thought to assist Demeter, as did I. In truth, they cast the first blow." He lied easily. "For the part we played in the tragedy that followed, we are heartily sorry, brother."

But Zeus did not look at him as he spoke, his attention was centered on Ares. "Are we?"

Poseidon glanced at Ares then, hoping for some sign of remorse of the God of War. And while Ares expression remained fearsome and his body taut with anger, Poseidon prayed the ever so slight nod Ares offered Zeus would be enough.

"Good," Zeus spoke. "Tell me, what was said that unleashed such a bitter punishment?"

Poseidon sighed, glancing at Ares. But Ares was no help. His pride was wounded, he would not speak to Zeus unless he was forced. Considering the mood in the Council Chamber, perhaps it was best if he told the whole of it.

"He was the fisherman Ione was sold to, when her father still lived. He was the man she was with when I discovered her." Poseidon admitted. "When she disappeared, he assumed she'd drowned herself. When he found her clothing tangled in one of his fishing nets, he had all the proof he needed. But several years later he saw her again."

Zeus' crossed his arms over his chest, listening.

"He said she wore the clothes of a lady and rode a fine mount. But when she saw him, she fled quickly. Later he was visited by a man he called a warrior and statesman. The man gave him a bag of gold to forget who he'd seen in the market." Poseidon shrugged. "But Demeter's bag was larger and the fisherman told all."

"And the cause of the dispute?" Zeus prodded.

Ares cleared his throat, shifting from foot to foot with repressed aggression. All eyes upon turned upon him as Poseidon said, "He said that Ares was either lazy or cowardly not to have caught the shade by now."

"Did he know whom he spoke to?" Zeus asked, aghast.

Poseidon shook his head.

"No," Zeus agreed. "If he had, he would never have dared speak such blasphemy." His anger thickened his words but his look had softened when he regarded Ares again.

Poseidon reached Ares' side as Zeus moved off to join Hera and Athena.

"You've a gifted tongue," Ares spoke. "I've never heard such… slippery truths."

Poseidon laughed.

"I confess, there was little glory to be found. I seek a skilled adversary, one that will challenge my arm and mind." Ares swallowed down the contents of his cup. "What say you, Poseidon? A raid? Far from Greece and Zeus' eye."

Poseidon stared into his goblet, considering. "I fear there are matters that I must tend to here first."

"Leave Erysichthon be," Ares warned.

He nodded. "This is of a personal affront."

"Ah. I wondered when you'd retaliate." Ares smiled. "Poor Apollo."

Poseidon snorted. "He'd no cause for such an assault."

"To you, perhaps. Yet I've never seen golden Apollo strike with such ferocity. Most impressive. I'd ask the cause, but I'm all too familiar with your version of the truth."

Poseidon held his tongue. Apollo had humiliated him before those that mattered. He would humiliate Apollo to the one he considered most dear. It would be an easy feat, far too easy as Daphne was most willing to assist him in exacting his revenge.

Chapter Thirteen

Coronis sat, her feet dangling in the warm waters of the Aegean while her face warmed beneath the rays of the sun.

"Coronis."

She shaded her eyes with her hand, smiling at the sight of Apollo holding a large fish aloft.

"Dinner," he called out, the fish thrashing in his hold.

She nodded. "Then do not drop it," she returned, laughing as the fish's tail slapped the water and splashed Apollo.

"You're turning as golden as the sun," Apollo said as he reached her on the sand. He shook his head, spattering her with icy drops from the sea.

She squealed, laughing as he fell atop her and soaked her exomie through.

Apollo's eyes swept over her. "I prefer you this way."

"Shivering and wet?" she countered.

"No," he glanced down at her tunic.

She followed his gaze. Her tunic was transparent in its sodden state. "Have you not tired of such a view?"

He frowned at her, tugging her beneath him. "I have not." His lips were soft upon her, searching and firm. "And you, wife? Are you done with me then?"

She reached up, wiping the water from his brow before twining her arms about his neck. "I shall endure it a bit longer."

His teeth nipped her lower lip, his hands sliding beneath her tunic. "Endure it?" His hand clasped her breast, his thumb and forefinger caressing her nipple 'til she gasped and arched into his touch. "Indeed."

She sighed as he entered her, welcoming him as she had countless times now. Her body had never known passion or desire but now it sought it out. When he was near, she would touch him, kiss him, and stroke the strength of his arm or the line of his back. Her hands gripped his hips now, loving the clench of muscle as he thrust deep into her. She gave in to him, the pleasure and torment of his touch on her skin.

"I love you wife," his whisper filled her ear before his lips latched onto her earlobe.

She shuddered, wrapping her legs around him and piercing his skin with her nails.

He came with a groan, grinding against her and shattering her in an instant.

He fell to his side, pulling her against him. She burrowed closer, loving the gasp of his breath, the pound of his heart. She loved him...

"What is it?" he asked, tilting her chin up to face him.

"Nothing." She'd not meant to stiffen or react but-

"Tell me," he rasped.

She stared into his golden gaze, wanting to confess what was in her heart but fearing the result. It was selfish perhaps, but she would keep him as long as she could.

"What is in your mind?" It was a plea, she heard it.

Could she not resist him? First her body would not be denied, now she would bare her soul to him-for him? "I miss your skin upon mine." She swallowed. "Even joined as we are, I want-"

"All?" he asked, his voice husky and deep.

She leaned into the hand he pressed to her cheek. "I... I ache for you," she admitted, a discomfiting pressure forming in her chest.

"Yet still you resist me?" A look of anguish creased his face.

"I have not resisted, husband. I will not. I have known what it is to be a warrior. I've much to learn of becoming a wife, or accepting the wants—the needs—of a woman." She paused. "Passion is new, something to be cautious of. How many women have lost themselves to it? Their dignity and pride?" She waited but he did not answer. "How many women have you loved passionately? And now love no more. A woman's desire and love is nothing unusual for you." She swallowed. "But for me, to feel such things so deeply and with no control, it is a dangerous thing."

"You confuse passion with love, Coronis," he murmured, his brow furrowing.

"Do I?" she frowned.

"I have bedded many women. Wanted many women." He held her head still, forcing her gaze to his. "I love you apart."

Her chest hurt, demanding she speak. She swallowed.

"Come," he rose, holding his hand out to her. "I am hungry—for something other than you." He winked. "For now."

"For now," she agreed, taking his hand and standing.

His smile warmed her from within. In time, she suspected her physical need of him would fade. She'd not counted on the friendship they'd forged. He was jovial, witty, and generous with his humor. He listened when she spoke, considering her thoughts and words without condescension. And no mortal had ever matched her so physically.

She was the better archer, but she no longer felt the need to tease him over it. In all else, he dominated. But, as she made a point of, he'd had far more time to perfect his tracking and aim.

The climb from beach to the cabin had become another challenge of sorts. He would use his strength to force her aside or brush past her, but she'd learned her own ways to distract him. Ways that often left them stumbling into their chambers as soon as they'd reached the summit. She beat him this time and turned to tease him.

But he grabbed her up, throwing her over his shoulder as he carried her inside. She hung, her head facing his hip, laughing as Pina and Mara came forward to greet them.

"Is a bath ready for my lady and me?" Apollo asked.

"It is, master," Mara answered quickly.

"Good." Apollo announced. "Here, fish for dinner."

From her view, she saw Pina's smile and Mara's startled gaze as he thrust the large fish at her. Pina looked at her, shaking her head and patting her stomach before mimicking a rocking motion. She frowned at Pina, dread washing over her. Pina went through it all again, each movement clear and precise, assuring she'd understood the older woman's intent the first time.

"Put me down," her voice sounded hollow to her own ears. The old woman had to be wrong. She must. Coronis needed her to be wrong—she wasn't ready.

She was instantly on the ground. Apollo's arms came around her, a frown lining his face as he stared down at her. But she avoided his gaze and shrugged from his hold, heading towards the bath room and a moment's peace. The water was deep, a fine steam rising off its surface. The room danced in shadows, scented tapers surrounding the bath and lining the walls in ornately carved sconces. It was a room for calm... yet there was no calm in her heart. Shock still gripped her, numbing her through.

"Coronis?" Apollo's voice was soft, his hand upon her shoulder gentle.

She wanted to avoid his touch. She wanted to run far from him. If Pina was right... She ached to turn into him, to find the comfort and love she'd felt only moments before. She'd known it was an illusion but it was one she'd grown fond of.

"Tell me." His tone was gruff.

She spun, her frayed nerves snapping. "Tell you?" She bit back. "Is that a request or a demand?"

His brows rose high. "It was meant as a request." His eyes narrowed. "But I will demand it if need be." His fingers tipped her chin back, forcing her gaze to meet his. His hands rubbed up and down her arms briskly. "You're cold."

She was shivering. "You have the gift of prophecy?"

He nodded, his gaze wary.

"You've had a vision of me? Of our s-son? A prophecy?" She paused, unable to share Pina's news yet. Instead she asked, "Is that all you've seen of our future together?"

His frown grew so severe she would have stepped back, but his arm tightened around her waist and drug her close. His reaction startled her. What else had he seen? Her concern turned to dread. "Answer me," she murmured, her anxiety increasing every second he remained silent.

"I have had other visions," he spoke, his voice tight and gruff.

"Were they so terrible?" She searched his face. "You were eager to share the news of our son. To see you now I know the rest is not so joyful."

He drew in a deep breath. "My vision is what *might* be, wife." He shook his head. "The only prophecy that matters is the one that came true. You, in my arms, well-pleased and smiling."

"Two. Two visions... Pina says I am w-with child," she stammered. "That you must take greater... care with me." She waited, watching him closely. Would he be pleased? Or was it too soon? She'd not known what to expect, but such joy, such anticipation baffled her. His smile was blinding, his eyes fathomless and tender. She knew he'd fathered many children, with many women... Had he reacted so to their announcement? She shoved the thought aside as he knelt before her.

His expression was one of pure adoration as he regarded her stomach. Warm hands parted her tunic to grip her hips and pull her forward. His gaze did not wander, but his hands did, splaying across her abdomen and stroking the skin with a feather light touch. He kissed her stomach, murmuring something against her flesh, before looking up at her.

She could not resist sliding her fingers through his golden locks. "You are pleased?

He buried his face against her stomach, laughing softly.

"Apollo?" her hands tightened in his hair, tugging his head back.

He moved swiftly, standing and pulling her into his arms before she'd time to react. He spun them, his laughter ringing out in the tile lined bath room and echoing.

"Never," his voice boomed. "Never have I been so *pleased.*" He paused then, kissing her with an ardor that made her forget her concerns for the moment. His lips parted hers, his tongue and breath mingling with hers until she was limp in his arms. "*Never, Coronis. Pleased* is a sadly inadequate descriptor... I know you fear my devotion. What it is between us and the love I have for you. But I would ask one thing of you."

She could not deny the love and affection in his golden gaze as he looked upon her now. In the time they'd spent together, she'd come to know him as a generous, kind man. The few things he'd asked of her had led to great pleasure and happiness. Why deny him now? "Ask."

"Love me." It was a plea. Raw and broken, vulnerable and desperate.

She searched his gaze, awash in a mix of emotions—some too new and vast to comprehend. She loved him. She loved his stubborn nature and his easy laugh. She loved that one stroke of her finger made his thick chest quiver and his breath hitch. She loved that he found joy in her laughter and ease in her arms. She loved him too well. "I will lose you," she murmured. "I will lose you and there will be nothing left of me."

"Coronis," he spoke harshly. "I gave you my vow, before your father, the people of Delphi-even some of my brethren. So I give it to you anew. I am yours. As long as you remain true to me, I will never leave you or stray. You have altered me forever in ways you cannot know. To think of the future brings me a sense of contentment and peace I'd not known before." He kissed her. "You and our children will live with me, immortal and timeless, a strong family born of love."

She could not speak then. Immortal? Did she want such a thing? Yet the answer was there, waiting patiently with a smile that rivaled the sun. Speaking the words in her heart was one of the greatest challenges of her life. "You have my heart husband. You hold it so tightly it is lost to me forever."

When Apollo was a boy Hera had thought him a loud, wild thing. Her patient nature had been tested time and again, for he was not hers but the product of one of Zeus' many affairs. Yet, she tolerated him, charmed in spite of herself. Until he ran about the Council Chamber, yelling and laughing and too boisterous for such a lauded setting. It had taken time to learn to control such outbursts, to reign in powerful emotions...

He had the desire to do so now. To run and laugh and act a fool. His joy was that of his youthful self, unfettered by the cares and burdens he now carried upon his shoulders. In his existence he'd had many pleasures: women, music, art, philosophy, athleticism... but his time with Coronis was deeper—sweeter. He'd not known she'd become part of him, yet she was as necessary to him as the air he breathed.

And she loved him. This proud, strong woman who yielded for none loved him.

"It is not lost," he lifted her hands, pressing a kiss to each knuckle. "It is here, with me, guarded and cherished." Her nervousness was not lost upon him. She was reluctant with her words if not her body. Because her word was weighted, an oath, a vow—unbreakable. And she'd given hers to him. She'd given herself to him. "You and our son—children—will never doubt my fealty."

She drew in an unsteady breath. "Son?"

He smiled. "Or daughter. I've no knowledge of our boy's arrival, only that he will be. I saw him as clearly as I see you now."

"What did he look like?" her question was soft, uncertain.

"Me," Apollo laughed. "But he had your eyes. And you spirit. I am eager to meet such a boy, to hold him in my arms and hear his laughter." He kissed her hands again, pressing them to his chest so he could wrap her in his arms once more. "For now, I would show his mother how loved she is."

Her fingers stroked his chest, sliding along the ridge of his shoulders. "I will hold you to your vow, husband."

Such words pleased him, the beginning of some sort of trust between them. She'd spent the whole of her life guarding her heart from such tender affections. Was it any wonder that finding love in him troubled her so? Would he not have resisted her, if she'd had the past he boasted of? What confidence could he have in such a woman, no matter how fervently she declared herself to him? Yet she dared to love him. She was far braver than he.

He reached behind her, working the knot of her tunic lose so the fabric slipped free to pool about her ankles. And while her beauty was distracting, he did not turn his gaze from her face. He could not, she spoke to him—called to him—filled his senses and throbbed in his blood with unrelenting fervor. He'd once thought himself a gifted wordsmith, but he had no words for the affection he bore this mortal woman.

She smiled up at him—albeit fragile and wavering. Her hands kneaded the back of his neck, offering comfort or seeking it? He rested his forehead against hers, resisting the need to press his lips to hers so that he might bask in the glow of her love a moment longer.

"A bath?" he asked.

"Yes," she spoke softly.

He took her hand, leading her down the steps into the heated water. The air grew heady, scented by the bath's lavender and jasmine oils.

"Your tunic?" She released his hand to unfasten the brooch at his shoulder.

He stood, letting her unwind the fabric from his shoulder and waist. Anticipation gripped him, bidding his body rise with need. When he was naked, she circled him slowly—trailing one feather-light finger across his shoulder and back. He pulsed, his body clenching briefly as her finger dipped to caress the underside of his buttock. His wife grew bold... and he approved most heartily. She was smiling as she came before him, her finger sweeping over the ridge of his hip. She paused then, her fingers a hairsbreadth from the rigid length of his arousal. She was fascinated by his body, by the effect she had upon him—it was plain upon her face. Such an expression—curiosity, hesitation, and desire. Her eyes upon him were almost as potent as the tender caress of her fingers. But then her fingers wrapped about him and he found breathing difficult.

"Wife," he grunted, gripping her wrist. He wanted her too much to risk spilling his seed like some untried mortal.

"You've touched me so," her voice wavered but her touch did not. "And driven me mad." Her gaze turned to him.

"I heard no protestation." He frowned. "Did you ask for mercy?" he asked, hissing when her hand slid along the length of him.

"No." She shook her head. "I want all you have to give me." The husky timbre of her voice did little to dampen his hunger.

"I feel in a giving mood." His hands gripped her hair, his mouth descending upon hers. He waited 'til her arms twined about her neck before moving them into the deeper waters. He sat, cradling her against him, savoring the slide of her skin against him.

When he lifted his head, she sighed deeply.

"A sigh?" he asked. "After such a kiss I'd prefer a moan. Or perhaps a swoon."

She arched a brow at him. "I've never swooned."

"I believe you."

"I may moan." Her hand cupped his cheek, sending water droplets down his neck. "But it will require more than a kiss husband."

He smiled, shaking his head as he cradled her face. "Zeus may rule all, but you rule me, lady."

"I've no wish to rule or be ruled, husband." Again, she stroked his cheek.

"What do you wish, then?" he asked. Without her prayers he'd no insight to those things she desired, those she'd protect, or the troubles that weighed upon her. Whatever she asked for, he would give it to her.

Her gaze fixed upon his shoulder, intent and thoughtful. After a few moments of silence, her gaze lifted to wander the room. She seemed to note every detail of the room—assessing the carved sconces and flickering tapers, the intricate mosaic overhead, and the wispy gauze curtains that offered them some sort of privacy from the rest of the house. When her gaze returned to him, she shook her head. "What more is there? I am here, in the place I love most. I have the affection of a most attentive husband. Now..." She paused, her hands settling on her stomach. "I will be a mother."

He'd no time to appreciate the sweetness of her words—his vision wavered. Coronis face, the bath room, even the flickering tapers grew black. Before him lay destruction. His ears rang with an unknown roar, smoke scorched his nostrils and stung his eyes. The heat of the air was oppressive, making each breath a challenge. He was not alone, the cries and screams of people reached him then. Many people. They ran, stumbling in their frantic state. Those that fell were trod upon, their cries cut short by a deafening noise. He looked up, watching the mighty cliffs above crumble.

"Apollo?" He heard Coronis' voice, calling to him in the distance.

He tried to turn from the scene before him, to return to Coronis—but he could not. The ground beneath him shook, splitting wide to swallow those still scrambling for refuge. He reached out, hoping to catch the woman and child teetering on the edge of the rift. He knew it was hopeless—he could not intervene. It was a vision, for now, and nothing more. They fell, the child's wail clutching his heart.

"Apollo?" Coronis' voice was fearful now. "What is it?"

The vision faded. Coronis waited, a deep furrow marring her brow.

His heart was pounding, his arms spread wide—reaching

for the woman and her child. Coronis gripped his arm, her face concerned and anxious. He let his arms fall and took her hands in his. "I am here."

"But you weren't... Your body remained but you were not..." Her gaze was fierce, searching.

"A vision." He smoothed the furrow from her brow with a kiss. "It is very much as you described it. I am only vaguely aware of the present when I am overcome so."

She regarded him closely, waiting for him to go on.

"A gift from the Fates, to be sure." He smiled. "But it is not always well-timed."

"What did you see?" she probed. "May I... may I ask such a thing?"

He nodded. "An earthquake, large enough to decimate a village of no small size." He sifted through the images plaguing his mind. "But when or where is left unknown. I will puzzle over what I saw, search for answers... To know such a thing is coming without the ability to offer aid is vexing." He pulled her back into his lap, the contact soothing him somewhat. "Most vexing."

"A burden indeed."

He looked at her. Her words were true. "It is. But it is mine to carry."

"I would help if I could," she offered.

His stared at the surface of the water, sharing all he'd seen with her—his mind playing it out before him again. The terrain, the weather, the feel of the air. He spoke with care, stating every detail, every sound and sight that might offer assistance. And she listened diligently. When he finished he shook his head. "In time, I will make sense of it." He said no more. He'd rather savor the feel of his wife pressed against him, the softness of her skin and the touch of her lips.

"I have seen you so before." Her frown returned. "The day of the chariot races... Whatever vision gripped you then tortured you. I saw it in your eyes when you looked at me."

He felt the cold weight of that vision seep into his chest, threatening the peace and love in his heart. He would not think on that now—or ever again. Yet he must. If he was to prevent what he'd seen, he must revisit it.

"It brought you pain." She touched his face. "Your face... I'd never seen such pain." Her words were forced.

He squeezed her hand in his, wishing he had some pithy words to brush her worries aside. He could not tell her—that much he knew. She was strong and proud. Sharing such a thing could only bring anxiety to her. Until he knew how to prevent such things from happening, she need not know of his vision.

"You would worry over me?" he asked, smiling. "Apollo the Olympian or your husband Apollo?"

"You are both. And while I cannot pray to you, I esteem you as an Olympian," her words were soft. "And as a husband."

He kissed her cheek, releasing her hands so that he might explore the rest of her. The oil of the bath made her delightfully slick, inflaming his somewhat dampened ardor instantly.

Her eyes narrowed, yet there was no denying the husky timbre of her voice. "I'm not a fool, my lord. You would distract me from my purpose."

She was far too shrewd. "What purpose is that?" he asked as his hands caressed along her ribs, resting just beneath the full roundness of her breasts.

"Your vision," she continued, bracing her hands against his chest. "That day, at the races, what was it?"

He hesitated briefly. "I saw an attack... on those that assist Demeter with her Eleusinian Mysteries. A deadly attack." It was true, he'd seen as much. But not at the races. Or again on his wedding day.

Coronis' eyes went round. "There is some time yet before Persephone returns from the Underworld, is there not? You can prevent such a thing from happening?"

He nodded. "I can. I will."

"This attack... Was it by this Erysichthon?" She shivered.

He nodded.

Her amber eyes held his. "Would Demeter kill Ione?" She paused. "If she found the mortal, that is. Would she kill her to get even with this shade king?"

Apollo would have dismissed her questions if not for the desperation on her face. "Perhaps. But Demeter will not find her. It has been too long and the mortal woman has taken pains to hide herself." He cupped her face. "What troubles you, Coronis? Do you worry for those mortal women? They know their purpose and the risk they face, yet serve freely."

"Such loyalty is admirable..." She drew in a deep, wavering breath. "Yet... such suffering..." She blinked against the moisture in her eyes. "It saddens me that there is no hope of a peaceful resolution. And no end."

He studied her, running his fingers through her wet hair and smoothing it down her back. "You have a generous heart."

"No," she argued. "Not at all. Does it not trouble you?"

He nodded. "In my time there have been many... inequalities. Many times when the demand for justice went unmet. I've no answers for this matter, none that will give Demeter the satisfaction she needs. Or stop the shade's attacks." He paused. "Even if Erisychton is brought to heel, Demeter would not have what she wants."

Coronis frowned. "Th-then what does she seek?"

"Her daughter. She would have Persephone restored to her. She chooses to forget the bargain made with the Fates. Or that Persephone chose—most eagerly—to marry Hades. If she does capture Erisychton or his poor daughter, then what? The threat of Persephone being stolen away is removed, but it does not bring her home. I fear Demeter's need for revenge will make her forget the possible consequences..." But something in the play of emotions across Coronis' face gave him pause. Her distress clawed at him. "Coronis, forgive me." He stroked through her hair again and again. "Wife, I would set these things aside. Today should be joyful, a celebration. Today, you have given me the greatest gift, Coronis. I beseech you, smile for me, wrap your arms around me—let us celebrate our news instead."

She leaned into his touch, her gaze locking with his. He watched her eyes clear, sharpen and come alive, before him. It was when her amber eyes crackled with heat that he felt her yield, her shoulders easing and posture relaxing. He could stand it no more, he wanted more. So he stooped to drop soft kisses to her temple, her cheek, and—finally—the corner of her mouth. Her breath tickled his ear, making his insides tighten and clench.

She was slow to return his smile. "And how would you celebrate?"

"Buried inside you, wife." He turned her so that she sat astride him, the length of his arousal pressed hard against her inner thigh. She shivered anew, but this time it was from passion. "I would lose myself in the love I have for you."

"Come then." She moved over him, a groan slipping from her lips as he slid deep inside her.

Chapter Fourteen

Coronis crouched in the underbrush, her eyes fixed on their prize. Apollo knelt at her side, silent. She glanced his way, but he drew no arrow. He would let her finish the hunt with no interference from him. There seemed to be no end to his thoughtfulness. And no end to her love for him.

Her sickness had prompted his suggestion to hunt, a sort of distraction from unrelenting nausea and weakness of her condition. She'd rallied. Her days had been focused on Apollo, the giving and receiving of pleasure. And while she had no complaints, she was aware that relying on him as her sole source of companionship and entertainment was perhaps not the wisest choice. She'd sprung from their bed, dressed in her short tunic, and found her bow. As remote as their hunting cabin was, the abundance of game roaming the region was too great a temptation to deny. She'd felt invigorated, enough so that the now constant churning in her stomach was forgotten. He'd deferred to her, letting her track their prey through the thick forest without a sound. It had been easy enough.

But when she'd drawn the cord tight and aimed her arrow, a woman stepped from the tree line and the deer darted off. Coronis blinked, stunned by the rapid movements of both the animal and the woman. A woman with wild hair, huge golden eyes, and the barest scraps of fur covering her body. "You should ask," the woman said, her golden gaze finding their hiding spot.

The eyes were familiar. Coronis glanced at Apollo, who was

smiling broadly.

"I'd no knowledge you'd claimed this forest, sister." Apollo rose and made his way to the woman in the clearing.

"She knows," the woman said, looking beyond Apollo into the trees.

Coronis understood then and hurried from the trees to make amends. "Forgive me Artemis, I beseech you." It was unlike her, to hunt without asking for Artemis' blessing and permission. She'd not anger the Goddess of the Hunt—especially now that she was her sister. Words lodged in her throat as the roiling of her stomach returned. She swallowed, fighting the bile that burned her throat. She wrapped her arms around her stomach and bit back a groan. "I'd meant no offense..." she murmured, pressing a hand to her mouth.

"She is breeding?" Artemis asked, her golden eyes sweeping her from head to toe. Yet Coronis could sense neither approval nor disapproval when their gazes met.

"She is," Apollo agreed. "My wife, Coronis. My sister, Artemis. I am pleased to have you meet." His arms wrapped about her, cradling her against his side. "Sit, wife, rest."

Coronis frowned, willing her body to cease its revolt. Artemis was a Goddess Coronis revered. She understood the need to run free, to be strong and independent. To have no man own her. And yet they meet when she was as weak-limbed as a newborn fawn. It did not sit well with Coronis but she had no choice but to do just that. She sat on a fallen log, resisting the urge to lie on the leaf-covered ground until the nausea passed.

"I know this mortal," Artemis spoke.

Coronis regarded them, drawing in slow breaths to ease her stomach.

"Do you?" Apollo asked.

"I have watched her grow. She is a hunter—strong, precise, and fair." Artemis' tone remained so emotionless Coronis marveled the she spoke words of praise. "You did well, brother."

"I did," Apollo agreed, smiling at her. "Though I fear growing our child is no easy task."

His words brought a smile to her lips. "Why would it be, husband? This is your child... The babe will grow as he will live. Causing mischief while charming those he torments..." She swallowed, waving Apollo away when he stepped forward.

Artemis laughed then. And the clear melodic sound was so surprising that Coronis stared at the Goddess in wonder. "You've no illusions about my brother then?" Artemis sat beside Coronis, blatantly assessing her. "That is good. Do not love him too dearly for he is a fickle brute. Give him only a piece of your heart."

Coronis glanced at Apollo then, knowing it was far too late for such advice.

Apollo was frowning, his brow marred with a deep furrow. "I have vowed to love her and no other sister. Your words-"

"Have you?" Artemis interrupted, looking back and forth between them. "Well... That is a most interesting development."

Coronis met Artemis' gaze without flinching. It gave her time to assess the Olympian that was now her kin. And what a splendid immortal Artemis was. Apollo's twin, Artemis had none of Apollo's charm or refinement. Wild, to be sure, her eyes held the same wariness of the wolf or the lion—ready to pounce or run as needed. She was all but naked, though the furs she wore covered enough. Her hair was not as blonde as her brother's, it was similar to her own. Light brown, with gold and blonde woven throughout. But while Coronis' fell in long waves, Artemis' was a twisted mass of knots and curls-adorned with twigs, leaves, and berries.

Artemis cocked her head to the side, arching a brow as Apollo did. "What I know of you has always been careful and deliberate." Artemis spoke. "Why, then, did you marry my brother?"

Coronis smiled, considering Artemis' question. It was true. She would never have chosen to marry Apollo. She hadn't considered it a possibility, not really. If not for her parents' secrets... She stopped then, admitting the truth to herself. "I wanted him." Her confession was soft.

He knelt before her then. "Whether she wanted me or not, she was mine. She is mine." He glanced at his sister then. "Come back to the lodge with us for food and companionship—if only for the evening?" His voice was soft and coaxing—as if he were speaking to a skittish horse.

Artemis stood quickly. "No."

Apollo stood before her. "You are always welcome."

Artemis' gaze fell upon Coronis then. "As you are always

welcome here, to hunt or find shade beneath the trees. The babe too," she said, pointing at Coronis' stomach. "It pleases me to see you so well matched, brother."

"Perhaps you will find a fitting mate," Apollo offered.

Artemis' gaze dimmed then, her expression gone rigid. "No."

But Coronis heard both anger and pain in the single word and wondered at it.

"Sister," Apollo gripped his sister by the shoulders. "You are too often alone. I miss your laughter, your smile. Come, stay with us. Let my wife come to know and love you as I do. You would be most welcome."

Artemis' smile was small. "Perhaps. But not now." Her attention wandered high above them, into the trees. "The animals, the birds, all seem to prepare for something. Have you seen anything brother?"

Apollo glanced overhead. "I have."

Artemis nodded. "I thought as much. It will cause great unrest... for mortal and beast..." Her gaze bounced from Coronis to Apollo again. "The animals' instincts are sharper than man's, I think. We shall see. What will happen?"

"An earthquake. But where or when I know not," Apollo spoke, his attention searching the trees overhead.

"What does Olympus say?" Artemis asked.

Apollo said nothing.

"You have told Olympus?" Artemis snapped. "Or Zeus?"

Coronis watched them then. Of course he should tell Olympus— yet he'd not left her side since the vision had gripped him. Why? Why would he ignore his duties? And those that needed protection? Perhaps those on Olympus could determine where the earthquake would fall... Apollo's vision—the details he'd recounted to her— might prove more useful to his immortal brethren. Whether Artemis' thoughts were similar, she could not be sure. But disapproval lined Artemis' face as Apollo regarded her with a sheepish grin.

"She will survive without you for a few days, brother," Artemis sighed.

Coronis stared at Apollo then. He stayed for her? When a threat so grave as this threatened the good people of Greece? What if her parents, the people of Delphi, were at risk?

She stood then, ignoring the twinge in her stomach. "You must go. I would not stand in the way of your duty. Or delay Olympus' grace for those who need it."

Apollo glared at Artemis before moving to her side. "I thought it best to stay until the worst was over." He smiled at her stomach.

"And if you're too late?" She took Apollo's hands in hers. "Pina and Mara will watch over me-"

"No, Coronis. I could hardly rest easy with such little protection. I will take you to your father's," Apollo asserted. "No harm will come to you there."

She frowned. She did not want to return to her father's house. She would stay in a place full of their memories together. But she would not argue with him now.

His hands cupped her face, his frown deepening. Something in his eyes... He seemed troubled. He worried over her protection? Protection from whom?

No harm will come to you there.

Her hands covered his, searching his gaze. "You will hurry?" An uneasiness washed over her. The thought of being separated from him was most distressing.

He was no more pleased than she. Did he scowl at the thought of leaving her? Or was it something more? Too many questions clogged her throat—but they would keep until they were alone.

He nodded, swallowing. "When do you leave?" Apollo asked but did not turn from her. "Artemis?"

But there was no answer.

Coronis turned, searching the trees and bushes for some sign of the Goddess. She was simply gone.

Apollo sighed. "She chastises me but takes pains to avoid setting foot in the Council Chamber."

Coronis stood, staring up into the branches of the trees. "Why should she go, Apollo? I imagine Artemis has little affection for Olympus," she murmured. "This is her temple, where she feels most at ease." The sun spilled through the thick green pine needles, their acrid pungent scent filling the warm air and soothing her stomach. She closed her eyes. "It would be hard to leave..."

"Yes," he agreed, his arms slipping around her waist. "It will be. And I'd not go-"

"You must." She admired the ridge of his jaw, the line of his nose, and the solemnity of his gaze. "You are an Olympian, husband. Your duties extend beyond my wants and needs. I know this, as do you."

His expression did not soften. Indeed, the severity of his disquiet troubled her. "You are my wife, Coronis. No mere mortal. And soon no mortal at all." His hands pressed against her back. "I will not give you up, woman. You will be mine, now and for all time."

"What is it that troubles you so?" she murmured, touching his cheek. "At times you look at me as if you fear I'll fade away."

Apollo's gaze wandered, exploring every curve and plane of her face. "I worry over your fragility. You are mortal, vulnerable, and carrying my child. Many a mortal woman has passed into Hades' care while delivering new life to this world."

"As you said, I am no mere mortal," she soothed. "I am Coronis, strong, able, daughter of a king, wife to a God. Your babe will not be the end of me." She stared into his eyes. "You must go with the dawn, I demand it of you. I would never forgive you if so many died at my hand. Never. You are my husband, yes, but you are my favored God. A God that would not put his needs above those of his people. Your son has some time before he makes his entrance. I will make sure no harm comes to either of us. I swear it."

His gaze met hers, but worry still bracketed his mouth and clouded his golden eyes. "By the Fates, I believe you."

She ran her fingers across his brow and cupped his cheek. "Then smile, husband. Love me tonight so that I may travel to my father tomorrow—and you to Olympus." He need not know that she worried as well. Not that she would perish in childbirth or die of old age. No, she feared he would leave for Olympus and never return to her.

Apollo held her hand as they stood on Phlegys' steps. Delphi was quiet now, the crowd of the games long dispersed. She paused on the top step, her eyes trained on the distant horizon. He'd barely pulled the sun from its bed, wishing to delay the start to this day— and their parting.

He feasted upon such a sight, her beauty, her strength, the swell of his child in her gently rounding belly. He'd never known such peace. He'd never known such happiness. Or such fear. For the vision he'd had of Coronis, terrified and desperate, had visited him twice since his wedding. Each time he endured it, he saw something new—some new slight detail that had him crippled with fear, clinging tightly to her for hours, before his heart would ease and his lungs would once more draw in breath.

He was lucky the prophecies found him at night. True, mingling his sleep with such nightmarish images—images he could not escape—offered him little rest. But if she'd been awake, she would have known he was keeping something from her. And she would have badgered him relentlessly until she'd learned the truth.

He would shield her from the things he'd seen, the images he could not erase from his mind. Sleep was no longer easy for him, for he dreaded what might wait for him. Better to savor the feel of her in his arms, the comfort of her heartbeat and touch of her flesh against his. He would protect her. He would not let any ill come to her. Her well-being was all that mattered—body, mind, and soul. That was why he'd been so negligent in his duty to Olympus and those that would suffer from the earthquake.

He could summon Hermes and ask him to deliver news of the impending earthquake to his brethren. Yet he knew that would not suffice. Even if he sent Hermes, Zeus would demand he follow. It was Apollo that had seen the earthquake, had studied each detail in his mind's eyes. He must be the one to recount it.

But leaving her... In his existence, nothing had made him question his duty to Olympus and to Greece. Until now.

She reached up, tucking a strand of burnished hair behind her ear. If he were a mortal, his worries would not extend beyond the care of this woman, the babe in her belly, and their home. He would wake with the sun, toil beneath its rays or serve as a statesman, spend each night in her bed, and grow old at her side—content to be husband and father. It was a gentle fantasy, one he found far too tempting.

"You've much on your mind," her words were soft but he heard the question. "But worry over us should no longer press upon you. My father will keep us safe. Put that from your mind and think only on matters of your people and Greece." Her gaze lingered upon his lips. "And hurry back to me."

The fire in her eyes instantly inflamed him. His want for her—and her for him—was more powerful. "A few days, no longer."

He opened the door to Phlegys' great house. He noted the guards Phlegys had placed inside and relaxed.

Coronis, however, frowned. "Is something amiss?" she whispered at him. "Father never posts guards inside..." They reached the inner courtyard then, to find more reinforcements standing in each corner. "Apollo?" she hissed. "Tell me this is not your doing?"

He shook his head. "I cannot. You are my wife now. I will do as I see fit to protect you-"

"Protect me from what?" she snapped, her eyes narrowing. "You treat me as a child, a careless one at that. One that needs protection in her own home. A home well-occupied by those who would tend to my every need-"

"Enough." He gripped her shoulders. "They will stay. And the crows, as well."

Sadness and disbelief tainted her features. Her whispered, "You do not trust me," clutched at his heart.

"I trust none as I trust you, Coronis." He assured. "It is my own weakness that demands such assurances. I... I have never had so much to lose. Please, appease me in this."

She nodded, but she would not look at him. "I fear you're keeping something from me," she whispered.

He swallowed.

"Kalimera," Talousa's voice reached them then. "I have never seen a brighter morning than this one."

Phlegys and his lady wife approached, regarding Coronis with such love. It was as it should be, for his wife deserved nothing but love in her life. And protection. Clearly, Phlegys had received the message he'd sent with a crow last eve.

When Talousa held her arms open to Coronis, she slipped from his hold and into her mother's. He felt the loss of her instantly. The air was cooler. His arms were too empty. His hands craved the feel of her. But he held himself still, offering Talousa a warm smile.

"While mine grows dim at the thought of leaving." He teased, knowing his words were true. "My only comfort is knowing she will be protected and cherished within these walls."

"She will. We have done all you asked." Phlegys' gaze was most searching. "Delphi has never faced an attack or threat before. But we are ready if the need arises."

He felt Coronis' gaze upon him then but refused to look at her. Instead he focused on the good king of Phlegys. "I would speak with you alone before I go."

"Of course." Phlegys nodded, patting Coronis on the cheek before turning to go.

Apollo knew better than to draw out their good-byes. She had questions, many questions, he could see it. So he pulled her close, pressed a hard kiss to her temple and forehead, and said only, "I love you woman. Do not wander from this house until I return."

The surge of anger brought color to her cheeks. "I will-"

"Do as I say." He did not spare the edge to his voice. Or the tightening of his grip upon her arms. "I demand it."

Her lips pressed flat and her brow creased.

"I do not understand-"

"You've no need to understand," he argued. "You must simply obey."

Her nostrils flared.

"Coronis?" He challenged her, his tone sharper than before.

She scowled at him. Her jaw clenched as her skin turned a dark red. He could only imagine what she sought to say to him, the insults she would hurl upon him... Instead she nodded, once, stiff and rigid with unspoken hostility.

He smiled then, kissing her pinched lips and caressing the swell of her stomach with a slow stroke. "Thank you." He whispered in her ear, "Miss me as I will miss you." He paused, pulling the gift he'd made for her from his cloak. "To keep you warm until I return." He offered her the lion pelt, taken the day he met her. He'd worked the hide himself, beaten until it was soft and fine enough to touch her skin.

Coronis took it, turning wide eyes upon him. Her smile was faint, strained. But it was enough.

He turned to his lady wife's mother then and offered her a warm smile. "I shall return soon, lady. Until then, I leave them in your care."

Talousa nodded, clearly bemused by the scene before her.

He followed Phlegys then, each step faltering as flashes of the prophecy plagued him. They'd barely reached the andron, a room in which women were not welcome, when Apollo spoke. "I've no choice but to burden you with matters beyond understanding. I've had a vision of Coronis, one that has robbed me of sleep and almost reason."

Phlegys froze in his tracks, the pitcher of wine in his hold forgotten. "She needs protection?"

"She does." He paced the room. "I have yet to see who hunts her, only that she is hunted." He would not tell Phlegys of her terror—or the arrow that protruded from her shoulder. "I go to Olympus on matters of Greece or I'd not leave her side."

Phlegys was greatly perplexed. "She will not be alone until you return. I vow it." He shook his head. "Have you any suspicions? Who would seek harm upon Coronis?" Something in the mortal's expression gave Apollo pause.

"Damocles?" He shook his head, watching Phlegys closely. "I know of no other who feel wronged by her. I hoped you might have some insight?"

In Apollo's time he'd learned a great deal about those he ruled. Mortals were driven by only two things: family or power. While Phlegys was a powerful man, Apollo suspected he would give all to keep his family safe. It was because of this that Apollo respected the mortal king so. That Phlegys was both direct and honest only increased Apollo's regard for the man. And yet, the mortal hesitated in such a way that turned Apollo's blood cold.

"No," Phlegys spoke softly, avoiding Apollo's gaze. "I know of no one."

In that moment, Apollo was consumed with fury. He did not stop to think as he cross the room, grabbing the front of the kings' tunic and lifting him off the ground. "And I know you lie. You lie to me." There was no denying the threat in his words. "Whatever you have to hide—you cannot begin to comprehend the punishment I will serve upon you. There will be no secrets concerning my wife. None!" The last word bounced off the marble columns and spilled into the morning air. No bird, beast, or insect dared speak. Nothing but silence.

And still Phlegys did not look at him.

"Would losing Coronis grieve you?" Apollo growled.

Phlegys glared at him then. The good king's features were so altered, his skin mottled and the cords in his neck taut as he fought for control. "I will kill any who threatened her."

"As would I." Apollo nodded. "Whether that being aims a knife at her heart or stands by while she is in danger—I see no difference. Both will be dealt with without mercy. So I ask you again. Do you know of anyone who would threaten my wife?"

"Demeter," Phlegys could scarce force the words out.

Apollo released him, so stunned by the king's declaration that even his temper faltered. "Why?"

Phlegys ran a hand over his face then stared blindly up at the ceiling overhead. "Talousa is Ione."

Apollo regarded the man silently. Ione. The mortal Demeter dared to challenge the Fates over. The mortal she thought would bring an end to Erysichthon's reign and bestow Persephone to her for all time. And Coronis was her daughter.

His stomach clenched, the horrid import of Phlegys' words clasping his heart. She knew... she knew Demeter sought revenge upon her mother. "Coronis knows?" He asked, looking at the man. Was that why she married him? It was no secret she'd not wanted the union... But now. He swallowed the bile that rose up. Was he so blinded by his heart that he would not see her deceit? Did she love him? Or did she do what needed to be done for her family. He remembered her declaration and felt the fool. It was only when he'd begged her to love him that she said as much. "She knows?" he repeated, more firmly this time.

Phlegys nodded.

He sat heavily, staring at the mortal.

"I know this news is unexpected," Phlegys spoke, coming to kneel before him. "But there is more. If... if you love her as I think you do, you will understand why I tell you now. I would spare her from the humiliation my wife endured—and such suffering."

Apollo nodded stiffly. "Go on."

"I am not her father," Phlegys mumbled, his face paling and his gaze fixed on the ground. "It is Poseidon."

Apollo stood then, his stomach roiling. Poseidon. Always Poseidon. Would he still have felled that bloody tree if he'd known Coronis was his daughter? He had no answer... Only unease. His vision. Was it Demeter? Or Poseidon? He was beset with such agitation he paced the chamber twice. "Why did you wait so long to tell me this?"

Phlegys stood then, his gaze wary. "I will speak plainly and confess I would not have told you if not for the troubling vision you've had." Phlegys stood then. He regarded Apollo with a weariness he'd not had only moments before. "But Coronis' life is of greater import than either mine or my wife's. We have lived our lives protecting her—worrying over her. To hear she will face such a trial..." His voice broke. "We cannot save her, but you can."

He stared at the man, grappling with all that was said. She would need protection if Olympus learned the truth—if not for herself then her lady mother. He would offer it but his heart was too heavy to forgive so much so soon. Love should not matter. She was his wife and she would give him a son. Yet her love mattered greatly. Not something born duty or honor or the need to protect her family. But love—freely felt and freely given. He simply wanted her love.

"Do not think harshly of her," Phlegys implored. "She had no idea until you asked for her hand."

He remembered it all too well. "She did not want it," Apollo spoke, forcing the word past the lump in his throat.

Phlegys seemed to sense his pain then, for there was sympathy in the mortal's eyes. "She did not know what she wanted. Knowing my daughter as I do, she would have denied you even if she wanted you above all—that is her nature. To fight against her womanly needs." He shook his head. "She is a loyal daughter. Now I see a loyal wife."

"Perhaps." How he wished that were true. "But is she a loving wife?"

"Do not doubt it." Phlegys frowned. "Or her love for you. She does, with all her heart."

His brow arched as he regarded the mortal, his anger rising once more. Who was this mortal man? To placate him with pretty words and hollow reassurances. "What else would you say? That she endured my touch to protect you? That she can scarce wait for me to be done with her? No, that would hardly suit the purpose of this alliance now, would it? To keep me well-pleased and willing to champion your family. You've placed your fate—those of the ones you love most dear—in my hands." He scowled at Phlegys. "Now I must go to Olympus."

Phlegys turned an alarming shade of grey. "I beg for your mercy. If not for myself, then for my daughter."

He thought of Coronis last evening, wrapped in his arms and well-sated from their love-making. She'd smiled up at him before staring down at his hand upon her stomach. She'd seemed delighted by his fascination with the swell of their child. Yet... she'd seemed pleased with many things. Was it all pretense? Was she so skilled at deception?

He shook his head. No, not his Coronis. He knew her well. He'd heard her prayers for years before their meeting. She was stubborn and unforgiving, opinionated and proud. She was too fond of competition, too strong and independent. She'd had no interest in any man and had come to him with no talent for seduction.

But did she love him?

He glanced at Phlegys, making his way from the room. "No harm will come to her," he spoke without looking back.

Chapter Fifteen

Coronis stared at the distant mountains. Five days. He'd been gone five days and she'd had no word from him. And every second of those five days had been a sort of torture. One look at her father's face told her what he could not. But why her father dared reveal such a long kept secret to her Olympian husband was a question he refused to answer.

"I had no choice," he'd mumbled. "I had no choice."

Her mother had fretted so that she'd spent the last two days in bed, suffering an ache in her head that near crippled her.

Her father had spent those two days checking the reinforcements Apollo had demanded. Another question he would not answer.

Ichthys had visited frequently, doing his best to cheer her. But his winning smile could not offer the same distraction or satisfaction as the one that greeted her each night in sleep. While her dreams gave her hope, her waking hours were plagued with questions. Did he understand? Would he protect her secrets? Could he forgive her? And, most importantly, was his heart still hers?

"Your bath lady," Mara's voice was soft.

Coronis glanced at the girl, then beyond at the servants Apollo had insisted join Phlegys' household. Two men carried a large beaten metal bath into her room. They were broad shouldered and well-formed men, able to fetch her bath or defend her from whatever unseen threat Apollo alluded to before he left. They left, without once looking upon her.

So many questions.

Her attention wandered to the woman standing just inside the door. She was a lovely creature, her wide mossy green eyes assessing the room with open curiosity. Coronis had never seen the woman before, she would have remembered. The woman was most comely, distractingly so. But there was something else, something more... An air of awareness—menace—that Coronis could not dismiss. When the woman's mossy green eyes settled upon her, the hair along Coronis' arms and the back of her neck rose. "Are you new to my father's household?" she asked.

"She arrived this morning, my lady," Mara offered.

The woman dropped into a deep curtsey. "I have a message for you, Princess."

Coronis glanced at Mara, surprised. Most messengers were left to wait in the main courtyard until they were received. Mara knew this. And from the way Mara stared at the floor, jaw rigid and hands fisted at her side, Coronis suspected something was amiss. Had this woman argued with little Mara? Her irritation, quick to rise these days, was sharp. "I shall hear it in good time," Coronis spoke. "After my bath. Mara will show you where to wait."

"It is a message from your husband, my lady." The woman regarded her with slightly narrowed eyes. "But I will wait, of course." Her smile was pinched.

Coronis paused, inspecting the woman once more. Apollo sent this woman to her? Was there not a message in that alone? She did not care for the sense of foreboding that washed over her. She did not care for the look on the woman's face—she did not care for the woman. "Your name?"

"I am Daphne." She spoke clearly, the angle of her head a little too haughty-a little too proud for Coronis' liking. Should she know the name, for she did not? Yet the woman carried herself with a self-importance that implied she had some sort of status.

"Leave us," Coronis spoke to the room at large.

"My lady," Mara's voice was entreating, "let me prepare you bath-"

"Your lady has spoken," Daphne interrupted, her disapproval clear.

Coronis was so startled by the woman's impertinence a rebuke did not instantly form. "You forget your place, Daphne. What right have you to reprimand my attendant, in my home, in my presence?" She regarded the woman carefully.

"Only that which you husband bestowed upon me—as your attendant. He was most concerned over your current attendants, as they lack training, experience... One is quite aged and cannot speak? While the other is but a babe." Her disdain for Mara was evident. "As I have served Hera herself, he thought I would be a more fitting attendant."

Coronis bristled. "Is this his message?" Five days of silence and then he sends this woman to her? Was he too blinded by the woman's large chest and round thighs to see that she was an impudent shrew with a most scheming gaze? She would not win a place in Coronis' heart, not after insulting those she held in high esteem.

She nodded. "Yes, my lady."

Exhaustion swept over her. She had no desire to keep this woman in her house. She was yet another pair of eyes to watch and report to Apollo. "My mother is ill," Coronis spoke. "You shall serve her."

Daphne smiled, her smug satisfaction galling Coronis. "Your husband sent me to you. And bid me wait until his return."

Coronis stared at the woman. "And I send you to my lady mother, Queen Talousa. I have all the attendants I need." She regarded the woman a moment longer. "I do not hold with high-handedness or cruelty amongst my servants and attendants. You are mine now, you are no higher or lower than those currently serving me."

Daphne's mouth thinned at Coronis words, but she said nothing.

"Mara will show you to my lady mother's chambers," Coronis dismissed them, smoothing her tunic over the swell of her stomach.

Daphne's mossy gaze fixed on her stomach with such intensity Coronis felt the need to shelter the babe within. She wrapped her arms around herself, disconcerted by the unconcealed aggression in the woman's eyes.

"Stop!" Coronis called out, her own anger rising. "Who are

you?"

Daphne blinked, flustered by Coronis' question.

"Answer me now," Coronis pushed. "No attendant, on Olympus or in Delphi, would dare look upon their master with such disrespect. I will have the truth from you."

Daphne's gaze locked with hers. "I have served your... husband for years, lady." She hissed. "He bid me wait for him here, so I am here—to serve him as he sees fit."

Coronis swallowed the fury choking her. "*Serve* him?" she managed.

Daphne's smile was taunting. "I have many skills, my lady. Skills he is most fond of. Perhaps that is why he sent me? So that I could teach you."

Coronis moved without thought. Yet the sound of the slap reverberated off the marble walls. Mara gasped, running from the room. Daphne cried out. And all the while Coronis resisted the urge to throttle the woman who dared to speak so.

"You will leave this house," Coronis could not stop the trembling of her voice. "You will leave and never return."

Daphne's hand covered her injured cheek, and though her green eyes blazed with fury, she was smiling.

"Go now or I will not be held accountable for my actions," she promised, still shaking.

"Until we meet again, fair Coronis," Daphne's smile was most unnerving... But there was naught Coronis could do. She stood there, shaking, as the woman hurried along the outer walkway and disappeared from her sight.

"Coronis?" her father's voice echoed.

"Are you well?" Ichthys as well.

Yet Coronis stood staring in the direction Daphne had gone, puzzling over the exchange. Why had the woman come? Why had Apollo sent her? Did he seek to upset her—to cut out her heart or taunt her inexperience? Was he so cruel?

"You are so pale, daughter." Phlegys peered down at her, frowning heavily. "Mara said you needed assistance."

"What happened?" Ichthys asked. "Where is this woman sent to torment you?"

"She is gone, I sent her away," she murmured.

"Good. Good," her father held her at arms' length. "What happened?"

"She... she came to taunt me, nothing more." She felt cold. "Whether Apollo sent her, I cannot know. If he did..." She shook her head, growing colder with each passing second. "I struck her, father. She said horrible things and I struck her."

Her father's eyes went round. "Who was she?" His eyes narrowed before he turned to Ichthys. "Go, find this woman and bring her back. I will learn the point of her visit and who sent her."

Ichthys nodded before hurrying down the hall, after Daphne.

She shook her head. "You will not find her."

"She is just gone," her father argued. "We will find her. And I will deal with her myself."

Coronis rested her head against her father's chest, seeking comfort in his arms. Yet she could find none. Coronis could not ignore the triumph in Daphne's mossy green eyes—or the delighted anticipation of the woman's smile—as she bid her farewell.

"You doubt her?" Hermes asked.

Apollo shrugged, turning to regard his closest friend. "How can I not?"

"Such news is most... unexpected, brother." The slight shake of Hermes' head was enough. "That Poseidon's seed causes such torment is no surprise." He clapped Apollo on the shoulder. "But that Coronis would lie to you? That, brother, is a surprise. She has no talent for subtlety or deception. In truth, I've never met a mortal woman so... so honest."

Apollo smiled. It was true. And one of the reasons he loved her so. His heart twisted.

"If she said she loved you, do not doubt it," Hermes was most emphatic. "Such words would be difficult for her-"

"They were," Apollo agreed. "She was reluctant to speak them."

Hermes nodded. "Because her word is her truth. I've no doubt she would have told you the whole of it if you'd asked her."

"How could I know?" Apollo sighed.

"No, no, how could one anticipate such news?" Hermes rested on his elbows. "I simply meant she would not have kept it from you if you'd asked her. Just as she did not keep her heart from you when asked. It was no trickery, more a matter of omission." He paused. "If she did deceive you Apollo it was before your time together—before she knew her heart and carried your child."

"Your mind is a most wondrous thing. And your use of... logic is staggering." Apollo grinned. "Go on, then. I am eager to hear your conclusion."

"I've drawn the only conclusion that makes sound sense, brother." Hermes bobbed his eyebrows. "You are an ass, a lucky one at that. Think of all she has done as a comfort, born from her unwavering loyalty. What a blessing she is."

Apollo drew in a deep breath. While Hermes employed a certain style to his speech, there was no denying the truth of his words. To have such a revelation thrust upon her the very eve he'd asked for her hand... She'd had no choice. She'd done what was right, her duty to her family. How could he expect anything less of his Coronis?

He stared into the cup of wine he spun restlessly in his hands. When would Zeus release him? He was done with waiting. With no knowledge of time or place, there was no guarantee this mighty earthquake was an immediate concern. But sitting here, near crippled with anxiety, was a waste of time. Time he could not get back.

He smiled, considering the swell of her stomach. He'd been gone a fortnight yet he wondered if she'd grown rounder in his absence. Did the babe move yet? And did she smile in delight to feel their babe thrive within her? He could imagine her smile—and ached all the more.

He would not lose her. He would find a way to change the vision, to protect her. He'd had time enough to realize the culprit was in this very chamber. No mortal would dare attack her so. Damocles was an oaf but he even he would not affront Apollo so. Her father would have told him if she'd another rival but none was mentioned.

That left Demeter or one sworn to help her cause. His eyes lifted, sweeping the Council Chamber slowly. Most were gathered, clustered together and talking amongst themselves. It was hard to imagine any of them willfully hurting someone dear to him. But for the love of a child, he knew anything was possible. He had the benefit of knowledge—it was some sort of advantage. As of now none on Olympus knew. He would keep it that way.

Those that did know—Hermes, Phlegys, Talousa, and Coronis—would never speak of it. He leveled a hard stare at Hermes then. "I ask for your word, Hermes, to guard her secret as if it were your own."

"You had it without asking." Hermes frowned. "I'd be offended by your request if I did not know how dear she is to you." He shrugged. "And I like her. I like that she can beat you and still you smile."

"Forgive me any offense. You are my dearest friend and brother," Apollo spoke quickly. "I've never had anything I feared losing. Now I am consumed by such thoughts. It is infuriating to be helpless."

"Rest easy knowing she is in her father's care. And your crows. They would come if she needed you." Hermes' attempt to ease him was of some comfort.

Until Zeus swept into the chamber, followed by Ares and Athena. There was no denying the change in the air, the sense of portent that followed the three. That Ares, God of War, wore his battle gear and a most eager expression could mean only one thing. War was coming.

Zeus speared each and every one with a lingering glance. "There is rumor of disharmony between Sparta and Athens. Two such powerful states could decimate our people. Go, intervene as you can. Encourage a battle of words and negotiations over one of sword and spear." He glanced at Ares then. "We must hope we have some time yet before Apollo's prophecy occurs. Dealing with both would be a messy business." He looked at Apollo, adding, "If more is revealed, come at once." Zeus' brow creased deeply, his mouth curving down at the corners. "We must, all of us, be ready for what comes next."

Apollo glanced at Hermes then. War. Perhaps his vision had less to do with his brethren than he thought. But he was little cheered by such knowledge. War amongst the kingdoms of Greece would demand Phlegys serve.

"You have time yet, brother. She is well guarded still." Hermes murmured, nodding. "But I can see that my words mean nothing so go. Go on."

"Your devotion to this mortal is most touching. To have her

guarded when you leave? Are you afraid she'll run away? I confess, she was not so tempting that I would steal her from you." Poseidon stood smiling, leaning against one of the pearl white columns that surrounded the Council Chamber. "I'd have thought her well bedded and forgotten by now."

Apollo swallowed back his ire. Poseidon was a master at taunting and baiting, pushing and tormenting his chosen target until he'd broken them. It was one of his favorite past times, Athena his favorite target. Best not to take the bait Poseidon offered—for Coronis' sake if nothing else. Poseidon was a most cruel adversary. "Her father is a great man, one I rely on most heavily when I'm away from Delphi." He forced a smile. "And while his daughter is not to your taste, she pleases me. For a mortal."

"For a mortal." Poseidon's eyes narrowed ever so slightly. "I've had to comfort Daphne these months. She was quite demanding, after having go so long with her needs unmet."

Hermes laughed. "You are too generous, Poseidon, to suffer the company of so lush and responsive a creature."

Apollo's stomach was leaden. Daphne's sweetness was often surrounded by nasty claws and a sharp tongue. She was vengeful and petty—like Poseidon. Together the two could wreak terrible mischief against a mortal... or an Olympian. He kept his features at ease, all too aware of Poseidon's assessing gaze. "Beware her bite, brother," he spoke. "Her pleasure is costly."

Poseidon rolled his eyes. "Why give a woman such power? Mortal, nymph, or goddess—use them as you see fit and move on."

Apollo said nothing, for Athena had joined them and her fury was obvious. "You are a malevolent cur," Athena snapped. "If you were mortal, people would travel from afar to see your head on a spear."

"You see," Poseidon scarcely glanced at Athena. "I find only one acceptable use for a woman's mouth."

Apollo shook his head. He should be thankful for the distraction Athena provided. Yet he could not deny the thrill of satisfaction that coursed through him when Athena reacted.

Her voice was brittle, "You shall pay for such insolence." If not for Hermes, blood might have been spilled. Yet he caught her arm, stilling the sword she'd pulled free.

"What now?" Zeus descended upon them. "I have just charged you with a matter of grave importance. And you stand about squabbling. From Athena's red cheeks to the sword clenched in her fist I would assume you've insulted her once again, Poseidon?" He barely paused. "Apologize. Now. And do as you've been told." With a parting scowl, Zeus stormed from the Council Chamber.

"I am sorry, Athena." Poseidon's brow arched high, his grin growing. "But you will never see my head on a spear. Only as it is now, smiling back at you." He nodded at the rest present then left.

"I would kill him with my bare hands," Athena muttered, sliding her sword into its scabbard. "What purpose does he have?" She regarded them with questioning eyes. "He is a sore that will not heal. A bite left to fester-"

"I think sparring with you is one of the few joys he has left in his existence, Athena," Hermes tried to placate her.

She regarded Hermes curiously. "Joy? No, Hermes, he simply hates me as I hate him."

Apollo shrugged, offering her a smile. "Perhaps he is meant to remind of us of our duties—of what not to be?"

Athena's gaze met his, as if she were considering his words. "Perhaps."

"Or he is for entertainment?" Hermes offered.

"Is menace amusing to you?" Athena frowned. "It saddens me to think you've become jaded."

"I shall leave you to puzzle it out," Apollo stood. "Or, challenge you to think on him no more. Put him from your mind as he doubtless has forgotten you—for now." He clasped Athena's arm in parting.

She smiled at him. "Wise counsel indeed. Safe journeys. Blessings to you and your wife."

"And the babe she carries," Hermes added.

Athena's brows rose and her smile grew. "Well, well, Apollo. Blessings indeed."

He bid farewell to Hermes and left, forcing himself to walk as he made his way to his waiting chariot. It was not wise to reveal his eagerness to Poseidon. He could not shake the unease Poseidon's idle comments stirred. No harm had come to her. No harm would come to her.

On his way to Delphi, he raced the sun. He peered down at

Greece, remembering Zeus' words. A war amongst their people, Greek against Greek. Such a thing could divide Olympus as well, for his kin were nothing if not loyal to those that served them best. As the people of Delphi served him. He was responsible for his realm and the mortals under his watch. He was blessed to rule over such beautiful country. Far reaching mountains, hidden caves, abundant hunting, and caverns so deep they offered entry into Hades realm. He felt at home here—more so now that he'd found Coronis.

Torches blazed along the columns of Phlegys' house, welcoming him. He did not pause, but pushed through the doors. He'd almost forgotten the guards inside, but the slide of metal on metal alerted him before any blow was delivered.

"Peace," he called out. "It is Apollo." He nodded at the men, buoyed by their presence and the knowledge that Coronis was safe.

He moved quickly then, making his way to the inner courtyard. Phlegys and Ichthys were there, reclining on cushion laden klines. Talousa sat in her chair, her fingers working some thread. And Coronis... She sat at her mother's side, her head resting against her mother's knee, twining balls of spun wool. He would run to her, grab her in his arms, and carry her from the room.

But Phlegys rose to greet him, his hand outstretched in greeting. Apollo clasped the man's forearm in return.

"Welcome," Phlegys spoke, smiling warmly. "You have been missed," he whispered, glancing at his daughter.

Apollo turned slowly, his nerves at odds with the surge of anticipation he felt. How he'd missed her smile, the warmth in her eyes and subtle huskiness of her laugh.

Coronis stood, the wool spilling from her lap and rolling across the floor. But she did not smile at him. No. She frowned and ran from the room.

She ran from him.

He looked at Phlegys then. "Missed?" he asked.

"Ah," Phelgys sighed. "She did not take kindly to the attendant you sent."

"Attendant?" Apollo repeated. "I sent soldiers. Many soldiers. Has something happened to Pina? Or Mara?"

Talousa spoke then. "No, Apollo, they are well and taking care of Coronis." She cocked her head, waiting. "If you did not send her, who did?"

"I shall find out," Apollo spoke, his unease mounting. He bowed quickly before heading from the courtyard and after his wife.

She was waiting for him. And all he could do was stare at her beauty. Even blazing with fury, she was exquisite. Her hair was loose, spilling down her back in browns and golds. Her tunic was thin, so fine that he could make out each curve, ridge, and valley of her body. He smiled at the sight of her stomach. His throat tightened, overcome by the love he felt, yet he forced the words out, "I have missed you."

She stared at him but did not speak.

"I have missed you," he repeated, closing the distance between them before she could move. She was shaking, her breath harsh and wavering. And her face... Her anger was tempered by something more... Disappointment? His hands cupped her face, his thumbs caressing the softness of her lower lip as his gaze searched hers. "Do not keep yourself from me in anger, Coronis. For I would love you." He lowered his head.

"No," she groaned, pulling from him and moving across the room. "Why do you play with me so?"

He followed her, refusing the distance she would put between them. "Tell me."

"Tell you?" She scowled, her hands clenched tightly. "That your... your whore came with her big breasts and her rolling hips and offered to teach me how to please you."

He froze then.

"You will be sadly disappointed. I did not let her tutor me. No, I struck her." Her voice rose. "I sent her away. I sent her away! I would send you away too." Her voice broke then, her chin quivering. "Damn you."

He caught her in his arms then, pulling her close. "Coronis, hush-"

"I will not." She pushed against his chest, her anger strong even as her eyes glittered with tears. "I will not be quiet. I will not forgive you for mocking me."

"I did not," he spoke harshly.

Coronis stared up at him. "Why would she come to me then? Why would she lie to me?"

"Why would you choose to believe a stranger's word over mine? I am your husband, Coronis, one who loves you more than life itself. I would no more change the way you love me than the stars in the sky. It saddens me that your trust is so easily shaken." He paused. "Did this vile creature have a name?" He knew who it was. Poseidon had said as much.

"Daphne," she murmured.

"She was most affronted when I rejected her for a mortal. She is a nymph you see, and prides herself on her prowess." He smoothed her hair from her face. "It seems she sought revenge upon me while we were parted."

"Revenge?" Coronis scowl faded, but a frown remained. "You rejected her... for me?"

His gaze wandered her face. "I've no need for another, woman. You are more than enough."

She blinked then, a single tear rolling down her cheek. "She... Her words." She shook her head. "My heart..."

He wiped the tear from her cheek, aching. Her words, garbled and broken from the weight of emotion, held such power over him. "Is safe. I told you, I will always keep it so."

She closed her eyes. "Forgive me."

He kissed each eyelid softly and rested his forehead against hers. "I have."

She looked at him then. "Forgive me... for all." She swallowed. "Father told me. He told me you know... our secrets." She shook her head. "Forgive me for whatever distress such news caused."

"I have," he repeated.

She stepped forward then, pressing herself against him as her hands covered his. "I have missed you."

He kissed her then, breathing easier once she clasped him tightly to her. His lips parted hers, mingling their breaths and driving him mad with hunger. She clung to him, her fingers twisting in his hair as he carried her to their bed. In her arms, he found the peace he'd been missing since they'd parted.

Chapter Sixteen

Coronis woke to his cries. Whatever tormented in his dreams, she would chase it away. She rested her chin on his chest and stroked the line of his jaw. "Husband," she whispered. "Wake up." His breathing increased, tearing from in deep, gasping shudders.

She rose, lighting a candle and returning to their bed. She crouched beside him, startled by the ferocity of his expression. As wonderful as their time together was, these passing weeks had seen him grow more agitated. It seemed unjust that his dreams would offer him no peace. "Apollo?" His hands tightened in their blankets, seeking something... But what? Was he in the grips of prophecy? Should she wake him? Yet she could not bear the sounds of his anguish. She leaned over him and pressed her lips to his. "Wake up, husband. Please. Wake up, my love," she murmured.

He froze suddenly, his hands winding about her arms. "Coronis?" He sat up then, all but crushing her against him.

"I'm here." Her words were muffled against his chest.

His hold eased somewhat, but he did not release her.

"Was it a vision?" she asked. She knew he waited for some further sign of the coming earthquake. The waiting, the not knowing, seemed to press upon him.

"No," the word tore from him. "A nightmare, nothing more." His hold tightened so that she had no choice but to protest.

"You crush our son," she teased. "And yet I suffer the consequences." She found his hand and pressed it to her stomach.

She was rewarded with several vigorous thumps of their child's foot.

Apollo laughed, cradling her gently in his lap. "He is strong."

"Like his father," she agreed, smiling up at him. "What is it?" she asked, startled anew by the intensity of his gaze.

"There are times I'm struck anew by your beauty," he murmured, stroking a lock of her hair between his thumb and fingers.

She arched her brow, staring at him in disbelief. "You will not tell me?" she asked. She'd seen him look at her with adoration, it warmed her through and through. This was different—desperate. She did not understand the haunted depths of his golden eyes. Whatever demons he wrestled in his dreams, they had yet to fully leave him. She shivered, longing to ease him in some small way.

He smiled, kissing her suddenly. His arms slid beneath her hair, holding her gently as his passion rose. She held his shoulders as her head fell back. She relished the feel of his mouth on her neck, the tensing of his hands on her hips and he lay back and lifted her over him.

She smiled down at him. "I love you," she whispered as he slid deep within her.

"I love you wife," his hands tightened on her hips, but his movements were slow and gentle. "I love your tight warmth when you hold me inside you so. I love the hitch in your breath and the arch of your back when we move together." His voice grew husky as she ground against him. "I love the toss of your head when your body breaks free. And the sound of your cries when your soul meets mine."

She shuddered, his words heightening her already inflamed senses. His gift with words matched that of his body and hands. His hands tightened upon her hips, for control or from passion, she did not know. He was a thorough lover, finding the soft spots and tender places that quivered and delighted at his touch. What his hands neglected, his mouth tended. She was only too happy to be consumed by his love, his passion and desire. It was the unguarded emotion in his golden eyes that unleashed her pleasure. Yet even as she fell over the edge, her body trembling and senses overwhelmed with a pleasure that left her reeling—she knew something troubled Apollo. His body tightened soon after. She watched him, mesmerized by the power of his release. Every muscle tightened, the look of carnal bliss on his face. He held her close, his ragged groan a wondrous thing. She had yet to fully understand the hold she had on this being, she only knew she was equally bewitched by him. But when his passion eased and his golden gaze found hers, she felt a moment's panic at the desolation she saw there. There was no warmth or happiness, only pain.

"Whatever it is, tell me." She stared down at him. "I am not so frail as you seem to believe. Perhaps it will help—to share your burden with me."

He stared up at her, the rapid rise and fall of his chest uneven. "I know few as strong as you, wife."

"Yet you shield me like a babe," she argued, shuddering when his hands slid along her sides to caress her stomach.

"If I shield you, it is because you carry my babe," his voice was low. "I have lived countless mortal lives, Coronis. Believe me when I say there are some things best left unspoken."

"It is no small task," she murmured, slipping from his hold to lay at his side. "It goes against my nature to do nothing. Especially when it concerns someone I love."

He rolled to face her. "You do enough, wife. That you love me is enough." He smiled, bringing her hand to his lips. "That you give me a child is enough."

She smiled, a yawn slipping from her before she could stop it.

He pulled her into him, tucking her head against his chest with a sigh. "Sleep, Coronis. It's too early to greet the day. I would prefer to stay as we are until the sun demands we rise."

She sighed, relaxing against him. The beat of his heart was steady and strong. "Apollo, will we stay in Delphi?"

"We do not have to," his voice was muffled against her head. "Where would you go?"

She looked up at him. "Where is your home? Do you reside on Olympus?"

"Sometimes, though rarely for long. I find I love my kin more with distance between us." He laughed softly.

"Father would make a gift of the lodge." She watched him. "It may lack the splendor you're accustomed to but it...my happiest memories are there."

He cocked his head at her. "Tell me."

"You know," she argued. "I told you. My father and I-"

"Ah. Childhood memories." His golden gaze held hers.

"No," she murmured, "Well, yes… The best of my childhood was there." She smiled. "But the ones I will savor 'til I am old and grey are those we created." The babe began to kick once more. "Your son wakes to reign abuse on my ribs." She rolled onto her side, sighing as the warmth of his chest, abdomen, and thigh fitted against her back and hip.

His arms slid around her, one hand cupping the weight of her breast. His words tickled her ear, "You will never be old and grey, Coronis, I forbid. You will stay with me, as you are, forever."

She stared through the gauzy curtains that surrounded their bed. "To live forever…" She paused, unable to comprehend such a thing.

"With me," his voice was low, entreating as his thumb traced round her nipple. "I will tell your father we accept his generous offer."

"Thank you." She looked back over her shoulder, accepting the quick kiss he pressed against her mouth.

He laughed then. "You've no need to thank me. It is through you that I've gained everything I've ever wanted. So I will thank you." His touch upon her breast grew feather-light, teasing her body and nerves with the promise of pleasure.

She arched into him, the evidence of his arousal hard against her hip. His mouth latched on to her earlobe, his teeth nipping the soft skin, and forcing a groan from her lips. While his fingers teased her nipple to a throbbing peak, his other hand drifted lower. He moved, thrusting into her while his fingers stroked the most sensitive nub between her legs. She cried out, welcoming the abandon his touch stirred.

"Coronis," his voice was raw.

She reached behind her, needing to touch him, to hold on to him. He was all that mattered, his scent and touch, the rasp of his breath against her temple, and the unrestrained thrust of his body joining with hers. The world seemed to shake, her passion was so great…

But Apollo froze.

Again, the ground seemed to move. Gently, the slightest tremor.

He moved from her, wrapping his tunic about his waist before she'd understood something was wrong.

"What is it?" she asked, then realized the likely cause. "The earthquake?"

"Not here..." He assured her. "Sparta. I see it clearly now," he bit the words out.

"You must go," she'd not meant to sound so forlorn. "Of course you must go." She attempted a more cheerful tone.

His smile was quick. "It pleases me to know I will be missed."

She stood then, not bothering to cover herself. "You will. Take this," she pressed a kiss to his lips before she continued, "and take care. I would have you here when our son comes into the world."

He drew her close, a scowl forming. "Do not venture from your father's house, Coronis."

She frowned in return. "I would prefer your parting words were of a more adoring nature."

His scowl lessened. "Promise me you will not venture from your father's house."

She sighed, nodding. "I promise."

He smiled then, kissing her. "Good. If I were a mortal man nothing could take me from your side." He cradled her face. "You make me wish I were mortal."

"Mortal or no, the love I have for you knows no bounds husband." She yielded to his embrace, the sweetness of his words warming her heart. "But, as you are an Olympian, you must go."

"An Olympian who loves you," he whispered against her temple.

And then he was gone. She stood, the air around her growing colder as a heavy emptiness replaced the joy she'd experienced only moments before.

She dressed quickly, haphazardly tying her tunic about her and hurrying to her parents' chamber. While they were not immortals, perhaps there was something they—Delphi—could do to help those in peril.

Apollo sat heavily in his chair, regarding the Council Chamber with heavy-lidded eyes. Exhaustion hung from him, a cloak he was eager to escape. But now, he waited on Zeus' word. Only then was he free to find his bed. And his wife. He would find solace in her arms.

The destruction was worse than the prophecy revealed. For three days he'd toiled along the coast, working to free those caught or trapped beneath the rubble. Fewer were discovered alive now and hope was waning. This morning, he'd felt utter defeat at a gruesome discovery. His attention caught on a flash of white in one of the many newly formed gashes that tore into the land. He'd moved closer, shielding his eyes against the sun. Water poured into the gash, near black in the shadows of the ravine, before racing back out to the sea to reveal a twisted mass of broken bodies. It was too late for them. So many... If any had survived the fall, they had not lasted long amongst the pull and surge of the frigid water.

He'd turned, his gaze sweeping what was left. The village was all but gone, no structure remained. Some were crumpled beneath rocks, others smoldered from a fire-pit upended in the quake. And yet those that remained had managed to erect temporary shelters. Large fire pits and drying racks were scattered throughout, another sign that the people would not admit defeat. It was the resilience that had him toiling alongside a handful of mortals, moving debris in search of any survivors—until he'd been summoned to Olympus.

"Apollo." Hermes arrived. "You look weary my friend."

"As do you," Apollo clasped his forearm in greeting. "I fear this summons bodes ill for my plans to return home."

Hermes nodded. "It is not over yet. There is talk of rebellion."

"Now?" Apollo scowled. "Who?"

"Chaos often brings rebellion." Hermes shrugged. "And Sparta's Helots see this as a time of opportunity."

Opportunity indeed. The people he'd left this morning would fall if war reached them. They had little in the way of food and fresh water, let alone arms to protect—let alone defend—themselves. An easy conquest, to be sure.

"I have little care for your precious mortals," Artemis came round his chair, her wide golden eyes sweeping the room. "As long as the woods are protected and my animals spared, let them thrash one another."

"Sister," Apollo smiled at her, knowing it troubled her to be here. But Zeus had summoned all and even she could not deny him.

Hermes laughed. "I've no doubt some would agree. Ares

perhaps. Tell me, Artemis, which do you favor more?" He leaned in, teasing, "Mortals or the Council Chamber?"

She glared at Hermes. While most thought his sister indifferent to Olympus and the Council Chamber, Apollo knew the truth. She was frightened. She regarded her brethren as more reckless than the wildest beast, unpredictable and dangerous. He'd laughed when she'd first voiced such thoughts but now he wondered if she had the truth of it.

"Perhaps the mortals," Artemis admitted, wrinkling her nose. "But only a few."

"Only a few," Hermes repeated, smiling.

Artemis snorted and sat on the ground at Apollo's feet. She leaned against his leg, her muscle's tense and ready for flight. When she glanced back at him, he smiled at her, offering her the comfort she sought. Her answering smile was nervous and quick.

"I know you have much on your mind, brother." Hermes sighed. "Perhaps this rebellion is the cause of your visions? War would explain much of what you've shared with me."

"And yet I pray you are wrong, brother." Apollo regarded Hermes with narrowed eyes. "Then I would be forced to battle an army of Athenians or Spartiates."

"Talk of war already?" Athena asked.

"I'd have expected diplomacy from you, Apollo," Hera chided him.

"Why must we waste time with talk of war?" Ares fidgeted. "War will come, I feel it in my bones."

"Let us hope mighty Zeus has some means to prevent it," Hera spoke. "Our people have suffered enough these last few days."

Apollo nodded. "Indeed."

"I fear there will be more in the days ahead," Zeus was resigned. "Most cities have pledged troops to help Sparta end this rebellion before it becomes widespread."

"And Athens?" Athena asked, a frown marring her brow.

"Four thousand troops, under Cimon's command," Zeus nodded.

"Then why have you summoned us here?" Ares frowned, his disappointment almost comical. "You pull me from sport across the Aegean for this?"

Zeus frowned at Ares.

Artemis rose, retreating behind Apollo's chair once more.

"Sparta accepted all the support it received. Save one. They have turned Athens back," Zeus waited, watching Ares face.

Athena's eyes went round. "They did what?"

"What has been done?" Hermes asked.

"They have broken from the alliance," Zeus continued. "All seem braced and waiting."

Ares nodded. "Waiting for the first blow."

Athena paced. "Why did they reject Cimon? What was their reason?"

"That Cimon and his men would rally against Sparta and join the helots and Messenians in the revolt." Zeus shook his head.

"While both Megara and Corinth poke and prod at one another," Ares added.

"Sparta will suffer if two of its states engage in war—while Sparta challenges Athens and its embassies," Apollo finished. "What shall we do?"

Zeus swept his arms wide. "That is why I called you here." His voice rolled throughout the chamber, listening to Athena's counsel and arguing loudly with Ares insistence that action was the best course of action. All the while, a queer uneasiness found Apollo. His sense sharpened, his eyes wandering the chamber the source of his disquiet.

It was only then that Apollo spied a crow, perched on the back of his chair. He stared at the crow, his heart in his throat. The crow stared back, his beak opening and closing once as the two merged, the crows messages spilling into Apollo's mind quickly—almost incoherently. Apollo gripped the arms of his chair, piecing together the images he collected.

What he saw was cloudy. Coronis—perhaps. Her face was obscured. Poseidon. She was crying when Poseidon pulled her into his arms. Coronis kissed him then—but not as a daughter... His stomach tightened. She was in his arms. Another image. Poseidon, removing Coronis tunic and drawing her into his arms.

No.

His lungs emptied, his heart twisting.

No.

This was false.

A peculiar knot formed in his stomach. What trickery was this? Poseidon was her father.

She would never betray him. Never.

He looked again, searching... It was not Coronis. This woman wore his wife's jewels—but she was not his wife. Where Coronis was firm and lean, this woman was round and lush. And this woman had no babe in her stomach.

But they were in his bed? And this woman was most pleased...

He puzzled over the images.

If he'd not known the truth, that Poseidon was her father, he might have believed what he saw as truth. He shook his head. No. He knew his wife too well, her body and her spirit. She was loyal and he trusted her.

What was the purpose of this deceit?

He drew in a deep breath, his stomach churning and his chest heavy. He blinked, severing the connection to stare around the room. Poseidon was not there.

A flash then, his vision clouding as divination gripped him swiftly. Coronis was running—terror in her amber eyes. "No!" The word tore from his throat. "No." He pushed from his chair, knocking it on the floor.

"Brother?" Hermes paled before him.

Apollo stumbled, still clutched in prophecy. He saw them clearly. The arrows that pierced Coronis. By the Fates, no. He spun round, willing the vision aside so he might find peace. "Where is Artemis?"

"She spoke to your pretty bird and left," Hera offered. "Some time ago... Yes, after Ares had arrived. He frightens her I think-"

"Apollo?" Zeus's voice was stern. "What is it?"

Artemis would have seen the birds' message, she spoke to all the creatures of her realm. But she could not know the truth as he did. While Artemis cared little beyond her beast, she loved him above all else. She would have believed Coronis was unfaithful— and sought a most brutal revenge upon his wife... Never had he felt such panic.

Apollo ran.

Coronis rose slowly, the ache in her back and knees making even the task of bathing a chore. She smoothed her hands over the enormous curve of her belly and smiled. "Not much longer, I think," she spoke softly. When she spoke, he kicked. "What will entertain you then?"

She let Mara dry her, accepting the loose flowing gown Pina had sewn for her. She slipped it on and let Pina brush her hair until it hung smooth down her back.

She stood, taking Mara's arm as they made their way to her rooms. Her parents were long abed, yet her son protested her attempts at sleep. Pina thought a warm bath might soothe them both. And while Coronis felt pleasantly fatigued, her son continued his assault on her ribs.

It was only when she reached her chambers that the smell of smoke filled her nostrils. She hurried to the hall that ran along the outer wing of the house, Mara and Pina in her stead.

"The stables," Coronis glanced at Mara. "Go, rouse my parents, quickly." Once Mara had hurried off, she turned to Pina. "I must-"

Pina shook her head, pointing at the ground with one emphatic finger.

"Pina," she argued. "Please."

Pina shook her head, pointing at Coronis' belly.

Coronis sighed. Pina was right. There was little she could do in her condition, save get in the way. But she would not stand idly by. She sent the guards out to help, with buckets, basins, and several thick mats to beat out the fire. Pina went too, once she'd made Coronis promise she would wait inside.

She paced the hall until she could no longer ward off the chill. She made her way to the fire pit in her room, unaware she was no longer alone until he spoke.

"You hesitate," his voice was low. "Perhaps you seek to draw this out?"

Coronis turned slowly, a flare of panic running down her spine. In the shadows of her room, she spied two shapes. "Who is there?"

Neither spoke.

"Why do you hide from me?" she asked.

A man emerged then. No, he was no mortal man. His pale eyes regarded her curiously. He cocked his head to one side and smiled, circling her slowly. "She is no different than one of your deer. She bleeds." His words were spoken softly, almost coaxing. But the knife he held left no room for misunderstanding.

She felt a coldness deep in her bones. "Who are you?"

The man looked into the shadows. "Why do you wait? She is not deserving of mercy. No, I'd thought to offer her comfort and she offered me her body. And mark me, she was most eager." He moved quickly then, grabbing Coronis hair, yanking her so that she would have fallen back. Instead her back slammed into his chest. "She deserves no pity. Think of her husband. This heartbreak will destroy him."

"The child?" a voice came from the dark.

"Is it his?" the man asked. "Would he want it? He cannot. No man would." His hand tightened, forcing her neck to arch awkwardly back. She felt the sting of his blade as he drew it lightly along her neck. He turned the blade, slicing through her tunic and baring her to the waist. She grasped the fabric, covering herself.

"Coronis?" It was Ichthys' voice that carried.

"Another lover?" the man asked.

Ichthys had scarce entered the chamber when an arrow flew, driving deep into Ichthys side. He crumpled, favoring his side and he fell to the floor. "Coronis?"

She felt tears on her cheeks. "Please, please-"

"She begs." The man laughed. "Let us be done with it before the house is full once more."

Coronis was released so suddenly, she stumbled forward into a cushioned seat. She glanced back to see Ichthys' blade buried deep in the man's calf.

"Run," Ichthys called out. "Run, Coronis."

She ran, supporting her stomach with her arm. No one was there. No one could help her. And Ichthys—she swallowed, hurrying through the inner courtyard to the front doors.

She heard the break in the air before she felt the tip of the arrow spear her flesh. Her right arms was thrown forward, the rod of the arrow buried deep beneath her shoulder blade. She did not look back, she did not pause, she could not. She pushed through the front door and ran.

She could not stop the scream that tore from her throat. The man was there, a visage of smoke and evil, blocking her path to the barn. She ran on, then, toward the competition fields and forest. She would find a way to protect them, she had to—for the babe. But with each step, her stomach clenched fiercely.

Another arrow lodged itself beside the other, making her arm tingle then go numb.

She glanced back over her shoulder. The man was gone, but the other ran easily—a dark hunter in a bleak night. She forced herself forward, willing her legs to move even as they trembled beneath her. But when her stomach clenched violently, she fell, stumbling to her knees. "Please, no. I beg of you..." She sobbed, true terror gripping her. "Apollo!" she called out, staring into the night sky for some sliver of light. She closed her eyes and prayed. *Apollo, my love, I cannot save him. Please help us.*

Chapter Seventeen

Her prayer reached him. Never had he felt so helpless, so afraid. The fire rose into the black night, twisting and winding above the tall trees and blanketing the stars in a thick grey smoke. He did not let Pyrios slow but forced his mount on. A sudden desperation clawed at his heart. He could not get there fast enough, could not ease the terror that consumed him.

A pyre rose, the logs twice his height, well consumed by the orange and gold flames. A funeral pyre, there was no mistake. He stared at the structure, a roar of anger and frustration tearing from him.

"Brother," Artemis' touch was light upon his thigh.

He slid from the horse, pushing Artemis aside as he made his way to the pyre. "This is Poseidon's work, Artemis. She did not betray me." He spared a moment's glance upon her before finding a hold on the pyre. He would have time enough to deal with his sister. His wife, his child, had no time.

"Coronis," But he could not cry out, the flames snuffed out whatever air remained in his lungs. His gaze shifted, searching the flames. "No..." He swung up, finding a foothold in the ladder that crackled and splintered beneath him. When it gave way, he clung to the fiery wood and pulled himself up.

He listened, desperate for some sign that she lived. But he heard only the roar of the flames and the thundering of his heart. He was mindless to the singeing of his lungs, the charring of his skin, he must reach her. He had hope. The platform above was unscathed... If he could reach her in time, he might save her still.

Her foot dangled, the skin charred and blistered. He reached for her, climbing atop the fragile platform as a beam gave way.

She was so still.

"Coronis?" he rasped. Her chest did not rise and fall, no breath stirred the air. He knelt beside her, drawing her to him. "Coronis?" He swept the hair from her face and began to weep.

Her heart had been pierced by a knife, spilling her blood before the fire could do its work.

"No." he cried, shaking her. "You will live," he yelled, placing his hand over her rounded stomach. "You must live for him. For me."

Her eyes fluttered.

"Coronis?" He whispered, lifting her.

Her eyes flew open then, her scream drowning all else. "Save him."

Apollo shook his head. "I will save you both."

She gripped his arm, her amber eyes boring in his. "Save him. I demand it of you."

Apollo shook his head.

"You will do this." Her voice was strong. "You will, Apollo. Or I will haunt you for eternity."

"I cannot." He wept anew. "Stay with me."

"In him, I will." She stroked his cheek. "Promise me."

His hand covered hers as he pressed a kiss to her palm. The platform shifted, the warning pop of timber reminding him how little time they had.

"Swear it," she cried out.

"You have my vow."

"He moves..." Her voice grew faint. "He would meet his father." A flash of something, pain, sorrow, creased her brow. Her amber gaze bore into his, wet with tears. "I was loyal," the anguish in her voice tore his heart out.

"I know. I never doubted you. Hush, now," he pleaded. "I should have saved you. Forgive me, Coronis, forgive me. For I will never forgive myself."

The slightest smile touched her lips as the spirit he loved faded from her fathomless gaze.

"No... No..." He pressed his lips to hers. "Coronis." He pressed her against him. "No!" The cry ripping him in two.

Her stomach rolled, pressing against his chest. The babe, his son, seeking escape.

She was gone, lost to him. But he would honor his vow to her.

He lay her back, gritting his teeth as he pulled the dagger from his belt. He would not fail her again. "I will save him." His fingers stroked her face. She was gone, he knew it, but it pained him to close her eyes. He wiped the tears from his face and, yelling out, cut deep.

In seconds the babe was free. His cry rang out, strong and loud. Apollo could not look at him. He wrapped the babe in Coronis tunic and called out, "Hermes! I need you!"

When his son was safely delivered to Hermes, he scooped Coronis close and jumped from the pyre.

"Apollo-" Hermes cradled his screaming son.

"Take him to Olympus, to Hera or Aphrodite." He did not look at the babe. "I will take Coronis to Hades."

"She is gone brother," Hermes words were soft.

Apollo rounded on him. "He will bring her back." He climbed atop Pyrios, cradling Coronis close as he nudged the beast into the darkness of the forest. He knew time was of the essence. She'd not made the journey into the Underworld yet, there was time. Yet with every step Pyrios took, Coronis grew colder in his arms. He could not quell the panic in his chest.

When the cave loomed before him, Apollo drew in a deep breath.

"Hades!" he yelled. He slid from the horse and crept inside, calling out again. "Hades!" He looked down at Coronis, at how still and pale she was in his arms. He bellowed again, his desperation mounting. She grew colder in his arms, while he stood waiting— clinging to hope.

"Apollo?" Hades finally emerged from the black, a torch held aloft. "What has happened?"

"You must save her brother," Apollo held her out. "You must."

"What has happened?" Hades brow furrowed deeply. "Who is she?"

"My wife." He heard the waver in his voice.

Hades stared at him for what seemed an eternity.

"Why do stand there while she grows cold in my arms? Heal her brother, return her to me. Whatever needs by done, I will do it, but save her." His gaze fastened upon her face, the blood at her temple, coating her neck. She had suffered so much.

"Apollo, her wounds are too great." Hades lifted what remained of Coronis tunic. "Her body is ravaged-"

"Heal her," Apollo argued, the panic he'd scarce held at bay devouring him. "Heal her, damn you. You must." He was seized with a trembling, so fierce he feared he'd fall or lose his grip on Coronis.

Hades reached for her. "I cannot heal her, Apollo. If it were in my power, I would—I swear it. Let me take her." His voice was soothing. "Let her find peace."

He shook his head, the tremors in his arms forcing him to tighten his hold upon her as he sank to the cave floor. He heard Hades' words and knew there was truth in them. But his heart was not ready to let go. "Do not tell me there is no hope, brother. I will go mad, I swear it."

Hades said nothing.

"You have your Persephone for some given time, Hades. I doubt it is enough, but it is some sort of gift." His throat tightened. "It is all I ask. The thought of never seeing her again is as near to death as I can imagine." He stared up at his kin, searching for some sign of emotion within Hades' guarded visage.

He was most rewarded by the twist of Hades' mouth, the clenching of his jaw. "I have lived such a life," his words were bitter. "I can offer no promises." He knelt beside Apollo. "There is one hope left. The Fates. You must bargain with them and find balance, as is their way."

"The Fates," he repeated, nodding. His gaze returned to Coronis once more. Her lips were blue. No matter how closely he held her, she would not warm to him.

"Leave her in my care. Persephone and I, we will watch over her," Hades offered.

"As long as I hold her, I hold my rage at bay. I would see those that had a hand in this suffer as I suffer. I would kill Poseidon for this," he murmured.

"Now is not the time for revenge, Apollo," Hades reached for Coronis. "We will keep her safe, I give you my word."

Apollo buried his face in her hair for a moment, breathing in her scent and blinking back the tears that blurred his vision. "I will come back for you," he whispered.

He watched Hades carry her away then waited. What he was waiting for he knew not. Only that he hoped Hades would return with Coronis, smiling and laughing.

His trek from the cave was slow, fighting against despair and welcoming the heat of pure wrath. By the time he reached Pyrios, his rage warmed him. He climbed atop the horse and urged him into a gallop.

One of his crows appeared, singing softly. It thought to offer him solace, he knew. But Apollo could not look upon it. He'd looked to their pure-white plumage and melodious song as a source of enjoyment. Now, he saw only the images it had delivered—and his anguish spurred him on. The crow sang on, desperate for Apollo's attention. He could not listen to its pleas for forgiveness. He waved it away, but the bird would not heed his warning.

Apollo could stand it no more.

He reached out, gripping the bird in his hand—the darkness of his soul staining the bird's plumage darkest black. Crows would forever be as black as pitch, as black as his heart this day. The bird fought against Apollo, but it was not enough. He would not hear the birds' song, never savor its' peaceful tune—so the crow should sing no more. A strange sound emerged from the bird. When its' beak opened again, a grating caw emerged. A far more suitable sound for the bringer of death. He released the bird, kicking Pyrios on.

He could not strike Poseidon down, but Daphne was another matter altogether.

He knew the copses and meadows she favored, with their soft grasses and fragrant blooms. She was not hard to find. And when he did, he slipped from Pyrios back and freed his dagger from his belt.

When her mossy green gaze discovered him, she smiled.

"You greet death with a smile, Daphne?" he asked.

Her eyes went round then. "Apollo–"

"Nothing you say will spare you," he assured her. "You may run, but I will catch you." He paused, shaking with fury. "Go on, run. Daphne. Lead me on a merry chase. Run!"

She ran. She was faster than she looked. But the hunt did him good.

He ignored her pleas and incoherent cries. It mattered not if she had regrets. When she stumbled, he did not hesitate. Yet she rolled away, running to the river's edge.

Her prayers continued, growing louder and more frantic, seeking protection from the lesser gods of the trees and the river. Apollo paid them no mind.

He reached her, his hand gripping the tunic that slipped about her waist. "She was stabbed in the heart, Daphne. Tell me, do you have a heart?" She was crying as his hand gripped her hair.

He struck swiftly, but hit nothing. He stared, dazed at the sight before him. In his hand he gripped a branch of laurel leaves. Before him, wrapped in Daphne's tunic, was a laurel tree. He cried out, the sound tormented and raw. He slashed at the bark of the tree, cursing whatever deity had stolen his vengeance from him. Again and again his blade bounced off the wood, until he crumpled at the trees base and gave in to his sobs.

Poseidon stood on the edge of the meadow, his eyes burning from smoke.

He'd seen all, transfixed and horrified. Never in his wildest dreams could he have predicted this days' events. Daphne wanted retaliation against the mortal that stole Apollo and then dared to strike her... She would be ecstatic to see how well things played out.

In truth, he'd never expected Artemis to go through with it. She was a wild thing, but her nature was to protect, not injure. Yet Coronis flight had triggered something in the huntress. And once Artemis let loose her first arrow, Poseidon saw the change in her. She hunted Coronis with a hatred he understood. But he'd known Coronis had done nothing to warrant such an emotion. Poor Artemis played the fool in a most tragic tale.

It was only as Apollo pushed past his sister to reach Coronis that Artemis realized her mistake. She covered her face with her hands and ran from the meadow.

And Apollo... Never had he seen his kin so. He felt a twinge of regret. Perhaps he and Daphne had been too careless with their games? Yes, Apollo had wounded his pride. And in rejecting Daphne, Apollo had crossed her as well. But was either offenses cause for the horror of this evening's events? He should have enjoyed the splendor of Daphne's body and cast her aside. Instead he'd let his cock lead, corrupting what had always been an easy friendship.

Apollo would never forgive him. For that, he was sorry.

Coronis' babe was crying in earnest now. Its pitiful wail grew weaker. No, Apollo would never forgive him. But forgiveness was not necessary. Time would go on and today would fade. In time, all would be forgotten...

Apollo stood before the Fates. The room was dim, for their eyesight was fragile—or so Atropos said. It was a large room, but the ceiling was low and the single window let in very little light. A large pendulum hung over their fireplace, ticking off some measure of time.

It had ticked thirty-seven times since he'd finished his tale. And yet they said nothing. Instead they regarded him curiously, their oddly brilliant eyes assessing him.

"You have nothing to offer," Clotho, the spinner of every mortal's thread, spoke first.

"Her string was cut short," Lachesis, the one who measured each mortal's thread, spoke to the other. "A waste of string."

"I had little choice," Atropos snapped. Her large sheers rested across her lap. She cut every mortal's thread. "Poor girl could not have survived such torture."

Compared to their ancient appearance, their voices were surprisingly childlike. As were their eyes. In their bright gazes, he found sharp minds and quick wits.

"Surely there is something I can give?" He paused, remembering Hades warning. He must remain calm. "Or perhaps, something I can do?"

"Would you sing for us?" Clotho asked.

"Or play your aulos?" Lachesis added.

Atropos shook her head. "Her thread is gone, boy." She pointed at the pile before the fire. "Her time is over."

Apollo stared at the mountain of thread and felt his control slipping. "I would sing for you—play for you—every night if I could see her again."

Atropos frowned. "Why?"

"Would she want to see you?" Clotho asked.

"Do you love her still?" Lachesis sighed, smiling slightly. "You seemed to love her so."

"More so than Cyrene the lion tamer. And she bore you two sons, not just one." Clotho looked at her sisters. "And Hecuba. And Manto. And Phthia. All gave you sons."

"Go back to Delphi, woo another." Atropos smiled.

"Oh, what of Thalia," Clotho asked. "And Urania. To love not one, but two Muses."

"Is there a woman in Greece unknown to you?" Atropos asked.

"I want no other," Apollo argued. "It is Coronis that taught me of real love. There is no other like her. Tell me what to do, I shall do it. I will not replace her with another."

The sisters looked at one another then.

"No other?" Atropos asked. "Ever?"

He pressed his hand to his heart but the ache would not ease. "No other."

The sisters leaned together, whispering between them.

Lachesis stood and hobbled to the pile of string. Her gnarled fingers lifted each strand with care, inspecting thread after thread before finding the one she sought. She carried it back to her stool and sat between her sisters. Apollo stared at the string, too frightened to hope.

"We have a bargain, Apollo," Clotho arched her brow. "We have no need of song or anything else you would offer us. But listen well, for the terms are steep."

"One night a month," Lachesis spoke. "The morn of the full moon to sunrise on the following day—no more."

"She does not have to come, mind you," Atropos interjected. "If she rejects you, you will let her go and she will live on, in peace, in Elysium."

"But if she comes to you..." Clotho shook her head. "If she comes, your burden is great."

"You will honor your vow, Apollo. She will remain your wife—and you will be loyal to her only. No other. For all eternity," Lachesis stared at him then. "None."

"If you break this vow, she is lost to you." Atropos paused. "And cast into Tartarus."

Apollo stared at them, grappling with their bargain. "And balance?"

The three cackled in unison.

"You offered us entertainment," Clotho shrugged.

"We have no need for songs or stories," Lachesis dismissed. "We have no need to see you again."

"This bargain promises to be far more amusing," Atropos finished.

Tartarus. Could he risk it? Risk her life and soul? "Would she know of the bargain?" he asked.

They frowned at him in unison.

"Of course." Clotho shook her head at him.

"You will agree to this bargain," Lachesis said softly. "But my sisters and I suspect she will not."

"One would hardly risk eternal damnation against this boy's desirous nature." Atropos paused. "Will she accept?"

He ached for her, the hole in his chest a constant torture. Yet, she was safe. Apart from him, but safe nonetheless. "I know not," he murmured. What right did he have to ask so much of her?

The three looked at him.

"She loves you," Clotho spoke.

Lachesis voice grew faint. "We wept at her loss."

"As did I," he agreed. "I do still. When I see the babe..." his voice broke. His son. The son he'd kept at arm's length. "It pains me to see him."

"She would chide you for such behavior," Atropos scolded.

"She would," he agreed. "And I would love the sound of it."

A strange sound escaped Clotho.

Lachesis took her sister's hand in hers. "What say you, Apollo? Do you accept our bargain?"

"A good bargain. Your loving wife, returned to you—whole and healthy—for one night a month," Atropos went on. "The rest of her days spent in Elysium. A good bargain indeed."

"Hers will be the final decision," Clothos spoke. "Do you understand the terms?"

"She will come to you in your home," Lachesis murmured. "The place she is so fond of?"

"Her father's hunting lodge," Apollo nodded. The place *he* was most fond of.

He nodded. "Could she see others? Meet our boy?"

Lachesis spoke quickly. "If you would share her with others—if she wishes it. I'm sure she longs to meet her son."

Apollo swallowed down the lump in his throat. To see Coronis hold their son, to hear her laughter. He nodded. "I accept."

Coronis turned her face to the sun. She'd almost forgotten the glory of its heat. The sun in Elysium was different. Warm, yes, but lighter. Her gaze fastened on the golden orb, resting on the horizon. On her trek from the caves, she'd taken her time stroking every leaf, inhaling the scent of the earth, and the kiss of the fresh breeze upon her skin. To feel so alive, so free, was a gift in itself.

She had tried to make peace with her new life, to forget those she'd left behind. But her heart was too loyal. Too much was left unknown and unsaid.

The bargain the Fates had offered her—that Hades delivered to her—was the greatest gift she'd ever known.

A breeze lifted her hair and cooled her skin.

"Coronis?" His voice.

Her heart raced, thrumming with excitement. Yet she was rooted in place.

"Coronis?" His hand trembled as it clasped hers.

She glanced at his hand wrapped about hers. At the strength of his arms and breadth of his shoulders. His hair rested on his shoulders, golden in the fading sunlight. And his face…

"Do not cry," she murmured, wiping the tears from his cheeks.

His crushed her then, pulling her so tightly against him she could not breathe. She did not care. "Coronis," he groaned, his face turned into her neck.

She twined her arms about his waist and pressed her ear to his chest. His heartbeat, beneath her ear, as it should be.

He pulled back then, cupping her face in his hands and peering down at her. His smile was a thing of beauty. He looked tired, haunted, his eyes were red-rimmed—smudged by dark shadows. She covered his hands with hers and lost herself in his golden gaze.

"I have missed you," his voice rasped. "I have missed you so."

She stood on tiptoe. "And I have missed you." She twined her fingers through his hair and pulled his head to hers. She was eager for his kiss, the firmness of his mouth. Her lips parted his so that she could breathe him in.

He broke away, gasping for breath. "Let me see you, wife. Let me feast upon the sight of you."

She stroked his face. "You look tired, husband."

He pressed a kiss to her palm. "I will rest easier now, I think." His smile faltered. "There are things that need be spoken."

She nodded even as her heart twisted. "Persephone told me what happened. Is Artemis well?"

He frowned. "You think of Artemis?"

"She was wronged. She believed the crows' sight. Why would she doubt it? It was Poseidon and Daphne that tricked the poor bird… She did not know and trust me as you. She thought to avenge you. Would you not have done the same for her?" She gripped his face and frowned. "You will forgive her. You must. I demand it."

"I shall." He sighed, resting his forehead upon hers. "What of Hades' fair Persephone?"

"She is a fine companion." She smiled. "And a good friend. As is Medusa. I am not lonely, if that is what you fear."

"It is." He smoothed the hair from her face. "I have never seen Elysium. I cannot cross into the Underworld."

She nodded. When she'd pleaded with Hades to see Apollo—to ease the torment she knew he suffered—he'd told her as much. "It is not so different from this land. It is warmer here, brighter." She rested her head on his chest. "You must tell me the rest."

"Your parents are well." He assured her.

"Ichthys?"

"Is recovered. But he misses you. As we all do." He drew in a deep breath. "Come with me," he spoke softly, leading her inside.

Pina and Mara were waiting inside.

Mara promptly burst into tears. "My lady."

Coronis hugged her. "Mara. It is good to see you." She turned to hug Pina, but found herself face to face with her son.

Her son, wrapped in the lion pelt Apollo had gifted her. She smiled. How she'd longed to see him, to hold him… She'd woken many a night, clutching an empty belly. Such things were nightmares now. For he was here, small and soft and within her reach.

She stared at him, overcome.

"Your son," Apollo shifted the babe from Pina's hold to hers. "Healthy and strong." Apollo's lips brushed her temple. "I thank you, wife."

The babe was warm and solid in her arms. She held him close, breathing in his scent. She could not stop the tears then. Her son regarded her solemnly. "What a fine boy you are," she murmured as she leaned forward to press a kiss to his forehead, his cheek.

She sat, unwrapping the child so she could explore every inch. He was perfect, with long legs and a strong grip. She laughed when his tiny fingers wrapped tightly about her finger. He yawned and closed his eyes, his grip easing as he drifted off to sleep. "He will be as strong as you," she whispered, her gaze meeting Apollo's.

Her husband stared at her with so much love. "He will be as strong as his mother. For she is the stronger."

She swaddled the babe and handed him to Pina. "Please bring him to me when he wakes," she asked. Pina nodded, smiling happily as she and Mara left the room with the babe.

"You risk much by coming to me." His hands clasped her shoulders.

"No, Apollo, my husband. I do not. I trust you." She shook her head as she stepped into the circle of his arms. It was a greater risk to stay, to lose him forever. "I could not survive, in life or death, without you."

He closed his eyes, his jaw tensing as he rested his forehead against hers. "Nor I," his voice broke. "Nor I," he repeated, strong and sure.

"You gave me your vow." She stared up at him, gripping the front of his tunic with both hands. "And I hold you to it." She smiled, pressing a soft kiss to his lips.

"You have it, wife," his tone was fervent. "You have it always."

Epilogue

"I would hear you say the words, Demeter," Zeus demand rang out in the Council Chamber.

"I will leave Ione be." Demeter sighed. "The woman has endured more than I can fathom. Even I am not so heartless." She smiled sadly at Apollo.

"No, Demeter, your heart is full of the love you bear your daughter," Aphrodite spoke, clasping Demeter's hand in hers.

"A mother's love." Athena shook her head.

"No less fierce than a father's love," Apollo countered, glancing at Hera holding his boy Asclepius. Hera doted on the boy. In truth, all of Olympus was most fond of him—Even Ares had carved him a small wooden dagger. Asclepius was most fond of gumming it.

"And Erysichthon?" Ares asked. "What of him?"

"We will go on," Demeter sighed. "What else can we do?"

Apollo smiled at Asclepius as he reached for one of Hera's jewels. He had a winning smile and easy temper. But he saved his best smiles for those days they spent with Coronis. For those were the best of days.

"We have more important matters to discuss," Zeus went on. "War amongst the Greeks will find us soon."

Ares smiled, slamming his cup on the table. "At last, *I* have something to celebrate."

Aphrodite leaned over the Ares' shoulder and refilled his cup. "Perhaps you should seek other pursuits to occupy your time?" The

Goddess' gaze lingered.

"War is the only fitting pursuit for man." Ares scowled at her. "What else is there, woman?"

Aphrodite stooped to whisper something in his ear.

Apollo watched, amused by the play of expressions upon Ares' face. When the Goddess walked away, Ares gaze was fixed upon her.

"And Poseidon?" Hermes asked. "What of our kin?"

"I think he is best left across the Aegean for now. It is an easy banishment," Zeus shrugged. "We can hope he will come back to us changed. An Olympian worth honoring."

Apollo held little hope for such a change from his kin. But he said nothing. Indeed, he'd promised Coronis he would spend no more time or anger on Poseidon. Instead she'd challenged him to cherish the gifts he'd been given as an Olympian and as her husband. And while he accepted his duty to Greece, he found his only pleasure waiting for him on the morn of each full moon.

Sasha Summers

Sasha is part gypsy. Her passions have always been storytelling, romance, history, and travel. Her first play was written for her Girl Scout troupe. She's been writing ever since. She loves getting lost in the worlds and characters she creates; even if she frequently forgets to run the dishwasher or wash socks when she's doing so. Luckily, her four brilliant children and hero-inspiring hubby are super understanding and supportive.

Sasha can be found online at sashasummers.com.

Acknowledgements

Thanks to my writing buddies for encouraging me to write not-so-traditional romance.

To my parents – thank you for nurturing my dreams & teaching me to love stories of all kinds.

Sincere thanks to Naj Qamber for the gorgeous cover and Grace Coronado for the super quick/super perfect formatting. You guys make my book babies look soooo good!

Very special thanks to my kids for letting me ask things like "What if your sister lit your wife and baby on fire? What would you do? But she was trying to help." Or "Can you guys enact this fight scene as I read it out loud – in slow motion?" You're the best and I love you more than you'll ever know!

Glossary Terms & Reference Index

Andron – the gentlemen's section of a Greek house, no women were allowed.

Chiton – men's tunic of lightweight fabric

Chlamys – a short cloak, worn by men and women, made from one seamless piece of material

Doru – a spear, 7–9 feet long, used by the Greek infantrymen

Ekdromos/Ekdromoi – skilled infantrymen used for special missions or close combat

Epiblema – a woman's shawl

Himation – thick cloak. Large enough to be used as a blanket or folded into a pillow

Hoplite – Greek infantrymen

Kline – a fainting couch or day bed used for social gatherings

Linothorax – armor worn by more military leaders or affluent soldiers. Made of thick padded leather, fabric covered in metal scales of metal – depending upon the soldier's ability to pay. Not all soldiers could afford armor.

Oikos – the household – not the house itself but the property, livestock, family and slaves

Peplos – a full length tunic worn by women, usually made from one large piece of fabric to be pinned, sewn or draped.

Peltasts & Psiloi – foot soldiers without extensive training

Shades – souls or ghosts

Strategoi – ten generals chosen from ten Greek tribes

Trireme – a ship, propelled by three rows of oars, possibly 25 or more oars, on each side.

Xiphos – soldier's short sword used as a secondary weapon to the spear/doru.

Myths Revisited in Eclipsing Apollo

Daphne & Apollo myth – According to most myths, Apollo was overcome with Daphne and determined to win her. He was so relentless that Daphne begged a river god to save her from his amorous intentions. The river god did so by turning her into a laurel tree—Apollo's favored tree.

Coronis & Apollo myth – A lesser known Apollo myth. Some say Coronis simply refused Apollo's interest in favor of a mortal. Others say she was involved with Apollo but dared to take another lover. Apollo or Artemis, depending on the version, the throw Coronis on a funeral pyre and save the baby she's carrying. It was Apollo's white-feathered crow that brought the news of Coronis' betrayal to Apollo. Apollo was so upset that he turned the crow black and cursed the bird to the bringer of death.

Made in the USA
Middletown, DE
22 July 2022

69868920R00119